T5-DGB-423

HER WILL WAS STRONG— BUT HER DESIRE WAS STRONGER . . .

She tried to twist away.

He held on firmly.

She could not do anything to free herself. He was too strong, too powerful . . . She could see that he meant business—although she was not quite certain just what kind—or maybe she was, and that is what frightened her the most. "Look," she started, then stopped. Her throat felt suddenly dry. She moistened her lips with her tongue. It was her first mistake.

His gaze slipped from hers to the subtlety of her movement, his eyes nearly glowing red-hot in the darkness. His hand moved to her waist . . .

"No," she breathed the word aloud. She had seen that look in him before. And as badly as she might want him, she could not let this happen again. She pulled away.

He drew her back, hard against him. His mouth came down on hers, searing her lips. His tongue probed into the recesses of her mouth.

She felt his fingers on her shoulder, loosening the lacings of her dress, and she groaned. Her mind fought against what her body would not . . .

Diamond Books by Deborah James

GOLDEN FURY
BELOVED WARRIOR
WARRIOR'S TOUCH

WARRIOR'S TOUCH

DEBORAH JAMES

DIAMOND BOOKS, NEW YORK

If you purchased this book without a cover, you should be aware that this book is stolen property. It was reported as "unsold and destroyed" to the publisher, and neither the author nor the publisher has received any payment for this "stripped book."

This book is a Diamond original edition,
and has never been previously published.

WARRIOR'S TOUCH

A Diamond Book / published by arrangement with
the author

PRINTING HISTORY
Diamond edition / March 1994

All rights reserved.
Copyright © 1994 by Debbie Bailey.
This book may not be reproduced in whole or in part,
by mimeograph or any other means, without permission.
For information address: The Berkley Publishing Group,
200 Madison Avenue, New York, New York 10016.

ISBN: 1-55773-988-9

Diamond Books are published by The Berkley Publishing Group,
200 Madison Avenue, New York, New York 10016.
DIAMOND and the "D" design are trademarks
belonging to Charter Communications, Inc.

PRINTED IN THE UNITED STATES OF AMERICA

10   9   8   7   6   5   4   3   2   1

To my sister, Lynn—

This one's for you. I know you'll find your own *warrior* one day, and soon, too. He's out there waiting for you. They say it always happens when you're not looking . . . so for goodness sakes, *take off your glasses*!

I love you, Sis

As always, I wish to thank my good friends and some of the toughest, yet most loving, critics anyone could ever have, Jeannie and Jamie. What would I do without your encouragement?

And, to my husband, Jim . . . there aren't enough words to thank you for all that you do, and how much you care. Your generous understanding is what gets me through all my insane days of distraction while I'm writing.

WARRIOR'S
TOUCH

ONE

Late Spring, 1878

Gretchen Samuels did not count on old memories moving in on her and overshadowing what she had hoped would be an exciting trip from Reno to Cedar Rapids. But after only a mile or two of her trek, here they had come dragging her down into the gloom of despondency.

Why *had* she testified against her husband at his trial? After all, she was his wife. By law she could not be forced to contribute to his conviction. A fragment of guilt slithered up her spine. If only Garret had not hated her Indian friends so much. If only he had not been in on their attack. If only the two of them had truly loved each other. If only . . .

It had been six long weeks since she had received word from Yuma Prison of her husband's death. Yet even now ghosts of their loveless marriage tried to shroud the single ray of cheerfulness she had managed to find this dazzling Wyoming morning.

The coach thudded over a rut in the road, jostling her into the driver's side. "Beg pardon, ma'am." The rail-thin man flashed her a bashful smile from beneath a huge handlebar mustache.

Gretchen nodded but said nothing. Holding onto the seat for support, she watched with interest as the driver handled the lines of the eight spirited horses pulling the coach. He drove the animals with all the confidence of a much stouter man, giving the appearance of a carefree soul out for nothing more than a leisure ride instead of a stagecoach driver forging across the rugged route from Laramie City to Cheyenne.

Why had the man invited her to sit up top with him today? She thought back to the previous five days and realized that each morning the driver had invited a different passenger to sit with him and converse. Today had been no different, and it was Gretchen's turn.

Maybe she should have taken the train, as her older sister, Elise, had suggested. She mentally shook her head. No. She had opted for the stage for a reason. She wanted to give herself a little extra time to sort out her feelings before butting emotions with Elise. But why go back to Iowa? She hated farm life.

Why not to Chicago—or maybe even New York? Maybe even try her hand at becoming a doctor herself. She had worked with Garret often enough. She had the training—at least hands-on. She allowed herself a weighty moment to picture what that life would be like. Did she have the stamina to endure the ridicule and hardships of entering into a *man's* profession? She took a deep breath. Let's just see how you do with Elise, then . . . maybe.

She knew only too well what her sister would be like now that her mother and father had passed on. Still, she needed to be with family, and Elise and her husband, Jacob, were all she had left. She knew her much older sister would undoubtedly indulge Gretchen's every whim. But not without making her pay the price of hearing over and over how Gretchen should never have married a self-absorbed man like Garret Samuels in the first place.

She glanced down at the gold wedding band on her hand. Without thought, she began spinning it around her finger as had become her custom since Garret's suicide. When she had seen him sent to prison, she never considered the possibility that she would become a widow. Now that she had, her entire life would be changed.

She had known the type of man he was when she married him. But she had been smitten, and so had chosen to ignore the flaws she saw lurking just below the surface of his dashing good looks and smooth way of speaking. She stilled her fidgeting, shook her head, and took a deep breath. No more. She could do this no more. Just how long was she expected to mourn for a man she had not loved for over a year?

Garret Samuels had proven himself unworthy of any grief, much less devotion. She had to put the past behind her once and for all. Mindful of the driver's watchfulness, she gripped the ring and slipped it off her finger. She squeezed it one last time, digging her nails into her palm as she did so.

Pain and heartache were all her husband had given her over the last twelve months. It was only fitting that they were the last things she should feel before dislodging him from her life forever. Opening her hand, she lowered her arm and allowed the band to fall from her grasp to the ground.

"Looky there." The driver's voice pitched with another lurch of the stage.

Startled, Gretchen flinched. She glanced up just in time to see a deer bound across the road in front of them.

Chewing on what to Gretchen seemed like the largest wad of tobacco she had ever seen one human male cram inside his cheek, the driver nodded to the side. "Mama's out to protect her young'uns."

Gretchen turned and squinted against the brilliance of the mid-morning sky.

The flattened bodies of twin fawns hiding in the hip-high grasses at the side of the road came into focus. The animals lay so still that if it were not for their large eyes glistening in the sunshine, Gretchen might have missed seeing them.

"Oh, Mr.—" Even after these many days of traveling with the man, Gretchen suddenly realized she did not know his name. But then, she had been so absorbed with her own situation, she had not gotten to know any of the passengers either.

"Cable, ma'am. No mister—just plain Cable."

Barely aware he had spoken, Gretchen shot a look over her shoulder toward the delicate-looking creatures as the coach flew past. "How beautiful they are."

"Yes'm," the driver called out over the horses' pounding hooves and the clatter of harnesses. "No matter how many times I make this here trip, I never git tared a lookin'. God's country, I call it. Shame we gotta tear it up like we do." He gestured to the ribbon of road whipping up toward the dark line of mountains ahead of them.

"Are those the Laramies you told me about?" Bonnet strings mingling with a few errant strands of Gretchen's hair flew up to tickle her face.

"Yes'm."

"Do we have to cross them to get to Cheyenne?"

He answered her with a dip of his head. " 'Fraid so. Just you wait, though. That Cheyenne Pass is just 'bout the purtiest stretch a road in all the Wyomin' Territory." Scratchy and rough, Cable's voice sounded like sand blowing through a rusted-out can, but his tone gave more than a note of warmth to his words. He flicked the reins, slapping the leather straps against the slowing horses' rumps. "Geeyup there now."

"Is it safe?" Gretchen eyed the mountains growing larger in size by the minute. Piled one atop the other, foothills clothed in shades of living green butted against forbidding black peaks. Dark as pitch, they jutted up straight out of the ground.

She braced herself against the teeth-jarring ride, growing rougher with the slight incline. She tugged at the green redingote jacket of her new traveling costume, securing it down over her blouse to her waist.

Ever watchful, Cable turned his attention back to her. "Didn't the stationmaster back at Laramie City ask ya if'n ya wanted to take the train into Cheyenne?"

"Yes."

"Didn't he tell ya this was a bit tougher goin'?"

"Yes, he did—"

"Well if'n ya was asceered, why didn't ya go that aways?"

"I'm not afraid. I just like to know what I'm getting myself into, that's all." She hoped she sounded composed and sure of herself, but the constant jostling made her voice pitch with an uncertain air.

"No need to work yerself up into a flurry of petticoats, ma'am." He flicked a glance down to the scarred old rifle lying across his lap. "Me an' my sweet Adele here, we can handle jist 'bout any kinda trouble."

"I'm not worried—really," she said, though in truth she felt much less confident of the driver's protective capabilities than he apparently did.

"Sure, ma'am, sure."

Gretchen looked out at the scenery sprawling before her and tried to relax. The sudden change from prairie to foothills overwhelmed her with beauty. As they came upon the narrow path that would see them through the mountains, she sucked in a breath.

She remembered the Sierras that she had called home these past four years. They had been a wondrous and majestic sight, but these ominous crags looming before her path sent a strange shudder through her being. It was almost as if something lay in waiting for her inside the rugged walls of earth and stone.

Along the edge of the evergreen forest, quaking aspens whispered a mournful welcome in a rustling murmur. Another sound, a lark's wing beats, added to the unfavorable mood.

She shivered. Her gaze darted to the golden-yellow blossoms of arnica dancing on either side of the road, then slid to the paler blooms of buttercups wriggling in the warm breeze wherever the tufts of bluegrass gave way.

She took a deep breath. This was silly. There was nothing out here to frighten her.

The stage road, hardly more now than two wagon-wheel ruts, took a steep upswing, causing the horses to pull at a slower pace. In the distance, cascading a higher wall, a shimmering waterfall spilled down into a pond barely visible through the thick forest crowded with pine trees.

"Coming into some purty country, folks." Cable banged his hand on the side of the coach. "Best take a gander afore we pass on through to Cheyenne."

Immediately, Gretchen heard the murmuring voices of her fellow passengers as they poked their heads out the windows below her.

"What'd I tell ya, ma'am?" Cable relaxed against the back of the seat, allowing the heavily breathing horses to continue at a more leisurely pace. His gaze swept up and down the steep sides of the pass, as if the land were a beautiful woman that he alone were allowed to cherish. "Ain't it jist the grandest sight ya ever seen?"

No less caught up in the tender manner with which the gruff man spoke than in nature's own beauty, Gretchen could only nod and smile. Reaching up, she untied her bonnet and pulled it down to her lap. She tilted her head back and closed her eyes, allowing herself a respite from the dusty trail they had left on the plains behind them. She breathed deep, filling her lungs with the spicy scent of wildflowers and the fresh fragrance of pine needles.

Sunshine beat down on her face and warmed the dry breeze feathering her cheeks. It felt wonderful. She felt wonderful. For the first time since Garret's trial and the news of his suicide, Gretchen experienced pure contentment, and tranquillity. She sighed.

"So, Miz Samuels," the driver's voice interrupted her repose. "You goin' to Iowa for business or pleasure?"

Gretchen opened her eyes and quirked a brow. She was not certain how to answer him—or even if she should.

"Beg pardon, ma'am. Didn't mean to step on yer personabilities and all. It's jist that I happen to notice ya tossin' away that weddin' ring a li'l ways back there, and well I . . ." He pressed his lips into a thin line and swallowed. "Well, I jist noticed's all."

Still uncertain as to how to answer the man, Gretchen remained silent. Embarrassed that he had observed her throwing away her ring, she shifted her gaze back to the scenery. How was she to justify what she had done? But then, why should she? It was none of the driver's business.

This Cable was certainly a nosy fellow.

With his free and easy manner, the man did not appear to be the lonely type. But with a job that kept him racing back and forth across the country, it was pretty likely that his passengers were about the closest thing he would ever have to friends.

Gretchen's resentment turned to pity. Still, it was not any of his business.

Obviously aware that he had stepped over his boundary, Cable allowed only another minute or two of uncomfortable silence to press between them before returning to his easygoing demeanor. He winked at her playfully. "If'n ya look real careful like, ya jist might git a li'l glimpse of some of that Black Hills's gold ever'body's scramblin' around to find."

"Gold!" Gretchen's eyes widened. She shot him a curious look. "But surely these aren't *those* Black Hills. You said they were the Laramies."

The bottom row of his stained teeth flashed beneath the fullness of his mustache, and he shrugged. "Well afore we got in 'em, they looked black to me."

Gretchen tilted her head to one side and studied him. Her lips spread into a small smile. "You're teasing me, aren't you?"

With an impish nod, his brows shot upward across his leathery forehead. "Yes'm. I s'ppose I was at that." He looked back to his team and shifted the lump of tobacco to the other side of his mouth. "Shore was nice to see you smile, though."

Apparently he was trying to ease the tension he had caused in her.

"Yer quite the picture of a handsome woman—if'n y'all pardon me fer sayin' so, Miz Samuels. And when you jist smiled, well it sure was a dazzlin' picture for this old man's eyes."

On in years as he was, Gretchen thought she caught sight of a blush flitter across his rugged features. Inwardly, she beamed. It had been a long time since anyone had paid her such a compliment.

"Thank you, Cable."

He shrugged. "Jist tellin' it like I see—"

A gunshot blast splintered the air.

"What in hell?" Brows furrowed, Cable turned around.

Gretchen followed his stare.

Bolting down from the slopes behind, riders charged toward them.

Painted faces—men clad in buckskin—terrifying war whoops—all registered at once.

"Damnation!" Cable's eyes widened. His attention darted back to the team. Body taut, he leaned low and cracked the reins. "Geeyup! H'ya!"

The stage jerked into flight.

Pitched into the floorboard, Gretchen scrabbled to right herself.

"Stay down!" Cable yelled.

Inside the coach, voices echoed fear.

Knocked from side to side, Gretchen managed to rise up enough to tuck herself into a protective ball. She peeked around the side of the stage for another look at the attackers. Wood split near her hand. She ducked down with a scream.

Why were Indians attacking them?

No time to think—little time to act—she braced her feet against the bottom of the seat and spun around. Gripping the dash with one hand, she grabbed the barrel of Cable's rifle.

His eyes met hers. He nodded his understanding.

Gunshots rang out from the coach below. Bullets whizzed past. Others pinged into the body of the stage.

Fear spurred Gretchen into action. Up on her knees, she shoved the rifle lever forward. She rammed the stock into her shoulder, steadied the barrel against a metal seam of the coach, prayed for skill, hoped more for luck, and squeezed the trigger.

She did not even check her aim before she repeated the action. Over and over, she fired the weapon. She did not see—did not care—if she had killed. She only knew she had to fight if she wanted stay alive.

Dust choked her lungs. Dirt flew into her eyes. The rifle jammed. Something hit her back.

Cable slumped over.

"Oh, God!"

He opened pain-filled eyes, then grimaced. "Grab the reins!"

"But you're—"

He pushed against her with his good arm and reached for the lines. But the jostling of the stage threw him off balance. He fell back.

Blood smeared Gretchen's sleeve.

"We gotta git them leads," Cable shouted.

Gretchen nodded. Her attention flew to the leather straps falling farther from reach with each pound of the horses' hoofbeats. She had to get to them. Dropping the useless weapon, she hefted Cable to a half-sitting position, then grabbed the dash and leaned forward.

Wide-eyed, she stared down at the ground passing in a dusty blur beneath her. She swallowed. Clods of dirt kicked up by the animals stung her hands and face. She squinted. Stretching out her arm, she reached for one of the lines. It lay just out of her grasp.

The coach bounced. The line vaulted away.

Despite the dash digging into her stomach, Gretchen pressed herself farther out. She had to try again. She felt a tug on her skirt and looked back.

With his uninjured hand, Cable held her secured by the hem of her skirt.

Gretchen returned her attention to the lines.

A rider thundered up beside the stage.

Spurred by fear, Gretchen spread her fingers and lunged farther out.

Cable's hold broke.

Gretchen pitched forward. A scream tore from her lungs. She grabbed the dash with one hand, the underside of the footrest with the other. She could not get up. She could only hold on and pray.

Beneath the stage, she could see the ground spread out only a few feet to one side of the wheels, then only sky. They were dangerously close to a ledge. Terror unlike any she had ever felt before ripped through her soul.

She screamed again. "He-lp me! H-elp!" The words fell useless in the roar of gunplay. She struggled again, gained some leverage, and swung up onto her knees.

Cable had disappeared.

She looked back at the attackers, then wheeled forward again. The coach ricocheted off a mound of rocks and tipped up on two wheels. The leads to the team snapped free from the tongue of the stage. Too late, Gretchen saw the edge coming nearer. She froze. She could not jump free—could not move. Half-tucked under the seat, all she could do was hold on . . . and scream.

On a high shelf of rock, perched atop his pinto, Elk Dreamer watched the chaotic scene below with curious eyes. He stretched tall on his mount and stared down at the stagecoach falling away from sight. Never before had he witnessed such a traitorous and sense-less disgrace committed by one white on another.

"Why do these men do this act of dishonor?" Elk Dreamer's closest friend, Buffalo Calf, gestured toward the riders below with a sharp upswing of his chin. "They bring shame to their own people."

"Not theirs—ours." Elk Dreamer did not have to look at Buffalo Calf to know the man thought he was angry. "See how they dress?"

Buffalo Calf grunted.

"You think they do not have purpose in this?"

Elk Dreamer's friend shrugged. "I find no purpose in most of what the white-eye does." He jerked back on the rope fashioned into a bridle, reining his horse away from the cliff. "I do not care what purpose they have. Let them kill each other—it will save me the trouble."

"Maybe it would be better if you did." Elk Dreamer studied the whites in buckskin. From this distance he could not be certain, but he thought he recognized the horses ridden by two of the men that had attacked the stage.

If he was right, they were miners looking for the yellow iron found in most of the mountain ranges in Sioux Territory. He had encountered their unwel-comed presence on a couple of occasions these past few months. He knew, too, of the hatred they felt for all Indians.

Buffalo Calf rejoined him. Neither spoke as they continued to watch.

The men below them hesitated on the ledge from where the wagon had just plunged.

Someone yelled for help.

All heads turned toward a pine some distance back down the stage trail.

Elk Dreamer squinted against the sun's glare.

Barely visible against the landscape, a man lay hollering in obvious pain.

At once, the attackers lifted their rifles and tore out in his direction. Their unchallenged cries of battle shattered the momentary quiet.

Swallowing back a mixture of rage and, strangely enough, a kind of pity for the innocent travelers, Elk Dreamer shook his head.

Somewhere below, a man screamed in agony.

Carried on the chinook, the strong scent of blood filled Elk Dreamer's senses. He narrowed his eyes, envisioning the undoubted deaths that were taking place beyond the rim.

He had been Gall's lieutenant beneath Sitting Bull for many years. He had been with him at the Little Big Horn and fought against Yellow Hair. He was a seasoned warrior, and he had seen the ride of the Death Horse trample many men. But that had been in battle—for honor.

There was no honor in this senseless slaughter. Yet if his suspicions were right, there was a reason.

The whites dressed in buckskin below were constantly trying to incite the soldiers into plaguing the mountains in search of the Sioux. The miners knew the Indians were hiding out, but alone they were too few against Elk Dreamer's people. The whites wanted to get rid of them so they could cut the yellow rock out of the earth without reprisal. They would do anything to see this accomplished. But as yet, the small band of Sioux had eluded the army. Surely this was only another of the miners' schemes.

If Elk Dreamer were right, he knew the soldiers at the many forts surrounding the mountains would not rest until they had sought revenge against this murderous act. Now nothing would stop them from finding and slaughtering every last woman and child in his group. They would not care if the Sioux were blameless. Where the Indians were concerned, the whites were like mad wasps with readied stingers.

Nostrils flaring, Elk Dreamer glared down to where he had last seen the enemy hiding behind Sioux clothing.

The hornet's nest had been shaken once again.

TWO

Lying at the bottom of the ravine, Gretchen struggled to rise, but fell back when a stab of pain sliced her head. She knew she was bleeding. She could feel the trickle of liquid heat seeping down from her hairline to her temple, but she smoothed her hand across her forehead just the same. Crimson covered the tips of her gloved fingers in a thick smear. It must be even worse than she'd thought.

She gasped, but the sound was muffled by another's scream. Her gaze flitted upward toward that sound. She could see nothing above the ledge from which the stage had fallen.

Someone moaned nearby.

She searched her surroundings. "Oh, my good Lord!" Her voice caught in her throat.

Scattered across the ground lay her fellow passengers and the remnants of the coach.

Another shriek, more terror-filled than the last, echoed down over the ridge.

Gretchen took a quick count of the bodies. Three men and a woman. They were all there. So who was being tortured? "No! Oh no!" Where was Cable? What had happened to him?

"Help me." A weak voice filtered through the recesses of her thoughts.

She looked up and met the pain-filled expression of the young gambler who had tried to coax her into conversation several times during their trip.

In his battered condition, he could barely move, but he managed to stretch out a bleeding hand toward her. "Help me," he whispered again.

Hoofbeats echoed from above.

Gretchen's mind whirled. They were coming back. The Indians were coming back to finish them off. Her gaze darted up to the ledge. Still, she could see no one. She looked back to the gambler. They had to hide. But where? She glanced at the stage only a couple of feet away.

Flipped up on one end, it had crashed into a huge pine. Some of the tree's limbs protruded through the windows. It was an obvious hiding place, but it was their only chance. Both she and the young man were too injured to manage much farther.

She pushed herself up. Pain tore through her left arm. She grabbed her elbow, but only for a second. She had no time to inspect it now. Using her remaining strength, she dragged herself to the gambler. "We've got to hide."

He peered up. "I can't," he murmured. "I think both of my legs're broken."

Gretchen's gaze shot down to his lower limbs. True to the man's words, his right shin bone protruded through his pant leg.

She grimaced. "You've got to try. They'll kill you if they find you."

Squeezing his eyes closed, he nodded. He reached for her hand.

She shook her head. "No. I think it's broken, too." She scooted closer. "Hold on around my waist."

He cut her a quizzical glance.

"Grab hold." Panic flooded Gretchen's being. They did not have time for such nonsense as proper formalities now. The Indians would be down on them in no time. "I can't do this alone. You've got to help."

He swallowed. "Where?" His entire body shuddered with the effort of the single word.

"The stage." Gretchen gestured toward the wreckage. "Now, come on," she grated between clenched teeth. She had not meant to sound so harsh, but her arm and head had begun to throb. If she did not move now, she was afraid she might black out. And if she fainted, there was no telling what the Indians might do to her.

Gripping the material of her skirt, the young man fought to hang onto her. But with every movement he groaned.

Gretchen could feel his agony, but she had neither the time nor the strength to fret over his pain. They had to hide themselves and fast. Digging her fingers into the earth, her injured arm held limp at her side, she half-crawled, half-dragged herself to the coach. Reaching the stage, she wriggled in through one of the windows.

Whoops filled with blood lust reached her ears. Oh, Lord. They were coming! She pulled herself inside, then sat up and tugged on the man's arm. "Come on. You've got to get in here." Her pulse hammered in her temples.

He glanced over his shoulder, then shook his head. "They're too close. I'll never make it."

Gretchen scowled. She would not leave him out in the open. More than likely they *would* be discovered, but at least inside they might have a chance. She gripped him by the wrist and yanked. "You've got to try."

He reached down with his free hand and, with great effort and obvious pain, retrieved an object from his boot. "Take this." He shoved something metal into her palm.

Gretchen stared at the derringer. What did he expect her to do with that? But she knew all too well.

He closed her hand over it, then squeezed his fingers around hers. "Don't let them take you."

Their gazes met.

His sad blue eyes showed no fear, yet Gretchen knew he was afraid—knew by the imploring manner with which he gripped her hand. The thunder of her own heartbeat drummed out the growing sound of approaching horsemen.

He released her and rolled away.

"No—don't!" She lunged out, but she could not reach him.

The mingled sounds of horses racing toward them and men's voices grappled with her attention. She pulled back and darted a look around the inside of the coach. Behind her, the other windows were blocked by shrubs and boulders. She could not escape that way. But if she could not get out through there, the Indians could not get inside by that means either. Still, if they knew she was there, they could get to her by the same entrance she had taken.

Male voices echoed louder.

Blood pumping wildly, Gretchen searched for a hiding place. She could hear them fumbling around the dead bodies. There was nowhere inside where she could not be found. What was she to do? She could not just sit and wait for them to discover her. She listened to their movements. All the while her gaze flitted around the interior, searching, probing, looking for—

What was that they were saying? Her breath caught in her throat. She suddenly realized she could understand them. They were speaking in English. English? Her eyes flew wide. She flattened herself against one of the upturned seats. They were not Indians at all, but white men.

"Hey, now. Would ja looky here?" A gruff voice called out above the others.'

Gretchen flinched. Had they found her? She clutched her hand to her stomach and knotted the material of her jacket in her grip. She cringed.

Someone groaned.

"This un's alive, too."

No—not her. They had found the young gambler.

"Finish him," someone else called out. "We can't leave any witnesses alive."

Gretchen swallowed. God in Heaven. What was she going to do? It would not be long before they found her, too.

She heard a sound—like rocks or dirt being thrown against the outer shell of the coach.

"Son of a—"

The young man yelled in pain.

"Damn it, Oren. Quit messing around. Just get it done with." This time it was another voice that leapt out from the pillaging noises.

"He threw sand in my—"

"Damn you! Do it or I'll do it to *you*."

Gretchen's heart felt as if it had just lodged in her throat. She felt sick to her stomach. What were they doing to the poor man?

She heard a brief scuffling.

The gambler screamed in anguish. Then, death-filled silence.

Gretchen clinched her eyes closed against an onslaught of tears. The young man was dead. She knew it. He had given his life for hers. But all in vain. She had only moments before they would find her as well.

Find her? Her thoughts whirled. That was inevitable. She had to save herself. But how? She gripped the small pistol tightly. No. That was not the answer. She might get one of them, two if she were lucky, but she had no way of knowing how many there were out there.

She had to do something else. Oh, God. Her mind tortured her with scenes of what was sure to happen. She was going to die.

An idea sparked. Maybe not. It was not much of a plan, but it was all she had. Quietly as she could, she lay down and inched her head out through the bottom window, shrouded with bushes. It was hard to push through the thick shrubbery without being heard, but the bustling of the men's activities was enough to conceal any noises she made.

Wedging herself between a large boulder and the body of the coach, she winced as another shard of pain sliced through her forearm. She forced her breathing to a shuddering whisper and waited, the gun clutched tightly in her palm. She would have to play dead. But would it be enough?

Footsteps echoed nearer, and clinking—hollow and metal—like spurs or a buckle.

From her position, she could just see the ground through the opposite window. It would not be long now. She swallowed.

Legs clad in buckskin, feet covered in dusty rubber boots, suddenly appeared.

Gretchen sent a small prayer of hope heavenward.

A man squatted down.

She tried to see him clearly, but the shrubs concealed his face.

"There's another un in here." It was the same man who had spoken first. "This un's a woman."

"She dead?"

"Don't know. Looks like it. Least ways she ain't movin' none."

Another man knelt down beside the first. He leaned inside.

Looking through slitted lids, Gretchen could see his face no better.

He yanked on one of her feet.

She took a deep slow breath, hoping the action would secure her tighter in place. Her heart slammed against her chest. Her body slipped closer to them. They had her.

Something scraped the back of her hand. Though she was unable to see what it was, she let go of the derringer and grabbed what she thought was the scratchy foliage of a bush. It held her fast.

"Ya ain't gonna get her outta there, Palmer." The gruff man chuckled. "She's slapped in there tighter'n a slab a ham b'tween bread."

"Well, we can't take any chances."

A long pause ensued.

"Make sure." The second attacker moved from view.

"Sure thing." The first man's hand moved to the gun in his holster.

A cold shudder rippled through Gretchen's soul. Despite her efforts, she was still going to be killed. Releasing the branch, she searched blindly for the gun. At least she would get this one. She felt the handle, picked it up—

A gun blasted. White-hot pain bit into her side. She had been shot. Her body went limp. "God be merciful." She barely heard her own voice. Then, all faded to darkness.

Careful to conceal their movements, Elk Dreamer and Buffalo Calf followed the white men down as far as the edge of the cliff. There was no use in examining the man who had been thrown from the stage. They had heard his screams and knew there was no hope for him. The white savages had obviously tortured and then killed him.

"Let us leave from here before they see us." Buffalo Calf pointed to the catch of prairie dogs hanging from a thong around his horse's neck before lifting a frown toward the hideous scene below. "Six little yappers make a poor feast for so many at camp."

Elk Dreamer remained indifferent to his friend. He was held entranced by the actions of the whites. He had seen evidence of taking scalps from Indian women—but from their own kind? How could they find *any* honor in this?

He thought of his sister, Snow Dancer, and envisioned the torture she had endured under the blade of another white dog such as these, two winters past. His eyes narrowed. Hatred coursed through the entire length of his body. He had ridden up in time to save her life, but not before the man had managed to cut into her throat.

"Why do you make an angry face?" Buffalo Calf leaned into Elk Dreamer's line of vision. "They are nothing to us. Let them kill each other. It will save us the trouble later." Turning a fierce scowl in the direction of the whites, he clutched his tomahawk tighter.

"It does not matter to you that this will bring trouble for our people?" Elk Dreamer kept his gaze fixed below, yet he would have his friend understand that this attack would most likely place them in a dire situation.

"Until we reach the Canadas and are again united with the others, we must walk carefully within the bounds of danger. The people know this—they have known from the beginning. Why does this single matter put us at greater risk now?"

Elk Dreamer turned a sidelong look toward his friend. At an age of twenty winters, Buffalo Calf was not so much younger than Elk Dreamer. One would have thought the warrior would have learned to see with wiser eyes after such a span of time. But now, as in the past, Buffalo Calf allowed only the fiery passion of his heart to rule his thoughts.

"Why do we sit here? I grow weary of watching these dogs fight over the bones of their dead." He made as if to leave, but when Elk Dreamer remained squatting behind the boulders where they had been watching, the younger man turned back. He touched his friend's arm. "Elk Dreamer—"

"They are leaving."

Buffalo Calf hunkered down beside him. "Good. Now we can finish our hunt." He hesitated a moment, then turned away again.

When the last of the white men had mounted their horses and ridden off, Elk Dreamer rose. He scanned the area littered with the dead. Strange. Where was the woman that had ridden beside the driver when the coach was attacked? He had forgotten about seeing her until now.

He took a step toward the ledge.

"Where do you go now?" Buffalo Calf asked, his tone impatient.

"I do not see the woman with yellow hair."

"What woman?"

Elk Dreamer did not answer his friend. Curiosity prompting his actions, he traversed the slope to the floor of the ravine. He kept a watchful eye on the whites' withdrawal. Even though they had moved off a considerable distance, they could return at any moment and catch him off guard. At the bottom, he looked around.

"Why do you do this?" Buffalo Calf slid down beside him.

With a start, Elk Dreamer glared at his friend. He had not expected the man to follow him. "I do not see the woman."

Buffalo Calf searched the lifeless bodies lying around them. "There." He gestured toward a feminine form.

Together they moved nearer.

Elk Dreamer shook his head. He looked down at the patch of brown hair that still remained on the woman's head. "She does not have yellow hair."

Buffalo Calf shrugged. "She is a woman. You are wrong about the color."

Elk Dreamer felt a small pang of regret for the loss of the woman's life. Since he had gone on his first vision quest at the age of fourteen winters, he had been given the power of an Elk Medicine Man. It was his duty to protect the weak, the children, and the women. He had not been able to help this one. She had died a cruel and senseless death. And though he would not show it, he mourned for her. In his mind, he asked the Great Spirit to help her find the path to her ancestors.

"I do not see another woman." Buffalo Calf stepped over a young man dressed in finely woven cloth, then peered behind the overturned coach. "She is the only one."

"No. There is another." Elk Dreamer continued to scan the area. "I saw her."

"Maybe she is with the driver." Buffalo Calf

motioned back the way they had come. He began to move up the hillside. Obviously he cared little to continue the search. "She is dead, too."

Elk Dreamer strode closer to the man lying next to the stage. He squatted down.

Clumps of dirt and grass caked the toes of the man's boots.

Examining the body more closely, he saw that a bone poked through one of the man's leg coverings. He touched it to make sure. Puzzled, he felt the other limb and discovered that it, too, was broken. Soil and turf coated his clothing as well.

Elk Dreamer peered around more closely.

Tracks on the ground marked a path to the coach.

He leaned around and looked inside. The shift from light to dark affected his vision. He squinted, then bent inside and looked through one of the openings. He saw a foot—no, two. He touched one. It did not move.

As his eyes began to focus in the dim light, the fullness of a woman's dress came into view. This had to be the woman with the yellow hair. He tugged on her ankles. She did not budge.

He reached up higher, grabbed her above the knees, and pulled. He gained a small measure of space.

"What do you find?" Buffalo Calf knelt down and looked inside the coach.

"The yellow-hair." Elk Dreamer yanked harder.

His expression sour, Buffalo Calf rose up on one knee. "She is dead. Leave her."

Elk Dreamer ignored his friend. It had become an obsession. He had to see the woman's face. He did not know why, and did not care. He only knew that something drew him to bring her out into the light.

Her backside thumped onto the ground when she passed through the window. She moaned.

Elk Dreamer pulled back. He looked at his friend.

Buffalo Calf's brows shot upward.

Glancing back, Elk Dreamer clutched the woman above the hips and hauled her outside.

The instant sunlight hit her face, the woman's eyes fluttered open. She groaned a little louder. Blood and dirt streaked her skin from her forehead down to her cheek. "Please . . ." She spoke with the unnatural sound of the white man's words.

Buffalo Calf and Elk Dreamer exchanged puzzled stares. They looked back at the woman.

Feeling something warm and sticky on his hand, Elk Dreamer glanced down. It, too, was stained with red.

The woman screamed.

Elk Dreamer flinched.

"Get away! Get away!" Like lightning giving birth to thunder, she shrieked at them, flailing at their faces with her legs. She scooted her back up to the coach. She stared at them, the venom of pure fear spitting from her eyes.

"Shh . . . shh." Elk Dreamer chose a sound he thought she might understand. It had been a long time since he had had occasion to use the white tongue he had learned from his sister. And now, he could not remember even one word that might console this woman. He held up his hands, hoping she would see he would not hurt her.

It only caused her to scream louder, attacking him with the same unintelligible words as before. She shook her head wildly, the long strands of her yellow hair whipping back and forth against the earth.

Elk Dreamer reached out for her. He had to calm her.

Her cries grew more desperate—more terrified. She shot a frantic stare between the two men.

Buffalo Calf pulled back from the reach of her feet. With his aggravation apparent, the younger man shook his head and sighed. He pointed first to his own head, then the woman's. "The yellow-hair is crazy." He tossed a glower at Elk Dreamer. "Hmph! The people will surely cheer us with happy voices when they see what great prize we bring back *this* fine day of hunting."

Elk Dreamer paid no attention to his friend's scorn. Not wanting to frighten the woman more, he remained silent, and backed away. He could not make her understand his words. She would not let him near her. Confused, he sat back on his haunches and rested his arms on his knees. So how *was* he going to comfort her?

THREE

Gretchen felt the wood from the coach digging into her back, and her side ached, but she ignored the pain. Her only concern was the two Indians crouched in front of her, staring at her. She remembered the gunshot. Her gaze flitted between the two of them. Her chest rose up and down with her rapid breathing. Why did they not just kill her and be done with it?

Glancing to the side, she saw the lifeless form of the gambler. Terror lodged in her throat. A two-inch gap of blood and tissue coursing the top of his head left no doubt as to what had happened to him. He had been scalped alive.

Erect in his posture, the man to her left followed her gaze. Turning back to her, he shook his head as if he were denying the deed.

Gretchen looked away, her stomach threatening to heave. How could anyone do such a thing? She remembered the derringer. What had become of it?

"*E-i-i-i.*" The Indian's expression held regret. He pointed to her head and side, then gestured to his hand. "*Wasicun kakis'niyapi?*" As he spoke, he waved toward the mountains.

Gretchen glanced to where he had motioned. What was it she was supposed to see? She could not understand him. There was nothing but trees and grassland.

The second Indian appeared a bit younger. Unlike the other one, his features were stoic and unyielding. He narrowed his eyes, then nodded toward her. "*Hinziwin bo-ton-ton.*" He moved closer.

"Stay back!" Gretchen pressed herself even harder against the coach. The action shot pain through her injured arm and side. She flinched.

"*Ahpe.*" The one to her left held a hand up to his companion. His gaze softened. Still squatting, he shuffled forward.

Again Gretchen stiffened. Was it her turn now? Would they do the same to her that they had done to the gambler and the others? She held her breath.

"*Ah-ah.*" He reached up to her forehead, stopped mid-action, then moved toward her again.

At the feel of his hand, Gretchen's pulse jumped. She knocked his hand away. "Don't touch me!" She tried to sound forceful, but she was shaking uncontrollably. The motion hurt her forearm. She grimaced.

"*Ah-ah,*" he repeated, his voice low and soothing. He brushed her brow with his fingers.

Again, she tried to push him away.

He clasped her wrist.

"Ouch! Let go!"

Firmly, yet gently, he held onto her arm until she stilled. He grasped the sleeve of her jacket and yanked the fabric, splitting it up the seam, then repeated the action to her blouse.

Gretchen gasped.

Running a knowing hand up the length of her forearm, he appeared to be searching for the injury. Why should he do such a thing?

As if he had read her thoughts, he thumped his bare chest with his thumb. *"Pez'uta-wicas'a."*

Furrowing her brow, Gretchen shook her head. It seemed as though he were trying to comfort her, but she was not certain. What was he trying to tell her? She glanced down at his chest plate of quills and beads.

His shoulder-length hair gleamed russet-black in the sunlight. He cocked his head toward her and a small hoop made of a quill dangled out into view below two feathers at the back of his head. By his simple garb of breechcloth, buckskin leg coverings, and moccasins, it was evident that he was one of the many Plains Indians. But which tribe? Yet it made no difference. Gretchen could only speak Maidu and Paiute. How would she communicate with him?

He stood, pulling Gretchen up with him.

The sudden action startled her. Pain shot through her side.

He looked down to where blood had soaked through her dress. His features contorted into an angry scowl. *"Kakis'niyapi!"* He repeated his earlier words.

"I've been shot." Gretchen knew he did not understand her, but he appeared to be puzzled by her wound, and this angered her. He acted as though he had no idea what had happened to her. She held herself rigid in his grasp. "Which one of you did this to me?"

She knew how much Indians admired fearlessness, and though frightened beyond anything she had ever known, she held firm. She glared at each of them in turn. But in searching both with a quick look, she saw that neither had a gun.

Somewhere in the back of her mind, she remembered hearing men speaking in— That's right. It had been English. Her attackers had been white men. She looked back at the two Indians before her. So who were they? And what did they want of her?

The younger man stood. He leaned nearer. Apparently he wished to inspect her side as well.

The Indian holding her suddenly released her.

She buckled.

He grabbed her again, supporting her around the waist. Clasping the hilt of his knife, he whipped it up, then sliced the material sticking to her wound.

Gretchen recoiled. "Stop that!"

He cut through the waist-band of her skirt and shoved up the hem of her blouse. He bent down.

With the material now loose, her heavy skirt fell silently to the ground. "Oh, no! You can't mean to—" She slapped at him, but her hand only slipped across the top of his head.

He jumped. His black eyes spit fire.

"Let go! Let go!" He had another thing coming if he thought he was going to be able to take advantage of *this* white woman. She fought him with every ounce of strength she had left. *She* was not as helpless as he might think. He would *not* take her. She kicked his shin and dug her nails into the flesh of his arms.

"*Oowes'ica*." He shook her.

Gretchen struggled harder. She would not submit. "No! Let me go!"

A gunshot blasted. A bullet tore into the stage to the side of them.

Gretchen blanched. She sucked in a breath.

Ducking down, the Indians yanked her to the ground with them. They looked up to the ledge.

She followed their stares.

Another blast sounded. A pale wisp of white rose into the air.

"I'll save ya, Miz Samuels." The man's voice boomed loud but shaky.

Gretchen's eyes flew wide. Cable? She searched the spot where she had seen the smoke. Barely visible behind a mound of boulders, a head bobbed into view. "Cable," she shouted.

She jerked free from her captors. She lunged upward. Someone grabbed her foot. She hit the ground. Pain shot through her body. One of the Indians pounced atop her. Kicking and fighting, she managed to roll over.

The man who had been holding her earlier imprisoned her with his full weight. He shouted something, but she could not hear his words.

Forgetting her injuries, she flailed wildly. She had to get free. Cable was still alive. There was still a chance—a hope of escape.

Straddling her hips, the big man raised his fist. His eyes burned into hers.

Fear stormed her brain. She screamed. The solid force of his hand struck her jaw . . . then nothing.

"Leave her!" Buffalo Calf yelled. "The man will kill you." He pointed up to where the white man continued to fire down on them.

Grabbing the unconscious woman under her arms, Elk Dreamer dragged her back to where the coach sheltered them. He did not want to hit her, but he could not get her back to safety any other way.

"Let her go!" a gruff voice called down to them.

Elk Dreamer laid the woman down beside him. He peered out from the side of the stage. What was it the man had shouted? He obviously knew this woman and thought she was in danger. "Buffalo Calf. Go behind the coach and make your way up to the ledge from the side. I will hold his attention here."

The younger man gripped his tomahawk and nodded.

After his friend had successfully slipped around the stage, Elk Dreamer called out to the man above. "The woman is hurt. She needs help." Though he knew the man would probably not understand his words, he waited for a reply. He had to keep the man's focus on the bottom of the ravine. "Do you not hear me, white man?"

Still, no answer.

He peeked over the top of the coach.

Buffalo Calf had only managed to get halfway up.

Elk Dreamer hesitated another moment. He could feel the sweat trickling down his back. Neither he nor

Buffalo Calf had their rifles. They had both opted for their bows and throwing axes, wanting to know this day the thrill of hunting in the ways of the old ones. Elk Dreamer shook his head. What he would not give now to have brought the rifles instead.

He scanned the horizon.

Buffalo Calf was near the top of the ledge. If his friend could not overpower the white man, they both would most likely be killed. And what if this one were not alone? What if the white man were part of the group who had attacked these people? They would not stand a chance. He sought out the heavens. It was a good day to die. Still . . .

He called out again. "Hear me, white man."

"Elk Dreamer!" The sound of his name echoed across the open ground.

He looked out and around the coach.

Buffalo Calf stood where the shooter had been only moments ago. He waved his arms. "Come."

Glancing down at the woman, Elk Dreamer held silent. What had happened?

"Elk Dreamer, come. The white dog runs away."

Even from this distance, Elk Dreamer could see Buffalo Calf puff out his chest as if he were the great force behind the white man's sudden retreat. Yet why did the man run off? And where had he gone?

Standing over the woman, Elk Dreamer scanned the terrain. No one. He knew the man had been scalped like the others. The only difference being that the driver had managed to live through it. Elk Dreamer shook his head. He could not help but feel a little remorse for the man. Without help, how long would he last in his condition?

He glanced down at the yellow-hair. What was he supposed to do with her? He could not leave the woman to die, and he could not tend to her wounds here. Making a quick decision, he shot a wary glance in his friend's direction. He would have to take her back to their camp with them. It was risky, but he had no other choice. He stepped out from behind the stage. "Buffalo Calf." He motioned for the man to come down. "Bring the horses."

When Buffalo Calf returned, Elk Dreamer mounted. Holding the white woman across his lap, he was careful to maneuver his animal so that she would not be jostled unnecessarily. It was only a short distance to his people's camp, but it was still a dangerous route along which to be taking an injured person on horseback.

He stroked the woman's face with a tender gaze.

Though slender in stature, her cheeks were plump, with a light speckling of tiny spots trailing across her nose like those found on the eggs of a meadowlark. Her features relaxed, her pale lips parted into a sulky pout. Those of her own race might call her a pretty woman.

Elk Dreamer cocked a brow. No, she was not hard to look upon, true. But pretty? He allowed his gaze a leisurely sweep down her body before returning his eyes to her face. He felt the firm tone of her frame. Balanced. Yes, balanced—perhaps even graceful in her appearance. He nodded in silent approval. It was a good description.

"The people will not smile on this deed, Elk Dreamer." Buffalo Calf pulled up beside him. He frowned down at the woman. "Why do you bring her? It will only make trouble."

He thought of the many wolves and mountain cats that hunted the land. "Would you have me leave her to be eaten by mountain dogs or tuft-ears?" Elk Dreamer could not believe his friend could be so unfeeling. The woman was an innocent in all of this—even if she was their enemy.

"The soldiers will come looking for her. They will find us."

"For two winters we have been hiding in these mountains. They have not found us yet."

Buffalo Calf's glower deepened. "We have never taken one of theirs before. This yellow-hair will bring much trouble—bad memories—I know." He gestured to her with a wave of his hand. "Who among us will care for her? Who will take her to their lodge?"

Elk Dreamer hesitated a moment. He had not considered this. "We will take her to my tipi. Snow Dancer will see to the woman's needs."

Buffalo Calf stiffened. "I do not think this thing you ask will sit well with your sister."

"I have made the decision, Buffalo Calf. *I* am Gall's lieutenant. Upon his return, you may call a meeting of the leaders. You may speak your words to them. But for now . . . it is *I* who will determine her fate."

Cresting a rise of hills overlooking a small river basin, he peered down at the thicket of trees hiding his people's camp. Buffalo Calf held much truth in his words. Bringing the white woman into their band would cause much talk—most would be angry. But as Elk Dreamer saw it, he had no other choice. He would not leave the woman to die in the wilds.

He looked back at his friend, stressing his earlier command with a dip of his head. "For now, we take the woman to camp."

FOUR

When Gretchen opened her eyes, she saw that she had been transported into a world she did not recognize. Frightened, she scanned the strange interior. A small fire crackled nearby, and poles supporting the hide-canvas walls of the dwelling reached toward the sky. Twilight poured in through the hole where the beams came together.

Her stare widened. She was inside an Indian lodge. How had this happened? She did not remember—Suddenly, she did. She touched the aching spot in her jaw. Now she remembered—only too vividly.

The attack on the stage, the gambler, the white men, the Indians and Cable—everything—especially the Indian that had hit her. Anger flooded her senses. She jerked herself up to a half-sitting position, but sharp pains to her ribs and head forced her back to the ground. She groaned.

Her entire body felt as though she had been bashed and battered by a horde with clubs. Her memory flicked back to a time not too long ago when she had witnessed a close friend forced to run through a Paiute gauntlet. She shuddered. She was certain after what she had just endured that she knew how he had felt.

Another shard of pain bolted through her temple. Closing her eyes, she massaged the spot with her fingers. "God in Heaven. Let this be a dream . . . a very bad dream," she murmured.

Praying with all her might, she lifted a hopeful gaze. Suddenly aware of the bare skin of her arm, her eyes flew wide. But even before she looked beneath the fur covering her body, she knew she was naked.

She raised the pelt. An ungodly smell assailed her senses. Her side had been tended with some kind of odious salve and bandaged with raw vegetation. She squeezed her eyes closed. "Lord, no."

The dark visage of the Indian man loomed behind her eyelids. What had he done to her?

A light breeze rustled the tanned walls of the lodge. Gretchen sensed a presence. Startled, she looked up.

Standing just inside the tipi, a young woman tilted her head and squinted.

Gretchen drew taut.

The Indian woman lifted her chin. She peered silently down at Gretchen, her narrow stare displaying instant disdain.

Why? It was Gretchen who had been taken prisoner.

Silently, the woman moved toward the fire. After

pouring into an earthenware cup something that had been brewing next to the flames, she came to kneel next to Gretchen. She held out the mug.

Wary, Gretchen looked at the concoction. She wrinkled her nose at the unpleasant odor. Lifting an indignant gaze, she stared openly. Did the woman truly expect her just to accept the liquid and drink it without question?

Above one of her crisp brown eyes, the woman shot a brow upward. She watched Gretchen for a long moment, her harsh expression sharpening to a glare.

More than a little startled, Gretchen tensed. She caught herself. Then, mirroring the woman's posture, she held herself rigid. Disturbed as she was, she would not be bullied. Narrowing her eyes, she returned the woman's stare.

Apparently surprised, the Indian shifted, causing a cascade of hip-length hair to spill forward over one shoulder. Black in color, its only flaw was the unusual birthmark of a single lock of pure white running from her scalp to the ends.

The woman's features appeared to soften—but only a little. She glanced down at the cup, then back at Gretchen before lifting the corners of her mouth into a strained smile. She nodded. She was obviously determined that Gretchen would drink the potion—if not by force, then by complaisance.

Hesitating, Gretchen tried to read into the woman's reasoning. Surely the brew would not be toxic. Why would she be taken in and cared for by these people if they meant to see her harmed? She lifted her hand, but the effort shot a sharp pain through her side. She winced.

With an exasperated glower, the woman groaned. It was the first vocalized sound she had made since her entry. At once, she clasped the back of Gretchen's head and shoved the earthenware to her mouth.

It bruised Gretchen's lip. She grabbed the bottom of the cup. Overpowered, she swallowed a gulp. The green liquid tasted even worse than it smelled. Coughing, she knocked the mug to the ground and grimaced, then lifted a contemptuous look at the Indian.

Reflecting the woman's menacing expression, Gretchen held onto every ounce of courage she could muster. Her heart drummed against her chest. She recalled the incident with the Indian men back at the coach, and how roughly they had treated her. But this woman was even more severe. Maybe she *was* trying to kill Gretchen after all. But why?

"Wahinhan Wacipi!" a man shouted from the only opening in the lodge.

Gretchen flinched. Her gaze flew toward the sound.

The same man that had hit her by the stage earlier stood glaring at the Indian woman.

Gretchen's stare riveted to him. So puzzled by the young woman's harshness, she had momentarily forgotten her situation. Now, with the intrusion of this man, her plight rushed in on her again.

"Hiyu wo." He motioned the woman with a brusque wave to come to him. The man's regal manner commanded attention.

The woman jumped to her feet. In one quick movement, she hurried to stand in front of him, her head slightly bowed.

Staring at the two of them, Gretchen hugged the furs tighter to her chest.

At once, the woman began making strange gestures.

The man nodded. Every now and then his large black eyes slipped past the woman to bear down on Gretchen. Slightly sinister, his features were softened by a sensual mouth and pronounced dimples, though he did not smile.

Gretchen's nerves jittered just below her skin. What were they talking about? Her, most likely. Then, another movement caught her attention. She peered lower to where a small child, of about two, peeked around from behind the man's legs. Where had he come from? Had he been with the man all along?

Gaping at her beneath a thick mop of dark curls, the toddler held tightly clutched in a pudgy hand a fistful of fringe on the Indian man's leggings.

One of Gretchen's many regrets from her marriage was that she had never had a child. Garret had not wanted any. He did not like them. She smiled at the boy.

He did not respond.

She tilted her head and offered him a playful pout.

One tiny thumb plugging his mouth, the corners of his lips slowly turned upward.

Gretchen grinned. One small victory.

With a shy expression, he ducked behind the man's legs.

"Is'tahota." The man looked down. His tone held a scornful edge, yet his expression appeared gentle. He cut Gretchen a quizzical look, then returned his gaze to the boy. He motioned toward the opening. "Iyaya unci."

Staring up at him, the child seemed upset. He obviously did not want to do as the man had instructed.

"*Is'tahota.*" Towering above him, the Indian grasped the toddler's shoulders, turned him toward the exit, then urged him forward with a light swat. He watched the boy leave before turning his attention back to the woman standing next to him.

His gentle but firm handling of the baby surprised and intrigued Gretchen. At least these people were compassionate with their children. Shifting her position ever so slightly, she studied the couple engaged in conversation again.

For what seemed like an endless amount of time, the two remained entrenched in their own communication, though only the man actually spoke. The woman merely made more of the hand signals.

Growing more curious by the minute, Gretchen continued to watch them. Intent on discovering the topic of their discussion, she strained to hear their words, though she did not know why. She could not understand anything they said. Yet somewhere in the back of her mind, something in the woman's movements did trigger another memory.

Of course! She blinked with the realization. She had seen both the Maidu and Paiute use such simple signals to communicate with other tribes who did not speak the same language.

The man spoke again.

The woman brushed a finger across her brow, then pointed back at Gretchen.

White man. Gretchen had seen that sign often enough. They *were* talking about her. But just exactly what they were saying she could not guess.

The man's voice grew angry.

The woman's signing became hostile.

Apparently lost in the heat of their own argument, the two turned their complete attention on each other.

With a heavy groan, Gretchen fell back to the ground. She felt a sudden rush of self-pity. "Perfect. Now the whole world's forgotten about me." She was not sure if that was good or bad—but somehow it seemed to make her situation more frustrating. She sighed.

The small interior became deadly silent. She froze. What now? She looked at the couple.

They returned her stare.

The man whispered something to his companion.

She replied with another gesture.

Cutting his gaze back to Gretchen, he grunted. Then, with a curt dip of his head, he said one last word and brushed past the woman. With three easy strides, he walked over to where Gretchen lay.

Their eyes met.

Gretchen shivered beneath his perusal. What did he want?

He squatted next to her. "We no forget."

Stunned, Gretchen carefully raised herself back up on her elbow. "You speak English? You can understand me?" Her gaze flitted between the man and the Indian woman.

"Small bit." He pointed to the woman, then turned his attention back to Gretchen. He reached out and touched her forehead. "Snow Dancer know more."

Gretchen jerked away.

He halted in mid-action. His gaze reached into hers.

"*Hau.*" He lifted his brows as if asking for her permission, yet he examined her wound, his obvious intent, without further hesitation.

Again she glanced at the Indian woman, hoping for—what? She did not know. But if this Snow Dancer really did know English, perhaps she could— No. Gretchen's hopes died. The woman could not speak. Besides. She appeared to view Gretchen with nothing more than distrust and hatred.

The man, too, peered over his shoulder toward Snow Dancer.

She gestured something to him.

He nodded. Touching his chest, he looked back at Gretchen. "*Pez'uta-wicas'a.*"

Though it shook uncontrollably, Gretchen found her voice. "What?"

"*Pez'uta-wicas'a.* I medicine man."

"You're a medicine man?" She was surprised by this information.

He nodded, then placed his open palm against his chest. "*Hanble Hehaka.*"

Gretchen frowned. As if it would help her understand better, she leaned forward. "What?"

He repeated the words.

She shook her head. "I don't under—"

The woman stamped her foot, drawing both Gretchen and the man's attention. She waved her hands furiously.

The man stilled her efforts with a stern look, before turning back to his patient. "*Hehaka.*" He looked away as if determining his next words. Like horns, he raised his fingers to each side of his head. "*Hehaka . . . Wapiti?*"

Gretchen had heard that word used by her Paiute friends. "Deer—Elk?"

He nodded. "I am Elk—" He hesitated. Closing his eyes a moment, he tilted his head as if in sleep. "Dream-er."

"Elk Dreamer." Though Gretchen thought the name to be quite charming, she did not want to appear too impressed. She still had no idea where she stood with these people, or why they had brought her into their camp. What if they *had* taken her hostage? But for what purpose? She could not allow herself to be too taken in by this man's sudden friendliness.

"Who you?" The man's voice jumped out at her.

He wanted to know her name? She quirked a quizzical brow. Still, no sense inciting trouble. She could try to be a little congenial, too. Anything to keep things on the friendly side. "Gretchen Samuels."

Like matching bookends, both Elk Dreamer and the woman scowled. Apparently, neither held much appreciation for Gretchen's name.

She thought of her Paiute name. Maybe that would be better. "Moon Dove." She glanced at each of them in turn. *"Muha Ihovi."*

"Winnemucca!" Obviously shocked, Elk Dreamer cut his companion a puzzled look. *"Coo-yu-ee Pah?"*

Gretchen could not believe her good fortune. This man knew of Chief Winnemucca. What else had he said? The forgotten words came back to her. "Fish-Eaters—yes!" She nodded. How could she have been so lucky as to stumble across another people who knew Paiute? "I'm Moon Dove," she repeated in the foreign tongue.

The man shook his head. "I not speak *Coo-yu-ee Pah.*

I only hear." He pointed to the west, then frowned at her. "You are of the Fish-Eaters?"

Happy to be making at least a little progress in communication, Gretchen smiled and nodded.

"*Hoh.*" He pointed down at Gretchen's wound. Then lifting the pelt, he pulled away the poultice and touched her side.

She flinched.

"*Oowes'ica.*"

Gretchen stared at him. They were still painfully lacking in their communication skills. Not knowing what he had said, she could only offer him an uneasy smile. And, too, the fact that he was a man—a stranger—boldly tending her like this, made her even more uncomfortable. She kept a modest arm held tightly atop the fur blanket, shielding as much of her body from his view as possible. "It only hurts a little."

He looked at the Indian woman and nodded toward Gretchen.

She signed something else.

"Ah." He turned to Gretchen. "Bad wound."

"Mmm-hmm." Gretchen had to agree. For the first time, she saw where the bullet had grazed her side. It really was not severe, but just the sight of it on her own body was enough to cause ample discomfort. "If I only had my medical bag, I could take care of this myself."

Again, the man looked to the woman behind him. She answered with her hands.

"What is me-tic-le bag?"

How should she put this? She was not a doctor, but she did have some skills. "Like you, I am a . . ." She searched for just the right word. "Medicine woman."

"You? Medicine woman?" He appeared quite surprised.

She nodded. "And if you would only go back to the wreckage and find my bag—it's black with writing on it—like this." She flipped one corner of the fur hide over and drew an imprint of the name G. Samuels, M.D., with her fingernail.

Elk Dreamer frowned, then shook his head. "You not need black bag. I fix scratch good." He dropped the edge of the pelt.

Scratch? Some bedside manner. Could he not see that it *did* cause her discomfort? After all, she had been shot. And he was supposed to be some kind of doctor. Hmph. Gretchen eyed him carefully. And what about her nudity? He did not even appear the least bit taken aback. Why? She watched him command the woman away.

Snow Dancer cut Gretchen a hateful glare.

"*Wahinhan Wacipi! Iyaya!*" Elk Dreamer waved her outside.

In a huff, she took her departure, throwing open the flap and leaving it gaping to the night.

Once she had gone, Elk Dreamer turned his attention to something near the far wall of the tipi.

Gretchen tried to relax. Lying back, she peered up at the stars winking steadily brighter through the smoke hole. This *was* a nightmare. How was she going to get out of here? How had it all happened? Slowly her mind began to replay the events of the day. She shuddered. Good Lord in Heaven, what was she going to do?

A solitary tear blurred her vision. She blinked it away. Did *anyone* know where she was—or what had

happened to her? Cable. She remembered seeing him
on the ledge. Where was he now? Had he gone for
help? Had the Indians killed him? Seeking an answer,
she looked back to the medicine man.

He stood beside her.

She gasped. When had he moved back to her? Lost
in her own sorrow, she had not noticed.

The weightiness of his stare grew increasingly
unbearable. Sitting beside her, he stretched out one
leg, but kept the other bent. He rested an arm atop
his knee. Without warning, he scooped up a handful
of her hair. "*Hinziwin* not look *Coo-yu-ee Pah*."

"*Hinziwin*?"

He fingered the blond length. "Yellow-hair woman."

"Oh." Gretchen offered him a nervous chuckle,
though she was careful to pull her hair from his
grasp. "They adopted me."

"A-dop—" He scowled. "I not know this word." He
wet his lips with his tongue.

The single action made Gretchen all the more aware
of being alone with a strange man in a strange place.
With careful effort, she rolled onto her uninjured side,
securing a little extra space between herself and the
man. She smiled weakly. "You know." She nodded
toward the small fire. "They took me into their lodge—
like daughter—sister?"

"Ah. *Hunka*." His lips spread into a thin smile. "They
take you as relative . . . by choice."

"Yes—choice."

"I, too, a relative by choice." He puffed out his chest
and smiled. "Snow Dancer."

Puzzled, Gretchen glanced toward the yawning entrance. She had thought that the Indian was his wife.

"She is sister of woman I wished for wife." He appeared to be studying her reaction to his statement. Obviously, he was quite pleased with telling her this.

So he *was* married. "Where's your woman now?"

"*Wakan Tanka*." His voice flattened, yet his eyes lifted to the opening in the tipi. When Gretchen made no further comment, his expression sharpened. "It is good I take her as sister. She not alone now."

What did he mean by that? She wanted to ask, but thinking of her situation, she changed the subject instead. "Does this Snow Dancer hate *all* whites, or do *I* just bring out the hatred in her?"

"Hate-red?" He tipped his head to one side, causing a quill loop to dangle out into view.

Searching her memory, Gretchen fanned the fingers of one hand and drew them down her face over a scowl.

"Ah." He appeared to understand. "Snow Dancer no like white man." He paused as if waiting for her to remark. He took a deep breath, his body visibly tensing when he continued. "Two winters gone, white men attack Snow Dancer and her sister."

"Your woman?"

He dipped his head, then took a slow breath. "They cut Snow Dancer—here." He drew an invisible line across his throat with his finger. "She not talk now."

Gretchen shuddered. No wonder the woman hated her upon sight. And after what Gretchen had experienced with that band of fiendish white men today, she could well understand Snow Dancer's bitterness. "And your wife? She was Snow Dancer's sister?"

He nodded, though he appeared to be looking through her, instead of at her.

"Did they hurt her, too?"

Elk Dreamer's expression hardened. He pinned a stare on Gretchen. "They kill." His nostrils flared. His demeanor shifted from friendliness to hostility. Leaping to his full height, he towered over her. "White-eye are blind like snake that rattles. They see red skin and strike."

Fear tore through Gretchen's being. What had caused his anger? A moment ago, he had worried over her injuries.

"Buffalo Calf speak truth," Elk Dreamer sneered. "I should not bring. *Hinziwin* cause bad memories—bad feelings." He looked away from her, his features filled with loathing. Jaw taut, he lifted his chin. Then, without further explanation, he turned and stalked from the tipi, slapping the covering closed behind him.

FIVE

Elk Dreamer faced the last hues of the setting sun with a scowl. He had not meant to lose his temper with the yellow-hair. She had only been curious, as people are when meeting. But her questions had brought back the rage he had felt when *Tacincala* had been killed.

Lifting fierce eyes, he saw Snow Dancer on her way back to the tipi with the healing roots he had told her to get. His temper shifted to her. Never before had she questioned one of his commands as she had in front of the yellow-hair. He could not let this go unpunished. With angry strides, he moved into her path.

Jerking her head up with a start, she halted.

"You forget your place, Snow Dancer." Grateful for the use of his own language again, Elk Dreamer thrust the full weight of his irritation upon her. It did not matter that others were watching. "When Fawn was killed and you were left alone, I took you to my lodge. No one—not even your own family would accept the burden of you and your unruly behavior. When your son was born, I accepted him without question."

Snow Dancer lowered her head meekly.

Elk Dreamer balled his hands into fists. He would have liked to hit something—anything—but it was not his way. Instead, he allowed the strength of his voice to dispel some of his anger. "You have done well to keep your usual discontent in its proper place these past two winters, but know this, you tempt much this day by abusing the goodness of my heart with your defiance."

Visibly chafed, Snow Dancer cut a shame-filled glance toward the tribe members gathered at a distance.

Elk Dreamer did not care whether or not her display of guilt was a ruse. He was too furious. He shoved his hand toward the tipi. "As with you, I have taken the white woman to my hearth. You *will* see to her care when I am not here. You will *not* mistreat her. If you do, you defy me." Leaning nearer, he took a breath, and his next words erupted from deep within him. "And you *will* show me the proper respect. Never again will you challenge my authority. Now go!" He motioned her away with a flick of his wrist.

Wordlessly, Snow Dancer scurried toward the tipi.

The crowd of onlookers murmured their obvious approval, then continued about their various chores.

But Elk Dreamer paid them little attention. Their favor did not matter in this situation. He would not have the woman—or any woman—challenge his decisions.

To punctuate his thought, he dipped his head, then started for the nearby stream that ran beside the camp. He had not been this angered in a long time. He needed the comfort of the cool water. But he had not taken more than a few steps before a movement drew his attention out of the corner of his eye.

His grandmother stepped into view.

He grumbled to himself. At this moment Elk Dreamer did not want to see anyone, least of all, *Wiyukcan Maniwin*. The old woman had a way about her—one that forced him to realize when he had handled a situation improperly.

No—not this time. Snow Dancer had overstepped her bounds with him. He had been correct in his manner of discipline. It was good that she lived under his protection. Another man might have beaten her for her insolence.

Without so much as another glance toward his grandmother, Elk Dreamer veered away from her and tromped to the stream.

Still angry, he stripped off his chest plate, leggings, and moccasins, then removed his prized flute from his waistband and laid it on the ground. Wearing only his loincloth, he dashed into the frigid water, and dove beneath the current. Icy cold from the snowmelt, it nipped at his skin. With a throaty roar, he bolted through the surface, expelling the energy of his temper along with the sound.

Usually it took a lot to irritate Elk Dreamer to the point of being fully enraged. Why had so little tonight provoked so much? Shaking his head, he tossed his hair from his face. He lunged forward again. Hand over hand, he swam upriver, pulling himself against the force of the flow with powerful strokes.

Finally, feeling the strain on his muscles, he cut across to a large, flat rock near the bank. Exhausted, he fell back against the cool granite and stared up at the night sky. Like distant camp fires, a multitude of stars winked down at him.

He sighed. It felt good to be tired. He did not get mad often, but whenever he did, the strength of his rage invariably took him off guard. He had always prided himself on his ability to think things through calmly. He did not like losing his reason to the potency of his temper. It made him feel as if another being lurked inside him—a monster lying ready—waiting to consume his thoughts and control his actions. It was the one thing that truly frightened him.

He thought of the white woman and how frightened *she* had appeared when he had pulled her out from the wreckage of the stagecoach, and again when he had entered the tipi and checked her wounds.

She had done her best not to display any pain or anguish, but he had known she felt both. It had shown in her eyes. Blue like flowers the color of summer sky, their delicate hue had reached out to him. He had seen many whites, but his dealings with these people had always been in battle. Before now, he had never been able to appreciate the fairness of the shade.

Shifting to a more comfortable position, he cradled the back of his head in his hand.

And her skin. It had shone pale in the firelight of the tipi—paler than any he ever remembered seeing. The memory of her lying naked beneath the fur pelts whispered across his mind, and with it, he felt a sudden tightness in his groin.

For a moment, he lost himself to the vision of the white woman's uncommon beauty—so different from the Indian women to whom he was accustomed. Earlier, when he had undressed her and tended her wounds, he had been too consumed by the tasks to give any thought to the softness of her skin. But now, in the privacy of his imagination, he wondered what would it be like to stir her womanly passion. To caress and fondle her to the highest peak of wonder, as was expected of a man.

Like a scornful apparition, the moon, fully rounded and bright, intruded on his thoughts. Elk Dreamer became suddenly aware of a murmur of familiar voices and an occasional titter of laughter coming from the opposite side of the stream. He sat up and squinted into the darkness.

A newly married couple from the tribe was apparently taking advantage of the balmy chinook warming the early spring evening. Obviously unaware that he watched, the pair eased down onto the ground and began to undress each other.

Elk Dreamer looked away. He moved as if to leave, but a heavy moan from the woman drew him back.

Clearly outlined in the wash of dusty-blue light, the couple embraced. Side by side, they touched and nuzzled.

The hushed tones of their pleasure-heightened sighs and words of love flamed the lust that Elk Dreamer's earlier fantasy had sparked within him. He brushed away a bead of sweat from his upper lip. Never had he encroached on any other lovers—he did not want to now. But he could not seem to tear himself away from the scene opposite him. Why? Rolling onto his stomach, he folded his hands beneath his chin and continued to watch.

The act of love was not something new to him. He had found many satisfying nights in the arms of Fawn. He missed her more than he had ever thought possible. He had discovered in her something wondrous— to make a man marvel with the thought of loving a woman.

If only their time together had not been so short. If only they had been able to marry and have a child before— He shook his head. How long would the pain of her death continue to haunt his mind?

Remaining focused on the couple, he felt a prick of envy. Why had destiny marked him to walk the earth alone and never know such wonderment again? At one time, he had even thought he might be able to find some small measure of this same wonderment with Snow Dancer. But she was nothing like her sister. She did not possess the warmth, or the caring heart of Fawn.

Over the flow of the gurgling water, another sound—a familiar song—pulled him out of his reflections. Remaining low on the rock, he looked behind him. He grimaced. *Wiyukcan Maniwin*. He would have known her humming anywhere.

Silver as a winter's moon, her gray head bobbed out from the shadows of the forest. She tottered to the bank nearest him and, with her usual amount of strain and effort, squatted with a labored groan.

Elk Dreamer darted a wary glance toward the couple.

In a flourish of erratic movements, they gathered their clothes and dashed into the concealment of the tree line.

Squeezing his eyes closed, Elk Dreamer clamped his teeth together and thumped his forehead to his hands. He hoped his friends had not seen him. It might prove to be embarrassing for the three of them when they came face-to-face again.

Elk Dreamer waited until the pair had completely immersed themselves in the darkness before rising. He did not know if *Wiyukcan Maniwin* had seen either him or the couple, but chances were she had. Very seldom did anything go unnoticed by the old woman.

Standing, he jumped down into the shallows, splashing the water as he waded over to his grandmother.

Undraping the thongs of the several waterskins she carried, she looked up, her expression indifferent. Then, one by one, she untied the leather drawstrings securing the pouches closed and poured out the clear liquid. Even after all of the animal bladders were empty, she still remained silent.

Elk Dreamer crouched beside her. He waited another moment before speaking. Ponders-as-she-walks Woman had certainly not come to this exact spot by accident. She wanted something. And he could pretty well figure out what. Cupping his face, he wiped away the spray, smoothing his hair back in the same movement. "It is dark, Grandmother."

Wiyukcan Maniwin lifted a keen eye and gazed at the sky. Returning her attention to her task, she nodded. "This is so."

Elk Dreamer let a knowing smile spread across his face. Her habit of maneuvering coincidence always amused him. Resting his forearms atop his knees, he tipped his head to one side and studied her. She had come with water in the sacks and drained them, only to once again refill them from the stream. Shaking his head, he sighed. "What is that I've done this time, Grandmother?"

Still, the old woman kept her focus on her chore. "Have you done something?"

"You came looking for me."

"I came for water." Filling the last pouch, she pulled it closed. Then, gathering the other thongs, she pushed herself up to a wobbly stance.

Elk Dreamer took her arm, steadying her. "The light is too poor for one on in your years to be out performing such a task at night. Why do you wait until dark?"

"The water is cooler."

Elk Dreamer grinned. He knew she would never admit to seeking him out on purpose. It was the game she always played. Yet he could not help but ask. How many times in the past had they assumed these same roles? Too many to count.

Since the death of his mother and father during a Crow raid, when he was but fourteen winters, Ponders-as-she-walks Woman and he had been each other's only family. She had lived with him in his lodge ever since and had always been good to him. She never questioned his judgment openly, but would instead suggest other means he might try under similar circumstances should the occasion ever arise again. He had always found her wisdom to be sound and helpful . . . even when he had not wanted it.

"Have I disturbed you, my grandson?"

Elk Dreamer thought of his friends coupling and of the fantasy. No more than they. He shook his head. "I came for a swim."

"You will sleep now?"

He nodded.

Taking a deep breath, *Wiyukcan Miniwin* hoisted the waterskins onto her shoulder. "Will you walk back with an old woman?"

Elk Dreamer gestured in the direction he had left his clothing. "I must get my things." He took the bags from her. It was not proper for a warrior to perform such a menial task, but he could not bear to see his own grandmother carry such a cumbersome burden.

They had only walked a short way through the forest of pines before Elk Dreamer chose to voice the subject he knew to be on the old woman's mind. "Snow Dancer challenged me."

Wiyukcan Maniwin did not remark, but continued to shuffle along beside him in silence.

"It was my right—my duty—to discipline her." Stepping around the opposite side of a clump of bushes, Elk Dreamer watched his grandmother for any sign of disagreement.

Her expression remained noncommittal.

He pressed for her opinion. "You do not think it wise of me to punish her as I did?"

She answered as she always answered. "I am not a man, my grandson. It is not my place to question your judgment."

As usual, he would have to prod deeper. "But you do believe I did not handle her properly?"

Picking her way through the underbrush, Ponders-as-she-walks Woman kept her eyes lowered to the ground. "You seek the counsel of an old woman?" She hesitated. "How do I answer this?"

Elk Dreamer knew she had already formed an opinion—it was her true reason for coming to the river. He also knew that in the end, she would deliver up her views. But, as always, he would have to coax them from her. It tried his patience to do so, but he loved and respected the old woman. He had learned from past experiences that he could only benefit from her wisdom. "Tell me, *Wiyukcan Maniwin*. I would hear your thoughts."

She did not answer right away, but when she finally spoke, her voice rang clear. "I am not a man. I have only the heart of a woman to trust. I can not think with the soundness of a man's judgment. But . . ." She hesitated again. "If I were such a man—especially a leader of the people—I do not believe I would need to humiliate to discipline."

Elk Dreamer had not even considered this aspect of his treatment of Snow Dancer. In fact, he had not given thought to anything except his anger and the violation of his authority. It was not his usual nature to shame or degrade another.

Coming upon his clothing, Elk Dreamer halted. He stared down at a single bead on his chest plate. Why had he done such a thing? Had he felt that threatened? He had rightfully earned his place as Gall's lieutenant, and his people respected him, yet this had not been the first time a member of his tribe had disagreed with him. Why *had* he been so harsh in his treatment of Snow Dancer?

"You will sleep now?" Ponders-as-she-walks Woman interrupted his thoughts.

He swept a tender gaze over her wrinkled face. Truly the woman was wiser than many of the council members of his tribe. Reaching out, he caressed the softness of her cheek with the back of his fingers. "I will think for a while yet."

Marking her obvious approval, she smiled in her customary knowing way. "It is good to reflect on one's own thoughts, my grandson." She moved as if to leave.

But, grasping her arm, Elk Dreamer halted her steps. He slipped his hand down to hers and squeezed gently. His eyes met hers in a loving embrace. "You are a good woman, *Wiyukcan Maniwin*—a very good woman."

Her smile broadened, yet as was proper by tribal custom, she appeared embarrassed and cut her eyes askance. She shifted her gaze to the low-hanging moon. "The old grow weary early. I will go to my robe and sleep now."

Releasing her hand, he nodded.

She toddled toward their family lodge.

Remembering the waterskins, Elk Dreamer opened his mouth to call her back, but clamped it closed. He smirked. He knew she had not wanted the water. It had merely been an excuse to seek him out at the river.

He set the pouches on the ground, grabbed up his chest plate, and slipped it over his head. Then, after retrieving his leggings and moccasins, he picked up his flute and headed out to find a quiet place to be alone.

He cast another look in the direction of his grandmother's departure, but she had already disappeared

into the tipi. Her words made him think. Ponders-
as-she-walks Woman had shown him something about
himself he did not like.

Moonlight filtered through the trees, its paleness re-
minding him once again of the white woman. How he
must have appeared to her with his grisly display of
temper. But then, why did he care what she thought?
She meant nothing to him. He would see her mended,
but no more, then send her back to her own people.

Turning back the way he had come, he trudged
toward the flat rock in the stream where he had lain
earlier. The couple had run off; his grandmother had
gone to sleep—it would be a good place to be silent
and give thought to the true reason behind his anger
with the yellow-hair and Snow Dancer. He must know
the answer. He would seek a vision.

Fat and feisty, the moon seemed to mock his good
intentions. Shining proudly, it cast a bright beam on a
clump of spiderwort peeking out from beneath some
nearby undergrowth.

Halting his steps, Elk Dreamer bent and picked a
single stem. He twirled the cluster of delicate blue
blossoms between his fingers. "Flowers the color
of . . ." He barely heard his own voice. Invading his
mind was a vision of soft, pale eyes frightened and—
"Blue like a summer sky."

As if he thought to see through the thick line of
trees, he looked back in the direction of his lodge. Why
was the yellow-hair plaguing his thoughts? Moving
to the water's edge, he crouched down and laid his
possessions on the ground. He splashed his face.

He sat like that for a long moment, entranced by
the gentle fluctuation of the stream. Seemingly of their

own volition, his eyes moved to the blossoms. He picked up the stem and stared at it as if it held the answers he sought.

A single fragile petal fell from the spindly stalk into his palm.

Absently, he rubbed it with his fingers, dissolving it into a gelatinous paint. Tingeing the lines on his hand, the pigment showed dark against his skin. Why all of a sudden did the color fascinate him so?

The breeze lifted, whispering across his skin. Peering across the water, he heard the voice of his *Wanagi*, his spiritual self.

Buffalo Calf spoke with much truth. The white woman will cause much trouble—some good, some bad. Be careful what it is you seek behind the blue eyes. Great power lies in wait within the hue of their depths.

A shiver raced up Elk Dreamer's spine. With a disgruntled snort, he submerged his hand and shook it beneath the water. But when he lifted his palm, another tremor shuddered through his body.

The mixture had stained the center of his hand with a small circle of blue. He rubbed it, then dunked it again . . . but the color did not wash away.

SIX

Inside the tipi, lying on her bed of buffalo robes, Snow Dancer pulled her fur blanket up and over her face. She did not want to look at the white woman any longer. It was bad enough that she was forced to share the shelter and comforts of the lodge with her.

Though it had filled her with loathing, she had done all that Elk Dreamer had commanded of her. She had bathed and fed the yellow-hair, and seen to her needs, but nothing more. When the woman had made an attempt at friendliness, Snow Dancer shunned her. Elk Dreamer had not ordered her to be nice to the woman. *That, she would not do.* She hated the sight of the pathetic, whimpering female.

The yellow-hair's body and hands were too soft for work. And though the woman did not appear old, she looked beyond the years of childbearing. She was not good for anything.

Across the room, the woman groaned pitifully.

Snow Dancer smiled to herself. Her own people must have thought so, too. Why else would they have cast her out to find her own way?

Snow Dancer flinched. The nip of her shallow judgment mocked her pride. Had not *her* people discarded her in a similar manner? After her sister's death, they had gladly given her over to Elk Dreamer without asking for the price of even one pony.

Unwelcome, the memory stung her eyes with bitter tears.

At first, he had not taken much notice of Snow Dancer, but over the course of the past two winters, she had maneuvered her way into the role of a principal woman in Elk Dreamer's lodge. And though she had not yet managed to entice him to her bed, nor been secured as his wife, she felt confident that both were only a matter of time. After all, had he not taken Grey-eyes to his heart? He even called her half-breed child *my son* when he spoke to the boy.

She brushed away the moisture from her cheek. At least *he* had wanted her—yes, wanted her. But now, to force her to be no less than a slave to this . . . She thought of the small headed, short-horned female buffalo who were always the last to mate within the herds. Agreeing with the comparison, she dipped her head. "Puny, ordinary cow."

Snow Dancer ground her teeth together. Her eyes narrowed. She burned a stare through the furs as if she could see the woman. A wicked smile slid across her lips. She would have to do something about that one—and soon. She would not allow the wiles of another woman to be woven around *her* man. And he *was* hers. She had seen to that.

She took a cleansing breath. If only she could win herself back into Elk Dreamer's good graces. Then, she would be able to subtly coax him into seeing his error.

Yes. She could do it. She would show him a compassionate and obedient heart, then bend him to *her* will. Snow Dancer would convince him that though it was his duty as a medicine man to see the woman mended, he must send her back to her own people. If he allowed her to stay in camp very long, she would cause great trouble. The soldiers would come looking for the yellow-hair soon—that was a certainty.

A rustling of the door cover drew Snow Dancer from her scheme. Her stomach tightened. Everyone but Elk Dreamer had gone to sleep hours ago. It had to be him. Now was her chance.

She hesitated, then swallowed her resentment. She had to ask for his forgiveness—beg for it, if necessary. She would not have him displeased with her any longer. She loved him, and she would have him. Nothing would get in her way—nothing—not even her own stubborn pride!

She moved to rise, but a sound stopped her.

He crooned as if to a child. "Shh . . ."

Snow Dancer stilled. Lifting the pelt, she peeked out.

"You are safe." On his knees, Elk Dreamer bent over the yellow-hair and stroked her brow.

After only a few moments, her fitful moaning ceased, and she quieted.

Snow Dancer watched as Elk Dreamer examined the woman.

Emblazoned within the dark shimmer of his eyes, a strange look—a hunger—glimmered fiery hot when he raised the blanket off the white woman's body and exposed her to his view. He did not touch her—not even to check the dressing on her wounds—but what his hands did not perform, his gaze carried through.

A thing—dark and venomous—a nameless viper slithered through Snow Dancer's soul. Never had Elk Dreamer looked at her with such desire.

The woman groaned again. "Garret—no!"

Elk Dreamer crooned softly, coaxing the yellow-hair to relax with his gentle tone. He lowered the pelt and tucked it carefully around her body. Then, retrieving the cup of sleep potion Snow Dancer had left by the fire, Elk Dreamer gently urged the woman to drink.

Snow Dancer could do nothing but lie seething in silence. She would have liked to leap from her bed and tear the yellow-hair's heart from her breast. She gripped the robe tighter.

Digging her nails into her palms, she squeezed her eyes closed. She could not continue watching. She let the blanket fall down across her face, controlling her anger with slow, deep breaths. She had to keep her plan intact. She could not afford to lose control.

Long after she had heard Elk Dreamer slip beneath the fur robes of his bed, Snow Dancer remained awake. She had to think her plan through in every detail.

This white woman wanted Elk Dreamer—that was unmistakable. Even in her condition, she had already cast her womanly powers over the man.

Snow Dancer could not afford the luxury of time as she had wanted. She had to strike now. But how? She needed the guidance of her spirit self, but she could not relax enough to hear the voice. It was too close—too pressing—in here.

She looked out from beneath her covering.

All were asleep.

She needed the open sky and tranquillity of the night. With practiced silence, she rose from her bed and stole out into the darkness.

Heedless of any forest danger that might be lurking about, Snow Dancer stalked the timberland until she became weary from frustration and fatigue. Taking refuge beside a tumble of boulders on the edge of a cliff, she sat down to await the answers from her spirit self.

Not yet fully dawn, the sun clawed at the sky, raking its outstretched fingers across the nakedness of the earth.

Snow Dancer called to the spirit world, but it remained silent. She glowered at the golden hues lighting the morning. She had to free her thoughts and allow her guide to speak to her. But even daybreak mocked her wishes, with the meanness of its vibrant colors—colors not unlike the yellow-hair's.

She lifted her chin, leaned forward, and glared at the brilliant ball rising ever higher. "You will not be here long, Yellow-Hair Cow. I will see to that!" She spat out the words with a scornful curl of her upper lip.

It felt good to be able to use her voice without worry of anyone overhearing her. She had gone too long without speaking to ruin things now. If she expected to keep Elk Dreamer's sympathy on her side, she must continue with her deception of silence. But when he

had commanded she care for the woman, then public-
ly humiliated Snow Dancer, it had taken ever ounce
of willpower she had to keep her temper imprisoned
and remain quiet.

As if in retaliation, the sun radiated brighter.

Snow Dancer's eyes burned watery. Looking away,
she blinked the moisture gone. She took a deep breath
and folded her arms across her middle. Falling back
against the cool stone, she scanned the countryside,
recklessly swinging her legs back and forth below the
ledge.

How long did Elk Dreamer plan to keep the white
woman at the encampment anyway? Did he not know
how dangerous it was to have her among them?

"I would have left her for the beasts and forest
scavengers," she grumbled.

Snow Dancer remembered watching Elk Dreamer
examine the yellow-hair's wounds. His hands had
been so gentle and tender.

Cold and black, the coil of hatred returned, winding
itself tighter around her heart.

He had been the same way with her sister. Many
times when he had thought them alone, Elk Dreamer
had shown the same attendance to Fawn.

Awakening within her, bitterness stole upon Snow
Dancer's attempt at meditation. She had thought the
old hatred put to rest with the death of her sister. But
here it was again, rising like a serpent lying in wait.

Closing her eyes, she became lost in the tortuous
vision of Elk Dreamer's seduction by Fawn.

As she had so many times before, she had followed
them, hiding in the darkness like an animal stalking
its prey. Her stare had narrowed on her sister.

Except for the crackle of the small camp fire Fawn had built beyond the lights of her village, the night sounds whispered softly.

Snow Dancer had not heard his approach, but suddenly he entered upon the scene. Startled, she jumped. Her teeth clamped together as she continued to watch.

Elk Dreamer moved a step nearer, then halted.

Though she could not see his eyes, Snow Dancer knew he was entranced by her sister's beauty. How could he not be captivated? Even she, herself, had to admit that Fawn was more than a mere handsome woman of the Cheyenne. In fact, among her people, she had been the most sought after maiden in the village.

Silent as the wind, Snow Dancer moved in closer. She wanted to see everything as Elk Dreamer saw it.

Sitting on a blanket before the fire, backlit in a molten glow of golden-red, Fawn waited. Apparently sensing the man she loved, she turned to look in his direction. Her head was slightly tilted, her black hair cascaded around her shoulders, and her chin hovered invitingly above one bent and exposed knee.

Elk Dreamer all but ran to her side. He was like a quivering stud caught up in the scent of a mare—randy and waiting.

It sickened Snow Dancer.

Fawn reached out to him.

He took her hand and knelt beside her. Within his hand, he offered her a gift.

Snow Dancer's throat closed as she peered through the trees at two white hushed-wing feathers.

Elk Dreamer must have searched hard for the rare owl tufts. Leaning close, he wove the plumes lovingly within the dark strands of Fawn's hair. He slid his fingertips down to her cheek, then traced the line of her jaw and tipped her face up to his . . .

Jerking her eyes open, Snow Dancer yanked herself away from the old haunt with a start. She shuddered, but recovered quickly. Fawn had deserved to die. Her sister's behavior with Elk Dreamer had been dishonorable and wanton.

Snow Dancer would have liked to disclose the illicit meeting between the couple, but it would have brought great shame upon the memory of her family. And, too, Elk Dreamer would have been taken out and buried up to his neck near an ant mound, then left to be fed alive to the tiny short-necks.

Never could she have allowed such a thing to happen to him. She loved him too much. She had undergone much to insure her future with Elk Dreamer—even to the point of trading her maidenhead to a greedy white man for his promise of her sister's murder.

She shuddered with the memory of the man's abusive treatment of her. She had hated the way he handled her so roughly, and the way he groped her face and body with his slobbering mouth and bruising hands.

Though to gain Elk Dreamer's love and attention, she would have gladly given up more. It would be different once *they* were together. He had been gentle with Fawn. He would be even more loving with Snow Dancer.

After the incident with her sister, it had taken great strength to cut into her own flesh. She traced the scar on her throat with a finger. But it had been worth it.

She knew she would not have Elk Dreamer's love—not right away—but her self-inflicted injury would at least insure enough of his sympathy that he would accept her as a relative and take her into his lodge.

She smiled to herself. He had gone too long without a woman. It was only a matter of time before he came to her. Of that, she had been certain. But now this yellow-hair had emerged and interfered with her plan. She remembered the lust that had glimmered in Elk Dreamer's eyes when he tended the woman. The cow would have to be dealt with. But how?

Blindly, Snow Dancer stared out across the treetops swaying in the warm chinook below her. White men. The word began to drum in her head, growing louder until it thundered across her mind.

A twisted thought forged an idea. She chuckled.

Had she not overheard Elk Dreamer telling some of the other men of the tribe that the attackers of the yellow-hair's coach had been whites dressed as Indians? She smiled to herself. They had tried to kill the woman before. Would they be willing to do so again?

She arched a brow. She had used the white man's greed to her favor once before and enlisted their help. Would these white dogs be as easily seduced by their own lusts as the others?

A vision of Grey-eyes leapt before her. But at what price? She loathed the thought of another such vile animal touching her. No. She would not be so naive again. Reaching down inside her right moccasin, she clasped her bone-handled knife. She would kill if any dared take her like that ever again. She relaxed her grip.

Still. She would have to have something to entice their aid. Rising, she shaded her eyes with her hand and looked out over the vast tree line. She scanned the mountainsides as if she thought to see the group of men appear.

Only the warm breeze disturbed the forest.

She sighed. Before she could decide what it was they wanted, she would have to find them.

SEVEN

Gentle, but insistent, something tugged at Gretchen's hair. Startled awake, she opened her eyes to the unfamiliar interior of— Where was she? An instant later, an account of the previous day's mishaps poked through the jumble of thoughts crowding her mind. Now she remembered. The Indian, Elk Dreamer, had brought her to his lodge. She relaxed a bit.

Sunlight filtered through the smoke hole in the hide roof. She groaned. It was morning already? She had spent a fitful night trying desperately to rest, but had found little comfort on her bed of buffalo robes. Though she had somehow managed to sleep, intolerable pain in her head and side had kept her from all but snatches of solace throughout the hours of darkness.

And then there had been the nightmares filled with visions of Garret swinging from a beam in his cell.

79

She shuddered against the imagined sight. Why had he chosen to kill himself like that? She should have gone to see him—at least once. She was still his wife, no matter what he had done.

She shook the thought from her head. She could not think about that now. She had a more pressing worry to consider. She touched her head. She still felt a little woozy. What had been in that stuff the woman had given her to drink?

And the man. Elk Dreamer had given her some, too. At least she thought he had. She seemed to remember him at her side sometime during the passing of the night, and giving her some of that awful concoction, but she could not be certain. It could have been a dream.

She felt another yank. She looked around. Except for herself, the tipi appeared empty. Jerking her head to the side, she cast a nervous glance backward.

Beneath a rumple of sable curls, the little boy from the day before lay facing her, twining the ends of her hair around his plump little fingers.

Gretchen smiled. "Oh, it's you."

The child jumped. He sat up, ramrod straight, and stared. His smoke colored eyes rounded, and he scooted back a space.

So as not to frighten him more, she offered him a playful smile. Then, with careful effort, she rolled onto her stomach and tucked her hands beneath her chin. She studied the child's features.

Round and pudgy, he appeared no different than any of the babies born to her Paiute and Maidu friends back home. Yet there was something unusual about him.

She tipped her head to one side and peered deeper. How strange. His eyes were grey. "Well, hi there, little grey-eyes."

Seemingly spellbound, he remained still—only blinked.

A movement off to the side drew Gretchen's attention. She tensed. Even before she looked, she sensed it was the man called Elk Dreamer. She peered up.

He watched her for a full moment before he spoke. "You meet *Is'tahota*?" It sounded like more of a statement than a question.

"Who?"

Crossing the room, he pointed to the boy, his own eyes, then the child again. "You say Grey-eyes."

Gretchen glanced at the toddler before returning her gaze to the man. "You mean that's really his name?"

He nodded, then sat beside her. "*Is'tahota.*"

Immediately, the boy crawled over to the man and plopped his bottom onto Elk Dreamer's lap.

He shifted, giving the little guy more room, then rested his hands atop his thighs. "You feel more good, this day?" Elk Dreamer directed the question at Gretchen.

The man's sudden nearness closed in on her. She became all too aware of her condition of dress—or lack thereof—beneath the fur blanket. Hesitant to trust her own voice, she carefully turned onto her uninjured side to face him. A dull pain shot through her middle. She grimaced.

Elk Dreamer leaned closer, his face hovering above the boy's. "You still hurt?"

"A little," she answered honestly. It was not bad, but it was enough to cause her to be uncomfortable.

She lifted her gaze to his and smiled weakly. Subconsciously, she secured the pelt tighter across her breasts.

His expression remained stoic, though his eyes followed her movements before returning once again to meet her gaze.

A timeless minute of silence stretched between them.

Gretchen's breathing turned rapid.

The baby squirmed.

Thankful for the distraction, she dragged her stare from Elk Dreamer. She looked at the boy. "H-o-w—" Traitorously, her voice faltered. She cleared her throat. "How did you say his name again?"

"Is'tahota."

Endeavoring to make a good show of pronunciation, Gretchen repeated the name.

Elk Dreamer smiled, deepening the dimples that creased his cheeks. "You talk Lakotah good."

Gretchen held back a smirk. That was more than she could say for his use of English, though she would not tell him so.

From somewhere outside, a woman called to the child.

He remained seated.

"Is'tahota, micinks'i." Elk Dreamer looked down at the boy. "Unci kipanna."

The child shook his head.

"Unci kipanna," Elk Dreamer repeated, his tone more stern, yet still affectionate. Before the little one could argue, the man hoisted the boy off his lap and pushed him toward the entrance.

Thrusting out his lower lip, the child toddled out through the open flap.

Following Grey-eyes's departure, Elk Dreamer chuckled.

"You have a beautiful son," Gretchen said when his eyes had returned to her. "You must be very proud."

Elk Dreamer shook his head. "*Is'tahota* not my son. He Snow Dancer's son."

A strange kind of relief rippled through her body. The unexpected emotion caused her to flinch. Why did it matter to her whether or not the child was his? He was a stranger.

He seemed close to the boy. Was he lying? She shrugged to herself. What a ridiculous thought. Why would he? Yet Snow Dancer *did* live here with him, did she not? A sudden curiosity flooded her. She had to know more about this Elk Dreamer, and why he had chosen to bring her here instead of leaving her to the elements.

Seizing the moment, she decided to see what she could find out. "Snow Dancer does live here—with you?" She shot a glance to where she had seen the Indian woman sleep last night, then returned her gaze to him.

Again, he nodded.

"But if you're not his father, then—"

He cocked his head to one side and studied her.

Realizing she had probably overstepped the bounds of hospitality, she clamped her mouth closed.

"His father was white." He seemed to read her thoughts, though he offered her no further explanation.

Gretchen's throat felt dry. She swallowed. Maybe

now was not such a good time to ask questions. After yesterday, she had no wish to provoke his anger. She wet her lips with a nervous flick of her tongue.

"You are thirsty?"

"What?" She blinked.

He mocked her action, then simulated a cup in his hand and the movements of taking a drink.

"Oh." She hid a chuckle behind a cough. Playing along, she looked at the pot of brew still sitting near the edge of the fire. "Not if it means I have to drink more of that."

Elk Dreamer smiled. "Good medicine. Make you sleep. Make you feel better when wake up."

"Maybe, but it tastes awful." She made a face. "And I don't want to sleep right now." With a hopeful expression, she raised her brows. "Could I just have some water?"

He grinned, then nodded. Standing, he crossed the interior and disappeared through the opening in the tipi. Moments later, he returned to her side with a small bowl. Kneeling, he tossed his hair from his eyes with a jerk of his head, then scooted up closer. With more gentleness than any understanding physician in the white world, he cupped the back of her head and helped her raise herself up on one elbow.

On reflex, Gretchen touched his wrist. She drank greedily. She could not remember plain water ever tasting so wonderfully clean and icy.

"Very slow." He tipped the container away from her lips. "Too fast, not good." His voice was edged with husky concern.

She drained the bowl. "Mmm. That was wonderful." She slid her gaze upward. "Thank you."

Elk Dreamer set the dish to one side, but he kept his hand beneath her head.

Becoming aware of the warmth that emanated from his fingers—more imperceptibly, the comfort that came with his touch—Gretchen felt herself relax into his hold. But she could not let herself feel the contact, or what it was doing to her. She stiffened.

She glanced down at her hand. A gradual buildup of energy surged through her arm, pulsing through her fingertips against his skin. Startled by her own boldness, she released her grasp. She snapped her head up and looked at him. Her face flamed hot.

Dark, thick lashes fanned his gaze. The corners of his mouth turned up—not quite into a smile—but enough to let her know that her embarrassment had pleased him.

A tremor of excitement tickled up her spine, and somewhere deep inside she felt a spear of longing plunge through the core of her being. Why did *he* not release *his* hold?

Suddenly he did just that.

Though she had wanted him to let go and move away, she now found herself wishing he had not.

He sat back on his heels and again slung his shoulder-length hair back from his face. Arching a brow, he folded his arms across his chest and watched her.

What? she wanted to ask, but could not seem to voice the single word. Why was he just sitting there staring at her? He appeared to be testing her nerve. Why? The weightiness of the following minutes of silence made her even more uncomfortable.

Again, her awareness was drawn to the heavy robe concealing her nakedness. Her stomach clenched. She tried to pull her gaze from his, but could not. Still resting up on one arm, she clutched the pelt more securely across her breasts.

His eyes never wavered from hers, yet she knew he had seen her movements.

Alluring, yet frightening, his black stare held her transfixed. There was something dangerously attractive in the way he looked at her. Like a ringing fire bell, alarm echoed through her body. Her throat tightened. She wanted to swallow, but would not allow even this small sign of fear.

Finally, he spoke. "Why are you alone, Gret-chen?"

What did he mean? Puzzled, she looked around the interior of the tipi, then back at him.

He seemed to read her thoughts. "You have not yet shed a tear. I do not believe any of the men killed in the raid on the stagecoach was your husband . . ." Apparently waiting for her to confirm his suspicion, he hesitated.

She shook her head. "No. None were."

"Why are you alone?"

"I was traveling out from Nevada to visit my sister."

"Ah. But you are someone's woman—yes?"

She felt a light pang clutch her heart. During all of this, she had not thought of Garret even once. She had not been in love with him for a very long time, but still, she should feel something. Even though they had lived as man and wife in name only for the last twelve months, they *had* been married for three years.

She studied Elk Dreamer's expression. He appeared very inquisitive about her marital status. Her mouth felt dry. Why did it matter to him? Why did it matter at all? She wet her lips. "My husband died a month ago." She hesitated before continuing. "He . . . uh . . . he killed himself."

Elk Dreamer lifted a brow. He did not speak, but all the while, he nodded his head ever so slightly, as if to say, I see. His demeanor suddenly changed from vague curiosity to impertinent criticism. "You did not make him happy? If this was the way of things, he could have taken another woman. He did not have to—"

Gretchen did not listen to more. How dare the man be so presumptuous. He had no idea how hard she had worked to make Garret happy. Her temper soared. She wanted to shout any and all of the obscenities she had ever heard, but with her luck, he probably would not understand. She held her anger on a tight rein.

"Your face shows bitterness."

Bitterness? She had never considered herself bitter, but in light of her and Garret's situation, the word seemed to fit. "Yes. I suppose I am."

"You did not wish to share his life?"

"For a while." Her gaze slipped from Elk Dreamer's, and for a moment, she remembered the short while she and Garret had shared a loving relationship. But all too quickly, that had changed. After the Bannocks had captured her, Garret had charged her with the most vile notions. He believed her a coward—and worse, no better than a whore.

"Any white woman would've killed herself rather than allow them to violate her." That was all he had cared about—that another man had touched her, nothing more. She remembered the angry, accusing tone in his voice as if she had heard it yesterday.

She flinched with the memory. She had thought the old pain gone, but it was not—only dulled by time. Garret had never believed that the Indians had not taken her—but they had not. They had stolen her for a slave, and treated her no better than an animal. She was made to labor the day's full length at strenuous tasks, and given little more to eat than was necessary to keep her alive. And when, after three months, she had fallen sick from near-malnutrition, they had cast her out in the wilderness to die.

If it had not been for the Maidu finding her, she would have perished with no one to know the difference. She had tried countless, useless times to convince Garret of the truth, but he never believed her. Finally, she just gave up trying. She felt the sting of tears blur her vision. Blinking them back, she could not help but look to see if Elk Dreamer had noticed. He had.

With his watchful and penetrating dark eyes, Elk Dreamer appeared sensitive to her pain.

Gretchen's face heated with embarrassment. "I'm sorry," she whispered, more for herself than him.

He nodded in an understanding manner. "Old wounds, they sometimes cause more hurt than fresh ones." He touched her hand gently. He seemed to sense she needed it.

She held his gaze. She had not thought him capable of such compassion. She shuddered beneath his stare.

"You are cold?" His voice broke the spell.

She shook her head. She did not trust herself to

speak, the ancient pain was still too near, as was this man. Lifting the fur pelt just high enough to move, she shifted uncomfortably.

The stink of moldy underbrush, mixed with the gamy smell of the medicinal concoction plastered on her wound, assailed her nostrils. She wrinkled her nose and nearly gagged. Was that really her?

Elk Dreamer must have noticed, too. He grinned. "It smell bad, but work good."

Gretchen blushed, then grimaced as the odor attacked her senses with more force. It was not just bad—it was terrible! What she would not have given for a bath right now. She pulled her lower lip between her teeth. Could she? Surely she could manage. "Do you . . . think it might be possible for me to wash up a bit?"

Elk Dreamer frowned. "You want to kill medicine?"

"I *want* to kill the stench," she answered without thinking.

He leaned nearer and sniffed, then shrugged. "Smell means working good."

"Maybe, but I can't stand it anymore." She did not mean to sound ungrateful, but it really was getting pretty potent.

"No need to stand. Lay is more better. You heal faster." He poked his finger at her with a meaningful jab. His eyes flashed with authority.

Lay? Was he teasing her? No. She did not think so. There was a finality in his voice that warned Gretchen to steer clear, but she could not help herself. She hated to be told what to do—or rather what she could not do.

With the realization that she might have to remain

unwashed for even a short while longer, the stickiness of her sweat combined with the healing herbs became even more unbearable. It had been nearly a full day since the accident. She had not brushed her hair. It was matted and tangled. She was sure her scalp was imbedded with dirt and she felt completely filthy. She suddenly could not bear her own smell any longer. Like a small child bent on rebellion, she gritted her teeth against the impending pain and sat up sharply.

He watched her settle the robe tightly around her body, moving his gaze from her bare back to linger on her breasts.

Glancing up, she saw the return of that strange, almost predatory flicker in the depths of Elk Dreamer's dark eyes. Her pulse quickened. Could it be that this man wanted her?

No one—not even Garret—had wanted her, or even looked at her as Elk Dreamer did now for a very long time. She felt a small fluttering of need shudder within her. God in Heaven. What was she thinking? Had she gone so long without the touch of a man that she had unconsciously seduced his attention toward her? Could she seriously consider— Her body warmed.

No! she railed inwardly. She pulled her gaze away. She could not. Swallowing, she forced her responses to remain in check.

She could feel his eyes burning through the fur blanket. She had to get out of there. One more minute and she would scream.

"Gret-chen."

His voice jolted her into looking back at him. She blanched. When had his gaze returned to her face?

"You feel sick?" His expression filled with concern,

he wiped away the moisture from her forehead.

His question—more his touch—triggered a dangerous idea. It was crazy. And she had no wish to incite his temper, but she had to try. Maybe . . . she could get him to leave long enough to put her plan into effect. She smiled up at him. "I do feel a bit fevered," she answered honestly, then fell back on the fur bed. Then, putting on her most pathetic, oh-please-feel-sorry-for-me look, she turned her head to face him and stole a glance upward.

His gaze sharpened. He touched her cheek with his palm. "Your skin hot. I get more water to cool you."

Yes. She took a steadying breath. It was going to work. Now, if she could just make it to the stream without being seen and stopped. She knew the water had to be close by. After the encampment had settled down to sleep the night before, she had heard the soft rush of the current.

He studied her another minute, then stood. "Rest. I will return soon." That said, he left her to the empty lodge.

Relief washed through her body. He had fallen for it. Watchful of the open tent flap, she sat up again. On weak legs, she struggled to a wobbly stance. She had to be careful if she wanted to do this. Savage temper or not, she could not allow the will of this one man to supersede her own. She had been in control of her life too long to let this or *any* man dominate it now.

Scooping up a multicolored blanket near her bed, she hitched it up around her body as tightly as she could, then shuffled toward the opening. She peered out. Only a few women in the distance were in sight, and they were busy tanning hides.

Good. She took a deep breath. Willpower and fortitude, courage and grit forged through her nervousness. You can do this, Gretchen. She listened for the sound of the water to gain her bearings, then took one last glance around and stepped into the sunshine. She wanted—needed—that bath. And nothing—or *no one*—was going to stop her from getting it.

EIGHT

After filling the two large gourds with water from the river, Elk Dreamer headed back to the circle of tipis. Normally he would never have performed such a menial task, but Snow Dancer was nowhere to be found this morning.

In truth, he did not mind getting the water for the white woman. He knew the odor from her wound was probably becoming overpowering, and, too, the washing would not really hurt. He needed to change the poultice anyway.

Tromping through the underbrush, he maneuvered through the thick stand of trees, to the edge of the camp. He peered up. Just where *had* Snow Dancer run off to? He shook his head. Any other woman would be praying, but not Snow Dancer. She was probably sulking about the public humiliation she had endured from him. Ponders-as-she-walks Woman had been right. He should have found a more discreet form of punishment.

Being from another tribe, Snow Dancer had continually endeavored to fit in with Elk Dreamer's people. She did not understand that living under his protection made her accepted. It seemed she was constantly trying to be better than any of the other women in camp. *That* had not set well with the Lakotah females. She was accepted rightly enough, but always kept at a distance—except in the case of Buffalo Calf. He had been infatuated with Snow Dancer from the start.

Elk Dreamer chuckled to himself. He had a feeling it would not be too far into the future before his friend brought a string of ponies to his lodge and asked him for Snow Dancer. It would be a good match.

Coming upon his tipi, he stopped short. The hide cover had been pulled closed over the entrance. Strange. He did not remember doing that. He thought he'd left it open.

He lifted it aside. Once inside, he waited a moment for his eyes to adjust to the dimness. He took a few steps forward and halted. Gretchen was gone. His heartbeat leapt. He looked around as if he thought she could be hiding.

The lodge was empty.

Where had she gone? Anger coursed through his veins. She had fooled him. She did not feel so bad after all.

How did she think she was going to make it on foot? Her wounds might not be bad, but she was in no condition to walk out of the mountains—not to mention making it to the nearest fort, more than a half-a-day's pony ride away.

Pony ride! He glared down at the pelts where she had lain. She would not be so foolhardy—would she?

Spinning on his heels, he tossed the gourds to the ground. With angry strides, he burst outside. He had to find her, and quick. He scanned the many faces in his path. Gretchen's was not among them.

He ran toward the group of horses that were browsing at the opposite end of the camp. He had only left her alone for a few minutes. She would not have yet had time to catch a pony and leave the encampment. He could still get to her before she caused trouble. Foolish woman. She would only hurt herself trying to leave.

"Let go of me!" Unmistakable, Gretchen's voice boomed over the camp's ordinary morning sounds.

Elk Dreamer froze. He cocked his ear to the winds and searched the grounds. Where was she? He could not see her.

"I was only going to the river." Her words pitched louder.

He dashed toward her voice, across the center grounds, to where a small group had gathered. He pushed past them.

"You were trying to escape!" Buffalo Calf challenged in his native tongue. He held Gretchen by one wrist. He yanked on her arm. "Come. We will take you back to Elk Dreamer."

"There is no need." Elk Dreamer held up a hand. "I am here."

Buffalo Calf's head snapped up. He blanched, but his expression remained enraged.

"What is it you do with the yellow-hair?" Elk Dreamer lifted a regal expression.

"I caught her trying to get away."

Elk Dreamer looked at Gretchen. He switched to English. "What were you doing out of my lodge?"

"I was only going to the river . . . for that bath we talked about?" Though still defiant in her stance, her eyes pleaded for his understanding.

Inwardly, he groaned. Did she have to set those blue eyes on him like that? He wanted to believe her. Turning back to his friend, he offered the man his most appeasing tone. "She was not trying to escape. She was going to bathe."

Still holding onto the woman, Buffalo Calf snorted. He glared at her. "I do not trust her words. She was going for one of the soldier's forts."

Elk Dreamer held back a smile. "Look at her, my friend. She is hurt. She has no clothing. Can you not see that she could not manage such a thing?" He glanced at Gretchen.

Though he knew she was unable to understand their words, he could see that she clearly understood his friend's anger. His gaze flitted over her defensive posture—more over—the way she nervously gripped the weave of the scant blanket concealing her body. The woman held herself rigid in an all too apparent attempt at courage, yet fear reigned heavily in her eyes. He had to admire her spirit.

Buffalo Calf shifted a scowl between the woman and Elk Dreamer, his features depicting his conflict. Suddenly, his facial muscles grew taut. He jabbed an accusing finger at Elk Dreamer. "No! It is you, my brother, who does not see. The yellow-hair must have strong medicine to have blinded you to her wiles. But *I* am not so blinded." He puffed out his chest, looked out at the people, and lifted Gretchen's hand. "See now the truth of my words. The sun has not set twice and already the yellow-hair seeks escape."

Elk Dreamer took in the scene.

Others from the tribe had obviously heard the commotion and had joined the crowd.

He had no wish to incite the disapproval of the council before he had a chance to speak to them about the white woman. He had to get her out of their sight before Buffalo Calf's temper sparked their anger.

Grasping Gretchen's arm just above Buffalo Calf's hold, Elk Dreamer gently, but firmly, pulled her toward him. "I will take her now." He slid his arm around her waist.

Though she still held herself visibly taut, he thought he felt her tremble against him. She all but clung to his side. He had always enjoyed being protective, but now, holding this woman so close that her hair teased the nerve-endings in his shoulder, his defensive prowess seemed heightened.

He flashed his friend a warning glower. "The woman was not brought here as a prisoner. Until she is healed and able to travel, I will see that she *does not* escape. And when the council has heard my words on her behalf, and if they do not wish to grant her further hospitality, then *I*, Elk Dreamer, will do with her as they command." He did not give himself time to think about what he had just said. He took a breath. "Until then, she will stay at my fire—under *my* protection."

A soft rush of murmurs bolted through the crowd.

Elk Dreamer held himself defiant against any impending challenge.

Slowly, the onlookers began to retreat.

Buffalo Calf held his friend's stare, then as did the others, he, too, withdrew from the scene.

Elk Dreamer released a breath of relief. He had no wish to fight the younger man, but if it had come to that, he would have done so to show the strength of his meaning. No one would hurt Gretchen, and she would not escape either. He had given his word. He glanced down at her.

Her posture slipped, and she leaned against him, one hand still clutching the edge of her blanket wrap, the other flat against his chest. Her lashes fluttered upward, and she smiled thankfully.

He could feel her anguish fade, yet he could not offer her comfort. He could not allow himself the pleasure. She had defied him. He had told her she could not go to the stream to bathe, and here she was, going against his will.

She opened her mouth to speak.

His anger returned. "Do not talk!" he commanded harshly. He thought of Snow Dancer. Had she not committed the same crime? He peered up to find Ponders-as-she-walks Woman busy, with other women at a nearby lodge, sewing some beadwork onto a shirt. He knew she had seen the disturbance, but he would not allow himself to worry about the old woman's views—at least not now.

"*Wiyukcan Maniwin.*" When she looked up, he motioned for her to come to him.

She rose and shuffled forward.

"I will take Gret-chen to the stream where the current pools. You will find her some clothing and bring it to her."

Eyeing first her grandson, then the white woman, Ponders-as-she-walks Woman nodded. But as she turned to do his bidding, Elk Dreamer caught sight of a knowing smile on her lips.

He shook his head. If she were anybody else— He had no wish to make the same mistake again. He would have to find a more prudent punishment this time.

"You're hurting my arm." Gretchen interrupted his musing.

He forced the return of his earlier scowl. Some of his anger had been depleted, but he did not want the woman to know that. There was still her punishment to consider, though he did loosen his grip.

"You don't have to be mad. I was only going to thank—"

"Do not talk!" He ground the words between his teeth. Staring into those disarming blue eyes was hard enough on his determination. A bead of sweat trickled down his spine. He did not want to hear the seductive lilt of her voice. Still, it could not hurt to be tolerant this once. She was, after all, a stranger and untutored in their customs. He smiled to himself. His grandmother would be proud of his decision. He peered down at the woman.

Like a wounded eagle, she stared up at him—beautiful to look at, deadly to touch.

On reflex, his thigh muscles contracted, rekindling the feverish tension in his body. Her every look

tempted him sorely. He cringed against the sudden
rush of need surging his groin. Buffalo Calf's previous
words pierced his thinking.

*The yellow-hair must have strong medicine to have
blinded you to her wiles.*

Was it true? Had the white woman used some kind
of magic on him?

He would have to keep his guard up, and his mind
clear. He would have to seek his spiritual self. He
would call to the elk for strength and knowledge
against her charms. He would turn his eyes inward
and fill his body with *wakan*. Only by gathering the
power of the great mystery could he find the might
he needed.

But for now, he would have to keep in control of
his wit and stamina if he was to keep his word to the
people.

Grasping Gretchen's wrist in much the same way as
Buffalo Calf had, he secured her at his side. Since she
wanted a bath badly enough to risk danger, he would
see she got one.

From his vantage point near the edge of the river,
Elk Dreamer listened to her enter the water. He did
not want to leave her alone, but he did not trust
himself to remain in view of her while she bathed.

Folding his arms over his chest, he stretched out his
legs and crossed one atop the other. He looked up and
watched the play of clouds tussling one another for
room in the sky.

His mind began to wander to the soft splashes
behind him. He envisioned her pale nakedness. Sometimes the gift of being an elk medicine man seemed
more like a curse.

Women—young and old alike—were drawn to him. And he to them. Even before he walked among them, they would appear to sense his presence and become blushing and flirtatious. The power of the elk had always walked strong within him. He had never minded before, but since the death of Fawn, he found himself wanting more. It was no longer enough to be with a woman for the simple act of sex.

So why did this woman plague his mind? What was it he thought to find in her? He groaned. He would not—could not—think about it now. Not while she was this near to him, and frolicking in *his* bathing pool.

Seeking distraction, he pulled his flute from his belt. Ponders-as-she-walks Woman would be there soon. Then he would be free to pursue his meditation.

He rolled the length of his flute between his fingers. There was much power to be found in the charm of his music. It would soothe his spirit.

Placing his fingers atop the instrument, he began to play the song of the eagle. Softly at first, the sound lifted through the forest. It traveled far, calling to the spirit of the bird. On the wings of rhythm, it soared into the heavens, coaxing the breeze to become its mate and take flight to its tune.

Like the talons of the birds of prey, lifting and diving, clinging one to the other in rapturous flight, the wind clasped the melody.

Elk Dreamer became lost in the enchantment of the music. He felt the energy of the spirits moving through his body, invigorating his mind and soul. If only for the moment, the song cleansed his heart of his restless thoughts and persistent longings. Never more than now did he appreciate the teaching of his grandfather on the flute.

Suddenly, a loud splash interrupted his pleasure. He stopped, listened.

A groan, a gasp, followed by a yelp. Gretchen!

Alarm shot through his body. He jumped up and ran to the pool just in time to see her struggling to the surface. Without waiting to discover what had happened, he lunged into the water. Reaching her, he hooked her legs and scooped her into his arms.

She gasped, then sputtered. "What"—she coughed— "do you think you're doing?"

Enormous and deadly, startled and fearful, the deep blue of her panicked eyes lanced his very core. "You are not hurt?"

Staring at him as if he were some strange creature, she blinked the water from her eyes. "Not until *you* charged in here and grabbed me."

Elk Dreamer scowled. He looked up and searched the area as if he expected to see— What? He was not certain. He felt her hands push against his chest, and he glanced down. She was saying something. He tried to concentrate on her words.

"Put me down!"

Still unsure that she was unharmed, he did not release her.

Her features contorted. "Put me down, Elk Dreamer!" Her face flushed, then reddened.

Their gazes locked.

He felt her breast crushed against his bare chest, the pressure of his fingers clutched beneath the soft underswell of the other. He could feel the firm muscle tone of a woman used to hard work. It surprised him. It aroused him.

Like butterfly wings kissed with dew, her lashes fluttered against the tiny rivulets of water on her face.

He had never imagined that a white woman could be so beautiful. Excited by the sudden scare, his panic turned to passion. Inches from her neck, he inhaled. He could not help himself. She smelled clean, like flowers after a spring shower.

It took all the restraint he could muster not to stroke his thumb across the undercurve of her breast. Water ebbed and flowed between them, doing little to cool the molten heat surging through his veins. Staring at her—holding her as he was—he had become aroused—fully and completely.

She shuddered beneath his stare, her breathing shallow.

He had stirred the embers of excitement within her as well. He could feel it. He bent toward her mouth.

Her fingernails bit into his flesh.

He tensed. He could not allow himself to do this thing. This was all wrong. Her panting breaths—enticing before—echoed frantically now.

He had to get out of this. He had to release her—quick—before he lost himself in the spark of passion that reigned in her eyes. He swallowed.

Her gaze slid to the movement of his Adam's apple, lingered a moment, then timidly crept back up to his eyes.

He relaxed his hold, then slowly—dangerously so—he lowered her feet to the rocky bottom.

A full moment passed before she moved. Her gaze flitted downward. She shivered. Her face reddened. Her expression grew into one of humiliation and disbelief. Standing in the waist-high pool, she shielded her breasts with her arms and grasped her injured side with one hand.

He clamped his jaws tight. He had forgotten about her wound.

She plunged her body beneath the surface. Only her head and shoulders remained visible. She looked around, apparently searching for safer ground. Backing away, she moved to the far side of the wall of boulders forming the pool beside the stream and braced herself in front of it. As if she thought he might attack her, she pressed herself against the mound of rocks. "Why did you do that?"

"I heard you make noise."

"No." She shook her head. "Not that. I mean—" Her cheeks turned a deep shade of red. She seemed to be struggling with herself.

"I thought you had been hurt. I thought you . . . needed?" He hoped he had chosen the proper word. "To be . . ." Not knowing how to continue, he imitated the physical act of holding her. He watched her pull her lower lip between her teeth. It was a tempting move.

"I wasn't hurt. I slipped and lost my balance."

"But you called out."

"I was surprised."

"But when I held you . . ."

She lowered her gaze.

"I thought you—" Realizing how foolish he must appear to her, he halted in mid-sentence. She had not been hurt; she had simply been taking pleasure in the soothing water. She had not wanted him at all.

Hands on his hips, he closed his eyes and tipped his head back. He sucked in a deep breath. Anger rushed his senses. He had been so caught up in his own reflections, he had acted upon impulse, instead of judgment.

"I'm sorry, Elk Dreamer," she offered in a timid whisper. "I shouldn't have—" It was her turn to falter.

Regaining his composure, he looked at her.

"Thank you for coming to my rescue." She smiled then, outshining the sun—unsettling him once more with the pale light of her eyes.

She was doing it to him again—wooing his baser instincts. It might be an innocent act, but even so, she was doing it.

The sky color on his palm prickled his skin. He flexed his hand against the imagined tingle. At this moment, he wished he were any other man in camp. He could take her then—use her for his pleasures and forget her.

He leaned back and sank into the comfort of the sun-warmed water. But he was not another man. He was Elk Dreamer, the elk medicine man of the *Cante Tinza* warrior society of the Lakotah. He was a protector of women.

Surfacing, he smoothed the sluicing moisture from his face, pushing back his hair as he did so. He was a man who treated women with respect and gentleness. He was usually very strong when it came to holding a woman's attentions away from himself. But now with this one . . . He had not expected to be seduced by her strange enchantment. Her mere presence caught him off guard.

"*Hanble Hehaka.*" As if prompted by his frustration, Ponders-as-she-walks Woman called out to him.

He felt delivered from himself. He had to get away from the yellow-hair. Her power was too strong. He had to seek help from his spiritual self. Without hesitation, he quickly waded to the edge of the water.

"Elk Dreamer?" The woman's voice broke nervously.

He did not look at her. "The old woman is *Wiyukcan Maniwin.*" He thought of the words in the white man's tongue. "You say, Ponders-as-she-walks Woman."

"But where are you going?"

"She brings clothing. She will see to you." He swallowed hard. He started to turn around, but stopped himself. If he looked into those eyes once more, he might give in to the urgency of his need. And right now, that need was too great. "You *will* do as she instructs?" It was a command, but he posed it as a question.

She did not answer immediately.

Would she defy him again? His entire body went taut.

"Yes."

Relief lifted his apprehension. He straightened. "It is good." Then, with a curt nod, he plunged himself into the solace of the forest, and away from the disturbance of the woman.

NINE

Uncommonly warm for this early in the season, the heat of the noonday sun beat down on Snow Dancer. She had been scouring the area near the sight of the stage wreck since early morning, but had not managed to pick up a trail that might lead her to the white men she sought. She had found many tracks of shod ponies, but she could not decipher which had been ridden by the men she was searching for and which by passing travelers.

Coming across a shallow stream, she bent down for a drink. Frustration marked the expression reflecting up at her. Where were they? They had to have a camp close by. How else would they have known who and when to raid?

She cupped her hands and splashed her face, letting the cool water refresh her heated skin. Maybe she had chosen unwisely. Maybe the spirits were trying to tell her that now was not a good time to seek cooperation from these men. After all, she had nothing of value with which to trade, except herself, and she would never do that again.

She thought of the white men. What would they want? They had attacked the stageline and killed all of the travelers . . . all that is but the yellow-hair. She snickered wickedly. That was the answer. She had had a great prize to trade with them all along.

Snow Dancer recalled overhearing a conversation between Elk Dreamer, Buffalo Calf, and some of the other men. The yellow-hair had seen all that had taken place in the raid. The woman knew that her attackers had not been Indian. And if she knew who they were not, chances are she could describe who they were.

On hands and knees, Snow Dancer leaned back and sat on her heels. Her heart pounded with a rush of joy. The white men would want to kill the yellow-hair as much, if not more, than Snow Dancer wanted her dead.

Hoofbeats sounded nearby.

Snow Dancer froze. She fell forward, pressing herself down into the waist-high grasses on the embankment.

A horse snorted.

Peering through the reeds, she watched a rider approach on the opposite side of the stream.

Something shiny, like brass, reflected the sunlight from a dark uniform layered in dust.

A soldier!

She held her breath. She darted a wary gaze around her. Were there more? Her heart hammered. Fear clawed at her throat. She had not been this close to a soldier since before the great battles with the white armies in her homeland. She could not let them find her. She searched the grounds for others, but the trooper was alone.

Having reined to a stop, the young man stepped down from his mount and knelt at the edge of the water. He took off his hat, then bent down and drank freely from the stream.

A rush of wing beats attacked the quiet.

Startled, Snow Dancer gasped. She squinted against the sunshine.

Off to one side, a flock of grass birds pitched into the air.

She looked back across the water.

The soldier, too, appeared alarmed by the sudden noise. Tensing, he gripped the handle of his gun. Then, just as quickly, he relaxed. He chuckled and shook his head. Still watching the retreat of the prairie grouse, he removed the yellow cloth tied around his neck and dipped it into the water.

Snow Dancer remained low. Unlike the man, she did not release the tension in her body. She kept her gaze pinned on the soldier, and her ears cocked to the air. Something had frightened those birds. Digging her fingers into the ground, she carefully stretched her body out until she lay flat atop the reedy land.

A sharp twig stabbed her bare knee. Ever so cautiously, she slid her leg to the side.

The stick snapped.

She stilled, her eyes fixed on the man.

Still clutching the yellow cloth, he tensed again. He looked across the stream—straight at her.

Had he seen her? A scream lodged in her throat, but she swallowed it back.

He remained poised for a moment longer, then eased up. Looping the strip of material around his neck, he tied it at his throat. "Pretty jumpy, ain't I, Suzy?" He glanced up at his horse standing beside him.

From out of nowhere, war whoops echoed from the forest.

Snow Dancer jumped.

Awash with paint and dripping with fringe and buckskin, a band of warriors charged out from the tree line.

Snow Dancer gasped. Who were these men? They were not from her tribe. She had never seen them before.

Drawing his weapon, the soldier leapt to his feet. He fired a shot, then another, sending his bullets hurling into the attacking group. He brought one down, but it was not enough. The others were on him in an instant.

Screeching animal-like, they pounded the man with war clubs and tomahawks.

Still fighting, he fell to his knees.

A swarm of wasps could not have moved as quickly as the riders. They jumped down from their horses and began to bash at the man's body.

Someone struck his head.

The force spun him around.

Snow Dancer covered her mouth to keep from screaming.

Blood spurted from the open gash slicing the middle of his forehead to his temple. He groaned, and collapsed on the ground. He lifted his hand in one last and obvious attempt at self-preservation, then . . . his hand fell limp. He did not move again.

Overwhelmed with fright, Snow Dancer remained hidden in the rushes. She could not believe what she had just witnessed. Why had these men attacked the young soldier?

"Does he have any papers on him?" one of them asked in English. Apparently the leader, the man still sitting on his horse glared down at the youth now covered in blood.

Another man, short and round, began searching through the soldier's uniform. "Nah."

"How about that pouch he's carrying?"

"Hold on, Palmer. I ain't had a chance to—yep, here's somethin' right here."

Snow Dancer blanched. These were white men. Could they be the same ones she had been searching for?

"What's it say?"

The man sitting on the horse read the paper. "It's a dispatch from Fort Laramie." He chuckled. "Well, our little raids're working. It says here that they're sending out a company of troopers to smoke out the renegades claimed to be holed up in these mountains. They want Fort Sanders to do the same from their side."

"The hell you say." The large fellow who had found the paper grinned up at his cohort.

"I guess we didn't kill everybody on that last coach attack."

What? Snow Dancer's hearing pricked up. How could the army know that the yellow-hair still lived?

"Looks like that driver lived long enough to crawl

out of the mountains and tell somebody what happened."

"Couldn'ta. I took his hair clean off whilst he was still screamin'. He couldn'ta made it outta these mountains like that."

The rider shrugged. "He's the only one it could've been. We killed everybody else."

The big man rubbed his bristly jaws. "Well, do they know who we are?"

"Don't be stupid. Look at us." Still sitting atop his mount, the rider wadded up the paper and tossed it down at the dead man. "Our own mothers wouldn't know who we are. All that driver saw was a pack of Indians swooping down on them."

The short man pulled a knife from his belt. He cackled with laughter. "Ain't that the truth of it." Straddling the soldier, he lifted the man's head by the hair and sliced off the top section of scalp. "Ya nearly sceered the shit outta me for a minute there."

Snow Dancer fought to remain in control of her emotions. Surprise, fear, excitement, and uncertainty rushed her senses. These *were* the men she sought. What was she to do? She had not yet figured out how she was going to approach them with her plan. Now, she reasoned, when they were still caught up in their blood lust, would not be such a good time.

Once they left, she would follow their tracks and present her scheme at a time of her choosing and on her own terms. Belly dragging the ground, she backed away. She would have to find a better place to hide. Here, out in the open, she was too vulnerable.

"Hey! Look there!" a man yelled. "Somebody's over there."

Snow Dancer's heart slammed against her chest. She looked up just in time to see the three men on foot race toward her. Bolting to her feet, she ran toward the woods with all her speed. It was her only chance.

Trampling footsteps threatened from behind.

With every stride, her breath tore from her lungs. She kept her eyes focused on the trees. She did not dare look back. She had to make it into the folds of the tree shadows. Her feet pounded the earth. Her arms and legs pumped with all her strength.

Something hit her from behind.

The force knocked her to the ground.

Rising, she did not look up. Instead she again made for the safety of the trees. But before she had even managed four steps, a horse blocked her path. Glaring upward, she stepped back.

Clad in buckskin, the leader of the pack of marauders grinned down at her.

She backed away, but bumped into the solidity of another man. She wheeled around with a gasp.

He, too, was smiling wickedly.

Then another of the group approached. And, finally, the fourth. Like a pack of hungry wolves, they circled her, leering and pulling at her clothes and hair.

"Would ja looky at this purty li'l thing."

"Boy-howdy, ain't she, though." One of the other men pinched her bottom. "Have ya ever seen such a purty squaw before, Oren?"

Snow Dancer would not give any of them the satisfaction of hearing her so much as yelp. Still panting, she decided to stand her ground. Reaching inside her moccasin, she pulled out her knife and hunched down, ready for attack.

The effort did nothing to thwart their assault. Worse yet, it seemed only to incite a kind of fiendish revelry.

The fat one pulled out his own blade and stepped nearer. He flashed it near her face. "Ya wanna play, do ya, squaw-gal?"

The others fell back, giving them room.

Showing her teeth, Snow Dancer slashed her knife at him, but caught only air.

The others all laughed.

"Don't hurt her none, Oren. Leastways not too bad."

Snow Dancer no longer watched to see who was speaking. She moved to the right.

The man circled to her left.

Another called over the lecherous laughter. "Yeah. You know how long it's been since I had me a li'l taste of squaw meat."

A loud roar of snickers and jeering noises nearly deafened Snow Dancer. What was she going to do? Even if she managed to slit open the man's great fat belly, the others would surely pounce upon her an instant later.

A nearby horse stomped his front feet.

Distracted, she cut her eyes up at the rider.

The beefy man knocked her knife from her hand, grabbed her, and spun her around. He slammed her back up against his huge girth. He pressed his blade into the flesh of her throat. "Still wanna play, squaw-gal?"

Wide-eyed, Snow Dancer held herself still. Her mouth went dry, but she did not dare swallow. Once, not so long ago, she had known the sharp pain of steel slicing through her skin. But unlike the last time, this blade was not held by her own hand—and this time it would be fatal.

"Let her go, Oren." The rider approached.

Snow Dancer flicked a glance upward. With all that war paint hiding his features, she could not tell what he looked like, though he appeared to be a seasoned man, well on in his years.

"She's more good to us alive than dead."

"How ya figure that one?"

"Look at her clothes."

"Yeah, so . . ."

Snow Dancer could feel the sweltering heat of his vile breath as he leaned forward and swept a gaze down her body.

"She's Injun, so—"

"So did you notice what kind?"

"What'd ya mean, Palmer? Injuns is just Injuns," one of the men standing off to the side threw in.

The rider shook his head. "That beadwork on her dress looks Sioux."

Spinning around, Snow Dancer in tow, the one called Oren sneered up at the leader. "Hell, Palmer. There ain't no Sioux left this far south a the Tetons."

The rider quirked a brow. "You've been enjoying yourself so much these last couple of months, I guess you've forgotten who we're supposed to be pinning all of our raids on."

Oren squinted.

Snow Dancer prayed for deliverance.

"You tryin' to tell me this here squaw-gal is one

a them Sioux bastards we been trying to flush outta
these hills?"

The man did not answer. His smile was enough
to condemn Snow Dancer to more than just critical
stares.

"Well, hell. I oughta slit her throat just for being one
a them filthy varmints." He lifted the blade.

Snow Dancer stiffened. She was going to die. "Let
it be swift, *Wakan Tanka*," she said to the Great Spirit.
She felt the man's shoulder move. She could already
feel the knife. Of its own volition, her head tipped
back. She cringed.

"Holy shit! Would ja look at that?"

Oren stopped just short of her throat. "What?"

"Looks like somebody's already tried this go-
round."

Knife still tightly grasped in his hand, Oren grabbed
her under her chin and yanked her head back.

Snow Dancer stared at the cold steel so close to
her cheek. Inwardly, she winced. She could not allow
them to see her fear.

Oren's mood seemed to lighten. "I'll be damned."

"Probably." The one called Palmer chuckled.
"We're all probably damned."

Oren's grip loosened slightly, but he did not relin-
quish his hold.

"Let her go, Oren. Maybe we can get her to talk
to us."

"Ya think she can?" He dropped his guard and
pushed her away from him.

"Yeah, Palmer," a boy with hair the color of fire
asked. "I mean that scar looks like it was purty deep."

The rider shrugged. Then, stepping down from his saddle, he handed the reins over to one of the men standing nearest her. He pointed to her. "*Lakotah win?*"

Snow Dancer did not answer. She offered him nothing more than an angry, fixed stare.

He gestured to himself, then shook his head. "*Wicas'as'ni.*"

Snow Dancer glared at the man. He must think that she was touched by the spirits to believe such a lie. She looked around at the others. These were some of the most deceitful looking men she had ever seen.

"We—" He motioned toward the other men. "Great, uh, *wakan.*" He made a hacking motion with one hand atop the other. "We *wastay-ska* and *luta.* We *wahs'i icun* want to talk to *Lakotah otancan.*"

Snow Dancer gritted her teeth and listened as the man tore apart her language. She would have laughed out loud were she not afraid for her life. She swallowed, the bitter taste of her own panic as well as their false tales clogging her throat.

Half-white, half-red? Great messenger want to talk to Sioux leader? Did he believe her brain to be soft? The fool. It was he and his followers who were touched by the spirits if they thought she would fall for all of their lies.

She knew exactly who they were. Anyone with eyes could see they spoke with the tongue of a snake.

Apparently frustrated by his own pitiful attempts at communication, Palmer tried again. "We—"

"I know white man's talk." Snow Dancer could stand it no longer. She pulled herself up to her full height and challenged him with a glare.

"Hooo-leee shit! Did ja hear that, Pa? She talks American."

"Shut up, Willie."

Ignoring the skinny boy, Snow Dancer kept her eyes trained on the leader.

He folded an arm across his chest and cupped his elbow with one hand, then rubbed his jaw with the other. He smiled, not a pleasant smile, but one of amused curiosity.

"You think you're purty smart, don't ya, squaw-gal?" The great-bellied man stepped toward her.

"Hold on, Oren." Palmer moved in between the offensive man and Snow Dancer. "Maybe she is."

"Is what?"

Eyes fixed on hers, Palmer reached out and fingered the shock of white streaking the length of her hair.

Snow Dancer's body tightened. She slapped his hand aside. "Do not touch!"

"Ooowee! She is a feisty li'l thing, ain't she?" The man the boy had called Pa grinned. He snaked his tongue across his lips.

Instinctively, Snow Dancer took a step backward. She eyed the four men. Maybe she had taken on too many at one time. She should never have gotten up and tried to run. They might not have seen her if she had not. She should have remained hidden and followed them as she had planned. She could have watched and waited for a chance to speak to this Palmer alone.

But it was too late for that now. She would have to act quickly. She would have to choose her words carefully, and focus her scheme on the leader. The others were only out for blood—and maybe just a bit more. She fought the urge to shiver. She had to remain calm.

"So . . ." Palmer reached out again, but stopped and withdrew his hand. "What're you doing out here all by your lonesome?"

"I—" She faltered. She shifted her gaze from one man to the next, and back to Palmer. A single bead of sweat trickled down her spine. How would they react to her answer? "I look for white man—for you."

A guttural roar of laughter spewed out of the group of men.

"Ya hear that, Palm? The li'l gal came looking for ya."

"Ooowee, that's sweet. Ain't that sweet, Oren?"

"Hell, no!" He set a heavy glare on Snow Dancer. "Palmer's got a nuff gals back at Lilith May's. Ain't one a them whores that don't sashay up to him when he walks in that parlor." Oren moved up beside the man. He cocked his head toward the leader. "You got all them gals back in Cheyenne, Palmer. It ain't fair that you git this 'un, too."

Still smiling at Snow Dancer, Palmer turned just slightly and popped his friend in the chest with a playful thwack. "Let's just wait and see what the girl's got to say before we go making decisions about her. Okay?"

Snow Dancer lifted her head. Good. She had gotten the man's attention.

"No. It ain't okay." Oren moved another step closer; his eyes roved up and down the length of Snow Dancer's body, fastening finally on the side slit of her dress where it exposed her leg.

Palmer held him back. "Now, Oren . . ."

Snow Dancer did not listen to more. Panic regained its former hold. Careful not to move her head, she searched the ground with her eyes. Where had her knife fallen? Catching the blade's reflection, she saw that it lay only an arm's distance away. She lunged forward.

The men all jumped toward her.

Too quick, she grabbed the knife. It flashed in her grip. Shifting her weight from one foot to the other, she wielded the blade with the skill of a seasoned warrior. "Back!" With a lethal scowl, she forced them to retreat a step. Facing them head-on, she kept all four men in front of her. She could not afford to let them circle her as before.

"Well, now that ja got us, whatcha goin' to do with us?" The boy pumped his brows up and down, then cackled.

Palmer lifted his hands. "Hold on, boys. Can't you see you've frightened the little lady?"

"Hell," Oren sneered. "She ain't skeered—not yet anyways." Spreading his arms, he hunched over and stalked toward her.

Snow Dancer lunged, slicing the hulking fat man across the cheek. She jumped back, then repoised herself for another attack. Her heart hammered against her breastbone. If only she were a warrior, she could better handle herself.

She fought for control of her emotions. She wanted to run, but she knew they would only come after her. And when they caught her . . . She shuddered, then held up a defensive hand. "At the stream—" She tried not to pant, but fear sped up her breathing.

"You spoke of the driver seeing your . . . raid on the stage."

"What does *she* know about that?" The one called Pa hooked a thumb at her.

"I know much," she said a bit too loudly.

"Really?" Palmer folded his arms across his chest and pulled his lips into a half smile. "And exactly what is *much*?"

Snow Dancer swallowed. She had boxed herself into a blind ravine. She had not wanted to tell them like this. She had wanted more control. She had wanted to sway them to her side. But now she had little choice if she wanted to save her own life.

She took in the expression of each man.

Murderous and lust-crazed, all but Palmer leered at her, a wicked gleam in their eyes.

She singled out the leader with the one tidbit of information that she hoped would be enough to keep her alive. "There is another—a woman—with yellow hair. She was shot. And like the driver, she survived your attack." She gulped for air, and rushed on. "But, unlike him . . . *she* knows you are *not* Indian."

TEN

Staring at the small fire illuminating the interior of Elk Dreamer's lodge, Gretchen sat on her bed of buffalo robes and unbraided her hair. She combed her fingers through the thick strands still damp from her bath.

Where had Elk Dreamer run off to so suddenly? And why had he not yet returned? She, the old woman, and the child had already finished their evening meal of venison, and it was now growing quite late.

She glanced over at Ponders-as-she-walks Woman and watched her thread a bone needle through a tiny tin cone, then stitch it in place on a beaded pouch. The old woman began to hum softly, apparently content with her work. Lying beside her, Grey-eyes played with some animal carvings.

Gretchen smiled at the family setting. And most

whites believed these people to be savages. A tremor of envy rippled through her. How many nights so far away had she sat alone by the fire in her own home and wished for such a scene? Casting the unwanted thoughts aside, she sighed heavily.

Slowly, she allowed her gaze to move around the wondrous inner realm of the tipi. Taking in the different implements decorating the tanned walls, she became aware of the mixture of spiritual and commonplace that was the daily life of these Sioux.

A warrior's bustle of eagle feathers hung from one of the support beams, along with a colorfully beaded fan trimmed with matching plumes. On the floor, beside another pole, sat a painted steer skull. Resting across one horn, a long, beautifully handcrafted bag, depicting a scene of a brave on horseback, contained what appeared to be a pipe.

Clumps of sweet grasses, sage, and dried flowers were suspended from still other timbers, while in the rear of the lodge, stacks of animal skins, gourd rattles, and masks sat awaiting use. There were baskets of every description and size, and dishes of wood and clay alike.

And everywhere, on everything, she saw the symbols of beauty and power that proudly reflected the persistent belief in nature and the divine source that guided the lives of these magnificent people. No more finely furnished house could have displayed more splendor or loving care than this well-ordered yet primitive home.

Returning her gaze to the small fire, Gretchen shivered, partly from the chill of her hair, but mostly from the return of another tremor of bittersweet envy.

This was all she had ever truly wanted—a home, a child, and—catching a movement off to the side, she looked up.

Ponders-as-she-walks Woman motioned for Gretchen to join her nearer the flames.

Reluctance held Gretchen immobile a moment. The need for warmth coaxed her forward. Gathering a blanket around her shoulders, she scooted closer, though she still chose to remain a discreet distance back from the fire. "Thank you," she said, stretching forward to warm her hands.

Grey-eyes glanced up at her and smiled.

"You are . . . welcome?" Deeply resonant, Ponders-as-she-walks Woman's voice reached out to Gretchen.

Gretchen blanched. She could not believe she had heard the woman correctly. "You speak English?"

Ponders-as-she-walks Woman nodded, though she did not look up from her task.

"I've been with you all day long, and you wait until now to let me know?"

"You have not spoken to me until now."

"Yes, but—" Realizing the truth of the old woman's words, Gretchen smiled to herself. "I suppose you're right. But if I had only known, I would've said something. I didn't know you could speak English."

"You did not think an old woman clever enough to master such a skill?" The barest hint of sarcasm edged Ponders-as-she-walks Woman's voice.

"No—of course not. I mean—that's not what I meant at all." Gretchen offered her an apologetic smile. "It's just that . . . well . . . you caught me off guard."

"Ah." Still, Ponders-as-she-walks Woman's eyes remained focused on her work.

"How is it that you came to learn our language?" Gretchen's curiosity got the better of her. It was remarkable that Snow Dancer could understand English, and even more so that Elk Dreamer, too, could communicate in the language. But now to find still another in this family that could talk to her astounded Gretchen.

"Many years ago when I was new to my husband's lodge, I had a friend. Her name was Lavinia Louise." Briefly, the old woman lifted her gaze to stare at the fire, then returned it to her chore. "She was of the Mormon tribe."

Gretchen nodded. She had met a few of these earlier pioneers who had traveled out west in search of freedom from religious persecution.

"It was she who taught me."

Gretchen felt a spark of hope. Maybe if these people still lived nearby, she could get to them and ask for help. "Do you still see her?"

The old woman shook her head. "That was when we still lived with our *tiospa* . . . our extended family?" She peered up as if seeking approval, then nodded and returned to her task. "Back in the land of our fathers, I have not seen my Lavinia Louise since my fifteenth winter." For a moment, it looked as if the old woman were about to shed a tear.

"Did something happen to her?"

She lifted her thin shoulders in a shrug. "I have never known. Our men were not so friendly. Her husband was very cruel to her and jealous of the close bond between the two of us. He accused us of unspeakable things. Not so with mine. He was only concerned for my safety. He did not trust the white man." She sighed, regret dulling her eyes. "They found us one day when we had sneaked out to visit each other. My husband was very angry. It was the first time he beat me."

"He beat you?"

Ponders-as-she-walks Woman nodded.

Gretchen knew of this method of punishment. She had treated the aftereffects of similar occurrences with the Maidu and Paiute, but to see this fragile old woman now, it was very hard to imagine her capable of withstanding such trauma.

"It was his right. I disobeyed him."

Gretchen's heart went out to her. Never would she understand how any woman could allow herself to be so mistreated. "Did he raise his hand to you often?"

"Sometimes—but only when I did wrong. He was a good man—a good husband." She smiled softly, as if remembering. "But that was the time before I learned to seek out my needs and wishes from him with wisdom."

"Wisdom?"

The old woman tilted her gray head to one side and looked up. "Is it not the same with the women of your people? When your men are thirsty, do you not find that there are times when you have to lead them to drink, even when the stream that they seek runs before them?"

Gretchen thought back to the artistry of her mother's undemonstrative manner with her father, and grinned. "Yes, I suppose we do."

Ponders-as-she-walks Woman dipped her head with

obvious approval. "It is the same for Lakotah women. Once they have mastered this knowledge, the marriage goes well."

"But whatever happened to your friend?"

"Her husband took her far away from the land of the Dakotah." Her earlier disheartened expression returned.

Sensing that the memories had become painful for the old woman, Gretchen let go of the subject. It would do her no good to know more. There was no Lavinia Louise anywhere nearby to help her.

Glancing down, she saw that Grey-eyes had fallen asleep.

Cuddled in a ball behind Ponders-as-she-walks Woman, the child had abandoned his toys for the comfort of his thumb, which plugged his little mouth.

Awash with a sudden urge to touch him, Gretchen stroked his brow.

He smiled in his slumber, then shivered, inching closer to the old woman's backside.

Removing her blanket from around her shoulders, Gretchen laid it over him and tucked it around his curled form.

"You like babies?" Ponders-as-she-walks Woman tilted her head to one side, though her attention remained focused on the beadwork.

"Mmm." Gretchen ran a tender gaze over the tot. She combed her fingers through the mass of dark curls around his cherubic face. She had always wanted a child, but she and Garret had never been blessed with one. It was probably just as well—the poor babe would have been fatherless now. "All for the best," she murmured under her breath.

Ponders-as-she-walks Woman raised a quizzical stare.

Embarrassed at being heard, Gretchen answered the woman's earlier question. "I love children."

"Ah." Ponders-as-she-walks Woman threaded another bead.

"Snow Dancer must feel very favored to have had such a beautiful and healthy baby."

"She cares little for *Is'tahota*."

"What?" Had she heard the woman correctly?

"It is I, and Elk Dreamer, that see to his care." Ponders-as-she-walks Woman tugged the needle through another tin cone. She frowned at the tiny decoration as if it were some great foe. "The woman does not accept him as her son."

Gretchen looked down at the baby sleeping so peacefully. "But he *is* Snow Dancer's child?"

The old woman dipped her head. "Upon his birth, she held a blanket over his face."

Gretchen gasped. Her gaze darted to the sleeping boy. Why would any woman attempt to kill her own baby?

"It was Elk Dreamer that found her before she could complete the deed. It was he who saved *Is'tahota*."

"How could she do such a thing?" Gretchen pulled the little guy's hand away from his mouth and brushed away the drool. "How could anyone not love such a beautiful child?"

The old woman shook her head in apparent bewilderment. "She was raped by a white man. She said she was told in a vision that she would be cursed with *Is'tahota* by the white man's god. It was that same night that she gave *Is'tahota* to Elk Dreamer. The child is his son now."

"Gave him to—" Gretchen was stunned. No one just gave their child away like that. "What a horrible thing to do."

Ponders-as-she-walks Woman peered up with a critical look.

Gretchen swallowed. She had not meant to sound judgmental. She had forgotten how strongly Indians deemed their dreams to be messages. "Our god is good and just. Children are given as blessings to their parents, not curses."

"It is so with *Wakan Tanka*." She glanced down and at the boy with a loving expression. "Still, no words can convince Snow Dancer of this truth." Ponders-as-she-walks Woman's voice held a note of skepticism.

Was it because she, too, doubted the child to be a blessing, or because she did not believe Snow Dancer's story that she had been cursed?

She did not know why, but Gretchen had a feeling it was the latter.

The fire had died down a little, and with it, she felt the return of her earlier chill. "Do you think we can add a bit more wood to the flames?" she asked, hugging her arms to her chest.

"You sit too far away." Ponders-as-she-walks Woman gestured for Gretchen to move up beside her.

Grateful for the invitation, Gretchen did as she was bid.

Setting her sewing aside, the old woman took a thick stick and stirred the embers beneath the small flame, then tossed a few more limbs into the fire. She chuckled. "It is truly as my husband use to tell me."

"What?"

Ponders-as-she-walks Woman looked at Gretchen as if determining whether or not she should share the story. "He used to say that the ways of the whites were strange and wasteful. He said, Indian man build small fire sit up close, white man build big fire sit way back." She covered her mouth with her hand and laughed into her palm. "It used to make me smile."

"It seems it still works." Gretchen joined in the woman's mirth. "I guess we are wasteful sometimes. And it really is silly to build such a big fire and sit so far back, isn't it?"

Returning to her labor, the old woman agreed with a bob of her head.

Gretchen watched for a long while before speaking again. She seemed to have run out of things to talk about, and, too, she found that her mind had now wandered in the direction of Elk Dreamer. She could see the twinkle of starlight winking through the smoke hole, and her eyes were beginning to grow heavy. Why had he not come back yet? Had something happened to him?

Her gaze slid to the bustle of eagle feathers. Was it a costume of war, or celebration? She suddenly wished she could see it on the man himself. What did he wear with it?

She thought back to the pool. Without a care for his own safety, he had jumped into the water to give her aid. Why? She was nothing more than a stranger to him. The man was a mystery.

"You like?" Ponders-as-she-walks Woman held something up to her.

Gretchen blinked. "Beg pardon?"

"You think this is nice?" She lifted the nearly completed bag she had been covering in beads.

Setting the man from her mind, Gretchen nodded with a smile. "You do beautiful work." She smoothed her fingers across the beaded surface.

"*Pila maye*." The old woman's chest swelled with obvious pride. "It is a tobacco bag for *Hanble Hehaka*."

Gretchen fingered the tiny adornments stitched into the neck of the dress that Ponders-as-she-walks Woman had given to her after she had finished her bath. "Did you make this, too?"

Like a road map etching out the many vast trails across the Great Divide, the old woman's face lifted at the corners of her mouth. "I had intended to give it to Snow Dancer. You like it?"

"Oh, yes, very much." Gretchen toyed with one of the beaded fringes. "But won't Snow Dancer be angry? I mean, if this was supposed to be hers—" She looked up just in time to see the old woman's expression turn sour.

"You do not like it?"

"No-no—I mean— Yes. It's just that, well, Snow Dancer has already displayed a dislike for me."

"She has another. It was mine to give." Ponders-as-she-walks Woman paused. "I choose to give it to you."

Wonderful! Gretchen rolled her eyes. Now she and Snow Dancer would really be off to a great start.

Something rustled outside of the tipi, and as did Ponders-as-she-walks Woman, Gretchen looked toward the sound. She gripped the buckskin hem of her dress. Her anxiety mounted. Any moment now, she expected the young woman to come charging inside and rip the dress off her body.

The flap whipped up, and Elk Dreamer stepped into the light. He peered quizzically at each of them, then nodded a greeting, but did not speak.

Upon his entry, Ponders-as-she-walks Woman set her sewing aside and, without another word, hurried outside.

As if she were a small animal and he a bird of prey, Elk Dreamer stared down at Gretchen. His gaze roved over every inch of her, from the top of her head to the pair of doeskin moccasins that covered her feet.

She shivered inwardly. Her breathing quickened. She tried to still it, but that only seemed to heighten her nervousness. She tried to avert her gaze, but she could not seem to drag her eyes away from his.

"I have brought your bag." Elk Dreamer held out her black medicine satchel.

Gretchen's eyes widened. All feelings of agitation fled her body. "You found it!" She grabbed it from him and hugged it to her chest. She was like a small girl with a long lost doll. "You actually went out and got it for me."

Apparently startled by her sudden excitement, Elk Dreamer's brows flew upward. He took a seat beside her. After crossing his legs, he gestured toward the bag. "This thing makes you happy?"

Gretchen smiled. Her one and only treasure had been returned to her. "Oh, yes, Elk Dreamer. Thank you. I can't tell you how happy this makes me."

Elk Dreamer frowned, an expression of puzzlement creased his features. "It is a good thing, then?"

Glancing up, Gretchen nodded. She opened the

latch. "Now, if everything has just survived the wreck." She lifted out a buckskin bundle and looked inside. "Oh, no," she cried softly. She lifted out the jagged portion of a green glass bottle.

Elk Dreamer leaned forward and peered into the gaping mouth of the bag.

"The laudanum's all gone. It must've broken in the crash." Barely raising her gaze, she handed it to Elk Dreamer.

Scowling, he accepted the container and sniffed. He grimaced and set the vial aside.

She pulled out two smaller bottles that had survived the fall, one with quinine, the other iodine. "Well, at least not everything was broken. And now I can sterilize the bullet wound properly." This last she said under her breath. She glanced up at Elk Dreamer.

He appeared very curious about the bundle she had pulled out of the bag. He fingered the beaded fringes dangling from the cloth.

"It's a dress."

Elk Dreamer watched as she unrolled it.

"It was a present from a friend back home." Shaking out the garment, Gretchen felt a sudden yearning to see Winter Magic again. It had been almost a full week since the woman had seen Gretchen off at the stage depot.

Something fell into her lap. Just as it hit her body, she remembered the atomizer of white heliotrope perfume and the bar of soap. She grabbed them. They were the only two luxuries she had allowed herself on this trip. Good. They were both intact as well. She set them beside her.

Picking up the atomizer, Elk Dreamer accidentally

squeezed the bulb. With the nozzle aimed directly at him, it sprayed. He flinched and scowled. Wrinkling his nose, he waved a hand in front of his face and coughed.

Gretchen laughed out loud. "That's perfume. Do you like it?"

Brows raised, Elk Dreamer nodded, though Gretchen had a feeling he was not being truthful.

Reaching back inside the bag, she rolled her eyes heavenward and sighed. "Thank you, God." She lifted out the hollow rubber tubing of a stethoscope.

Elk Dreamer tentatively touched the implement. "What is this thing?"

"It's a stethoscope." Proud to own one of the first expensive instruments of its kind, Gretchen held up the single earpiece and gestured it toward him. "Put this in your ear."

Elk Dreamer hesitated. He looked as if he thought something might squirt out of this device, too.

"Go ahead." Gretchen nodded, keeping a check on her amusement. She had no wish to offend the man. "It won't hurt you, I promise."

Cautiously, Elk Dreamer did as she instructed. He raised his brows as if to say, *So, now what?*

Gretchen placed the chest piece against herself.

Elk Dreamer flinched. His eyes flew wide. He tossed the earpiece away from himself. "It speaks—like a drum!"

Gretchen laughed. She shook her head. Then she handed the earpiece back to him. "That's my heartbeat. That's how medicine men in my world listen when a person has a sick heart."

Elk Dreamer accepted the tool again. He held it

up to his ear. "This is powerful medicine. The spirit speaks with a loud voice in this."

"Yes, I suppose it does." She cleared her throat, hiding another titter within the sound. Surveying the rest of the contents inside the satchel, she found that nothing else had been damaged. Satisfied, she sighed.

At that moment, Ponders-as-she-walks Woman rejoined them. She handed Elk Dreamer a clay bowl with venison strips and wild onions in it. But when she bent down, she inhaled and her brows knitted. She leaned closer to the man and sniffed again.

Elk Dreamer pulled back and scowled at her.

Gretchen bit her lip to keep from smiling. Obviously, Elk Dreamer did not approve of the old woman's attention.

Ponders-as-she-walks Woman rose up and peered down at Gretchen with a faint smile. Then, without a single word, she gathered up Grey-eyes and took him to her bed robes with her.

Gretchen watched the old woman as both she and the child settled between the furs. In only a short while she had grown very fond of Ponders-as-she-walks Woman. "Good night," she called out softly.

The old woman merely smiled again and nodded.

Gretchen turned back to see Elk Dreamer wipe his hands on his leggings. He had finished his entire meal already. He picked up the stethoscope again. He appeared fascinated with the instrument. "This called a steho—" The word appeared to frustrate him. "Do you use this thing much?" He held it nearer the fire and gazed at the tiny reflection of his face in the metal.

"Yes. All doctors have one." She *had* told the truth. All doctors did use one. Just because she was not really a doctor herself yet did not mean she could not use it as Garret had taught her.

"How does it talk? It does not live." Elk Dreamer examined every inch of the tool.

"The chest piece, there"—she pointed to the lower end of the stethoscope—"captures the sound of a person's heartbeat." She traced her finger over the tube to the earpiece. "Then it sends a tiny echo up through this tubing to the doctor's ear."

"How does he know if the heart is sick? Does it tell him?"

Gretchen spent the next half hour explaining the details and functions of the few precious instruments and medications she had left from Garret's practice.

Elk Dreamer listened intently. No finer Boston student of medicine could have taken in all of the information more quickly. By the time she had finished talking, he had memorized all the proper pronunciations, the doses of medicines, and the illnesses they were used for.

Gretchen was impressed with his astute learning abilities.

Elk Dreamer, too, appeared just as affected by *her* knowledge. "How did you learn these things?"

Gretchen hesitated. She was not sure she should tell him. "I was married—I think I told you that."

He nodded.

"My husband was a doctor."

"He was not a good medicine man?" Elk Dreamer's expression was one of concern.

"He was good—to his patients." Gretchen looked down. She had not meant to say that. She flitted a nervous glance his way. "I mean—yes. He was a very good doctor. Very well respected—and liked, too."

A moment of silence followed.

Elk Dreamer stared at her as if he were searching for a deeper answer—another meaning. The firelight flickered in the dark depths of his eyes.

Her face heated. She heard a buzzing in her ears as if he were inside of her head asking myriad questions she did not want to answer. That crazy excitement she had felt earlier at the pool now returned.

Boldly, he drew a finger down the edge of her jaw.

It startled her, yet incited her senses more. Warmth flowed through her body.

"Was he not good to *you*, Gret-chen?" Husky and low, his voice was filled with male ardor.

Her throat tightened. She wanted to pull away—to take flight before she weakened more—but she could not find enough strength even to drag her gaze from his. She had not had the attentions of a man in such a long time that his sudden closeness overwhelmed her. Her skin burned, melting any resolve she might have managed. She should have wanted him to stop, but she wanted him to continue even more.

His face came nearer.

She held her breath, anticipating the touch of his lips.

"Tell me, Gret-chen."

She loved the way he said her name, so sweet and childlike, yet hard and demanding. A whimper lodged in her throat.

As if he sensed this, he slipped his hand down to clasp her neck, then stroked with his thumb the throbbing pulse beating there.

The interior of the tipi pitched. She felt dizzy. It both frightened and thrilled her at the same time.

He inched closer, his mouth a mere whisper away. Sometime during his approach, he had touched her hand, and now he drew feather-light lines up and down the length of her forearm. His message was clear. Elk Dreamer wanted her.

She shivered uncontrollably. Her body went limp. Her eyes fluttered downward, watching his lips. Lord help her. She could not believe it herself, but she wanted him, too. So close now, she could almost taste his mouth.

"Was he not good to you . . . ?" He brushed her cheek with his. "Like this?"

"*Hanble Hehaka!*" A voice sounded from the shadows.

Gretchen jumped. Her heart bolted to her throat. She whipped her head toward the sound.

A man entered the tipi. Wide-eyed at first, he stared at the two of them still entranced by the fiery passion of the moment.

His gaze narrowed on Gretchen.

Elk Dreamer leapt to his feet. "*Wan!*" He crossed the interior in quick strides.

The man looked at Elk Dreamer.

They spoke together in hushed voices.

Then, without so much as a backward glance in Gretchen's direction, the man took his leave.

Elk Dreamer rushed to a group of baskets. He gathered some herbs and put them in a pouch hanging from his waistband.

What had happened? Why had the man barged in there like that? "Elk Dreamer?"

"Go to sleep, Gret-chen." Taking a larger bag from a hook, he kept his back to her.

What? Something must be wrong. Instantly concerned, Gretchen hurried to her feet. She peered over at Ponders-as-she-walks Woman.

Both woman and child slept on.

"What is it?" Gretchen insisted. "Has someone been hurt?" She thought of the Indian woman who had been absent all day. Moving up beside him, she kept her voice to a whisper. "Is it Snow Dancer? Has she been injured somehow?"

"Go to sleep, Gret-chen," he repeated. All the while he packed strange implements, then he crossed the room to the back of the lodge and retrieved a mask.

Gretchen stared down at the false face. What was he going to do with that? Her eyes rounded as she realized she must be right. Someone was hurt. She moved to the opening and blocked his passage. She gripped his wrist. "Who is it, Elk Dreamer? What's going on?"

He glowered down at her hand a second before he turned the same hard look on her.

She swallowed, but held herself firm. If someone was in trouble, she fully intended to know what had happened. She wanted to help.

His expression softened a little. "It is Buffalo Calf. He is sick with fever. He calls for his medicine man." He touched her face and almost smiled. "Now, go to your robes and sleep. I will return soon."

"But I can help." She wheeled away from him and dashed to her satchel. Happy finally to have something useful to do, she grabbed it up and rushed back to face him. "I'm a doctor, remember?"

Elk Dreamer's features hardened. He snatched the bag from her hand. He glared down at the satchel, then back at her. "*You* are not doc-tor here. *You* are only woman!"

ELEVEN

Face-to-face with Elk Dreamer, Gretchen could not believe she had heard what he had said. She had just showed him all of her medicines and explained how and why they were used. Did he not believe that she knew what she was talking about? "But I might be able to help him," she insisted.

Elk Dreamer carefully dropped the bag to the side. He placed his palm to his chest. "*I* am the medicine man here." His tone softened a little, and he gripped her by the shoulders. "Understand, Gret-chen. Buffalo Calf calls for me. He will not let you care for him."

Gretchen opened her mouth in protest, but just as quickly closed it. What good would it accomplish? She was acting like every other white man that had ever set foot in this country. Like them, she believed only her way was the best. She gave herself a mental shake.

These people had been caring for their own with ritual, song, and crude potions down through the centuries. Except where the diseases of whites had intruded, they had done all right for themselves. Why should Elk Dreamer allow her to interfere? She was in his territory. She should respect his wishes.

"Couldn't I just go with you?"

He shook his head.

"I'd only watch—I wouldn't say anything—I promise." She searched for better reasoning power. "I taught you a little about my medicine; let me see how you do yours," she pleaded quietly. "Maybe *I* could learn from *you*." She watched his face. She hoped she had found the key.

He hesitated. He looked down at the bag, then back at her. "Your medicine will stay here."

"But all of my—"

He pulled himself up straight, his features contorting.

Realizing her mistake, she quickly conceded with a nod. "Yes, of course."

He peered deeper into her eyes. He seemed to be contemplating whether or not he could trust her.

She held herself motionless. Would he let her go?

With a curt dip of his head, he finally relented. "Come, then. It is good to learn." Spinning on his heels, he disappeared out and into the night.

A flood of exhilaration rushed Gretchen's senses as she dashed after him.

Inside the bachelor's lodge, Gretchen found that both of the other two men that shared the tipi with Buffalo Calf were nervously pacing back and forth, waiting for Elk Dreamer.

The man who had come for Elk Dreamer bolted toward her. He yelled something at her in his native tongue and waved his arms in an angry manner.

Gretchen jumped back.

Elk Dreamer stepped in between them. He spoke softly, apparently telling the man that it was all right for her to be there. He motioned for the other to approach. He murmured something else, then gestured them both toward the tipi flap.

Together, they nodded and moved for the opening.

The one who had lunged toward her turned back at the hide covering and glared at her before taking his departure.

Staring after him, Gretchen wondered what she had done to make him so angry. Had Buffalo Calf convinced him that her being here would cause trouble for their people? Did he just hate all whites? Or was it what he had witnessed in Elk Dreamer's lodge?

None of those explanations set well with her. She would like to try and make friends—if only for the short while that she intended to be here. A pain-filled moan drew her attention. She turned.

But before she could take a step toward the man lying down, Elk Dreamer held up a hand.

Understanding his silent command, she remained where she was and watched as he knelt and began removing the things from his bag.

He poured some colored powders into what looked like clamshells, then mixed them with water. Next, he dipped his finger into each one in turn and painted small designs on Buffalo Calf's forehead, cheeks, and arms.

He held the fiercely carved mask he had brought

with him up to his face, then reached inside a small pouch and pulled out a pinch of thick powder. He mumbled something, then tossed it into the fire. With a blue puff, the flames hissed noisily.

Gretchen stared in awe, as she watched him place the false face over Buffalo Calf's.

He chanted some unintelligible words, then carefully set the glowering image upright on the ground above the younger man's head. He made a potion of some kind and heated it, then gave a swallow or two to Buffalo Calf.

Gretchen strained to see what herbs he was using, but in the dimness of the small firelight, she could not discern what they were.

Somewhere outside, voices lifted, as did the haunting drumbeat of a wailing song.

Gretchen shivered. She had never been invited to witness such a ritual with either the Paiute or the Maidu. She supposed that after they had discovered her knowledge for healing, they either had no more use for such superstitious practices, or they simply performed them before calling on her. She suspected the latter.

Paying no attention to her, Elk Dreamer removed a fully horned buffalo headdress from a bag, shook the length of his hair from off his face, and placed it on his head. He reared back on his heels and spread his arms wide. Tilting his head back, he closed his eyes and gave voice to the interior of the lodge. He sang with force and strength, apparently calling to the Great Spirit to heal his friend.

Gretchen clutched her arms over her chest. She knew it was probably just because she was caught up in the ceremony, but it suddenly felt as if a great power had flown into the room. She felt the pulsing tremors from the drums outside, vibrating up from the ground and into her body.

Without realizing she had, she closed her eyes and tipped her head back as she had seen Elk Dreamer do. Swaying to the rhythm of the chant, she found herself whispering a little prayer of her own. She hardly knew Buffalo Calf—and what she did know of him frightened her—still, she wished him no harm.

Elk Dreamer's song softened, though it did not end.

After a short while, Gretchen grew tired and sat down. Her side ached a little, but she forced it from her thoughts. There was another who was worse off than she. Facing the men, she could see that Buffalo Calf's face was beaded with sweat. The room was humid and hot, but she had a feeling his perspiration was do to more than the mere fire warming the lodge.

She stretched up tall, craning her neck for a better view. If only she could get closer and examine him herself, she might be able to help. She started to ask, but remembering her promise, decided not to— at least not right now.

For hours, the chanting and drumbeating continued, until Gretchen thought she would go mad from the strain of the monotonous rhythm.

Buffalo Calf groaned. His eyes fluttered wide. He called to Elk Dreamer.

Reaching out, Elk Dreamer clutched his hand.

Buffalo Calf grabbed the lower right side of his abdomen and winced.

Gretchen read the concern and fear in the medicine

man's eyes. He had labored long in ceremony, but it did not appear to be working. The mark of worry creased heavy lines in Elk Dreamer's face.

She looked at Buffalo Calf. She could see the war of strength battling the all too apparent pain in his eyes. Her heart constricted.

Clutching Elk Dreamer's hand tightly, the younger man whispered something.

Sadly, Elk Dreamer glanced down, over at her, then back at Buffalo Calf. Had he given up?

She could not stand it anymore. She had to do something—at least try. She jumped to her feet and hurried to the opposite side of Buffalo Calf.

Elk Dreamer glowered at her.

"I'm sorry—I know I promised, but—please, let me help." With pleading eyes, she rushed on. "He's not getting any better—he's getting worse. Can't you see that?" She reached out to touch the young man's forehead.

Elk Dreamer clasped her wrist. "You said, only watch."

"But I might be able to help him if you'll just let me try."

Buffalo Calf constricted into a tight ball. He grabbed his side again and gritted his teeth.

Above her hand still tightly secured in Elk Dreamer's grasp, Gretchen offered the medicine man a beseeching expression. "Just let me examine him." She knew she had overstepped her ground. She had broken her promise to him, but there was no help for it. It was not her nature to sit quietly by and allow someone to remain in agony when there was even a slim chance that she could save him.

Elk Dreamer stared at her long and hard, then, finally, he released her arm and nodded.

"Thank you." She smiled, but it was a small triumph. She felt Buffalo Calf's cheek and flinched. "My God! He's burning up with fever. I'll need my bag." She started to get up, but Elk Dreamer grabbed her again.

"No bag!" He sounded determined.

"But it has all of my medicines, and the stethoscope."

"Buffalo Calf has strong heart," Elk Dreamer argued. "He does not need your ste-tho-scope."

Gretchen wet her lips. She had to think of some way to get Elk Dreamer to let her have her things. She pulled down the fur robe that was atop Buffalo Calf. She watched the movement of his stomach.

His breathing was fast.

She touched his abdomen. It was tight. Carefully, she pressed in different areas until she came to the right side. She pushed down lightly.

He groaned fitfully.

Staring at him, she shook her head. "Lord, no."

Elk Dreamer frowned. His gaze shifted between Gretchen and his friend. "Do you know what is wrong?"

Sweat ran a course down Gretchen's spine. Resting her forehead in her hand, she nodded. She only wished she did not know. "It's his appendix."

"A-pen— What is this?" For the first time, Elk Dreamer's voice denoted fear.

She looked up and swallowed. This would be difficult. She clasped his hand reassuringly. "Elk Dreamer, I need to operate."

He frowned. "What is operate?"

Hesitating, Gretchen looked down at the younger man. "It means I need to cut him open . . . here." She indicated the spot, then glanced back at Elk Dreamer. "With the scalpel, remember?"

He stared at her with a look of shocked disbelief. He drew himself up straight. "No! You will kill Buffalo Calf."

"I won't kill him. I've assisted my husband several times in this same kind of surgery." She tried to ease his fears. "I know how to do it."

"No! You do not like Buffalo Calf. You would see him dead."

"Elk Dreamer." Any other time Gretchen might have been insulted by a statement like that, but not now. She did not have the time. She squeezed his hand. "I am a medicine woman. I will not hurt him."

As he had on so many occasions before, Elk Dreamer studied her as if he were seeking the truth of her heart.

"He'll die without the operation." Her brows knitted. "Won't you trust me?"

Slowly, as if he were suspended in time, Elk Dreamer removed the headdress and set it down beside him. He did not look at Gretchen, but instead peered down at his friend. "Buffalo Calf will die?"

She nodded. "Without the surgery . . . yes."

He glanced toward the sound of the drums still beating outside. "The people will not let you."

"They don't have to know."

He looked up. All too apparent, torment dulled the usual sparkle in his eyes. He appeared confused by her statement.

"You can stay in here with me and help."

Buffalo Calf began to pant. His stomach muscles tightened. The pain appeared to be almost continuous now. They would have to get started or it would be too late.

Gretchen pressed Elk Dreamer for an answer. "We can't wait too much longer."

Elk Dreamer pulled back. "I do not know your medicine."

"I'd need somebody. Please, Elk Dreamer." Taking his hand, she leaned forward and pressed his palm to her wound. "You helped me once . . . Help me again so that I can help your friend," she whispered.

At length, he expelled a rush of breath, and nodded. "Go and get your bag. I will help you . . . so that you may help Buffalo Calf."

Gretchen breathed a sigh of relief. She smiled. "Thank you." She rose, then started for the opening.

"Gret-chen." Hands pressing into his thighs, he stood.

She turned back.

He crossed the room and faced her. "I will get the bag. I do not want the people to know of this thing you do." He moved to the covered opening and halted. He hesitated, then cut her a glance over his shoulder.

She raised her brows, silently asking the reason for his delay.

"Do not thank me for this thing you ask."

"But why? It'll save his life."

He peered down at the ground. "You must know. If it does not go well—if Buffalo Calf should die, it will not be good for you." With anguished eyes, he sought out his friend, before returning a look of warning on her. "And it will not be good for me."

TWELVE

As was his custom when he wanted to be one with his inner self and meditate, Elk Dreamer set himself up in a quiet meadow surrounded by forest. He pulled off his breast plate and set it on the ground.

Peering up at the sky, he watched the frolicking of two sparrows. They reminded him of Buffalo Calf and himself. At twenty-four winters, Elk Dreamer was nearly five years older than his friend, yet the men had been inseparable since boyhood. He shuddered inwardly.

Never had he been so happy to see anyone open their eyes as he had a week ago, when Buffalo Calf awakened and smiled up at him. The surgery had taken until almost dawn, and not until mid-morning did his friend finally stir.

Although he had not admitted fear to Gretchen at

the time, he suspected that she had known, or at least felt it.

Unsure of the procedure, even more uncertain of the woman's skill, he had nervously sat by her side and allowed her to cut Buffalo Calf. Yet what else was he to do? *His* medicines had not worked. If the white woman had not been there to save his friend, the man more than likely would have died.

Shamelessly, he realized how much he loved the younger man. He was Elk Dreamer's brother no less than any blood relation. No loss, not even that of his own life, would have been a greater tragedy for him.

He exhaled a long, deep breath. Truly, the Great Spirit guided the white woman's hand. Never had he witnessed such a thing. Gretchen moved through the surgery as if it were an everyday occurrence. She did not talk much, only a few commands for "pressure here," and "hot water" for cleaning when she was through.

And he had been glad to do it. He had not been disturbed in the least that he was doing the bidding of a woman. His only concern had been for Buffalo Calf's life.

Gretchen's steadiness with the thin blade had amazed him. Not once the whole time did she complain of the tedious hours, or the awkwardness in his attempts to help her. She simply smiled patiently and waited for him to do as she instructed.

To watch her, no one would have believed that she, herself, endured great pain. Even *he* had almost forgotten. But afterward, when she had nearly collapsed from the effect of both her wound and physical fatigue, he had remembered all too quickly. Once the ordeal was over, she slept many hours.

Elk Dreamer picked up some pine needles near his pony blanket and rubbed them back and forth between his fingers, allowing the breeze to carry them a few feet away. With the reassurance that his friend was out of danger, a strange sadness had wormed its way into his heart.

He felt useless and unable to cope with his sudden inability to do his duty. Why had the Great Spirit chosen not to work through him? Had his power to communicate been dulled?

As if in answer, the warm chinook blew its soft breath across his face. He had to know. He would seek a vision to discover the answer. He needed the comfort of his flute. The music would help him open to the spirits.

Taking out the instrument, he closed his eyes and sent a soothing tune up to the heavens. As always when his heart was disturbed, he played the Song of the Eagle. But, again, he could not seem to focus. After the passing of nearly an hour, he finally relented. He had found very little peace, or comfort. For the first time in many years, the spirits did not answer his call. He felt even more dejected than before he had begun to play.

Sitting cross-legged, his body went lax. While he still held the flute in his hand, his head dropped forward. What was happening to him? He could not seem to concentrate. His mind was not on the spirits. Every time he sought to cleanse his soul, it seemed that his inner voice would speak of nothing else but the white woman. Since Buffalo Calf's surgery, Gretchen had plagued Elk Dreamer's thinking almost constantly.

And the people. They had suddenly grown quite fond of her. With the saving of his friend's life, she had captured their respect and admiration.

Counting himself, there were only sixty-two warriors in their group. The rest were old men, women, and children. Every capable brave was needed to insure the safety of the tribe. Even at such a young age, Buffalo Calf had already proven himself many times over in battle. All were happy that he had been healed and delivered back to them.

Over the course of these past seven days, most of the people had endeavored to speak with Gretchen and tell her of their gratitude. Some had even brought her small gifts of appreciation. None appeared to be even the slightest bit troubled that it had been she, a white woman, who had saved Buffalo Calf.

But Elk Dreamer was not so happy. Watching her among his tribe, he had found that his people seemed to have less occasion to call on him for their everyday needs—both spiritual and medicinal. With Gretchen's presence, they did not need him. She had learned to communicate and use their language very quickly. Upon Snow Dancer's return, even she appeared to have become more friendly—or at least tolerant of Gretchen.

Worse yet, after discovering what she had done for him, it was Gretchen, not Elk Dreamer, whom Buffalo Calf called for whenever he was in pain, or want of something. Not once during the passing of the last seven days had anyone asked for the tribe's own medicine man.

True, there had been no real need. No one had gotten sick, or been injured, but Elk Dreamer felt useless just the same. It seemed his fears for the white woman's safety among his people had been unwarranted.

Instead, he now found himself wondering if he should be concerned for his own security. Other medicine men had been run out of their tribes, or worse—killed—for not being able to fulfill their duties. It made him angry to think of being replaced.

Shifting to a more comfortable position, he lifted his face into the wind. This was ridiculous. The people would not shun him. He was too well liked. They needed his guidance and care just as much now as they always had. So why did they not show it?

Palms up, he spread his arms out from his body. He sought to alleviate his fear. "It is me, Elk Dreamer, elk medicine man to the Brave Heart warrior society of the Lakotah." He sang the prayer in his native language. "I am a spirit seeker calling to you, the old ones, for a vision. I try to walk in pleasant dreams, but evil thoughts crowd my mind. My blood, as does the blood of my fathers before me, runs deep throughout the land of the plains. It is my center, the reflection of my soul. It is what possesses me to speak to you now."

He hesitated, unsure of how to approach the Great Spirit with the trouble of his heart. "There is a woman—the yellow-hair—who has come among us. She brings great knowledge and power into our lives—" He paused. Shame bore down hard upon his soul.

But even as he continued, his mind raced with suggestive thoughts of Gretchen. "I am drawn to this woman, Great Spirit of the earth and heavens. My blood runs hot to be near her. My eyes burn to look at her. My heart races with want and need for her, yet I know this to be wrong. I am Elk Dreamer, bound by the blood that flows through my veins to join with one of my own . . ."

The sound of a woman's familiar voice softly stole upon his concentration. He turned his ear toward it.

She hummed his Song of the Eagle.

His heart leapt. Had the spirit heard him? He pleaded for it to be so, but it was too clear—too alive. He raised himself up on his knees and leaned back on his heels, fighting the growing lust battling against his prayer. "Help me, Great Spirit. I would know how to—"

The song grew louder—imposing on his resistance—stirring his desire even more. A vision of Gretchen rose behind his eyelids. A cascade of yellow hair fell loosely about bare shoulders. Pale soft skin beckoned to be touched.

His prayer forgotten, he reached out. His nostrils flared. He could almost smell the soft, heady fragrance of her womanly scent. His body reacted. Every muscle tightened. He felt himself grow hard.

Intense blue eyes, like a delicate summer sky, looked down upon him. Husky with passion, she called out his name.

"Elk Dreamer?"

Feather-light, a hand touched his shoulder.

"Elk Dreamer?"

There it was again. But this was no dream. The voice was too real. He blinked, forcing his eyes to open.

"Are you all right?" Holding a large acorn-shaped basket, Gretchen bent down to him.

Elk Dreamer's eyes nearly bulged from their sockets. This could not be. He was still entranced.

She squeezed his shoulder. "What is it? Are you ill?" Her voice caressed his hearing.

He stared hard at her. Was she real, or a taunting spirit sent to tease him? Uncertain, he reached out, clasping her hand in a tight grip. He groaned. This was no apparition. She *was* flesh and blood.

She blanched. "What's wrong with you, Elk Dreamer?" She placed her hand against his forehead.

Soothing and cool, her touch gave him more comfort than he had felt in many days, yet tempted him sorely. He fought the rush of need within him.

Headlong, his defiant pride rammed the maddening lust feeding on his senses. He jumped to his feet. "What do you want from me, woman?"

Wide-eyed, she flinched. "What do I— I don't want anything from you." Staring at him, she yanked her hand out of his. "I was out here with your grandmother and Snow Dancer looking for prairie roots."

He peered out across the meadow, but seeing no sign of either of the other two women, he eyed her with suspicion.

Her eyes rounded, and she expelled a haughty sound. "You think I came out here looking for you, don't you?"

That was exactly what he thought, though he did not answer her.

"Look, I'm telling you the truth."

Still, he remained silent. At that moment, he did not care whether or not she was lying. He only knew he had to get rid of her—fast—for the sake of both of them.

"I had no idea you were out here," she persisted. "I'm telling you—oh, I don't care if you believe me or not. When I saw you sitting like that, I thought there was something wrong with you."

"Why? Have you not seen a man pray before?"

Apparently confused, she snorted. "Well, I—"

Elk Dreamer glowered at her. Still caught up in the fiendish storm of his imagination, he had to get away from her. She was too close, and he could not trust his fevered emotions. Veering around her, he stalked off toward the trees.

"Don't you walk away from me!" Gretchen raced after him. Catching up with him at the edge of the tree line, she grabbed his arm and wrenched him back to face her. Panting lightly, she straightened, and flashed him a fiery glare. "Look, what's wrong with you? Ever since the surgery the other day, you've been walking around with that same brooding expression. You hardly speak to anyone—especially me."

He held himself rigid against her attack. The woman was bold, indeed, to speak to him with such force. His temptation grew stronger.

Her voice pitched. "I don't know what your problem is, but I haven't done anything to you!"

"You say this thing when you know that it is *you* my people are calling to?" The urgency of his need heightened. He did not like what was going through his mind, but he could not stop himself.

"Grey-eyes runs to you as if you were his mother. Ponders-as-she-walks Woman, as well as many others, no longer come to me. Now they seek *your* counsel. Even Buffalo Calf and Snow Dancer smile when they look upon you." His chest heaved with the force of his anger. The woman had cursed him— bewitched him with her powers. And now, here she stood demanding to know what was wrong and insisting that she had done nothing to him.

"So that's it." Her tone softened, as did her features. "You think I'm trying to replace you. You think your people don't need you anymore." She offered him what appeared to be an apologetic smile. "Oh, Elk Dreamer. I'm sorry. I didn't mean to—"

He peered deeper into her eyes. It was the wrong thing to do. His temper teetered.

With the softness of a butterfly's wing, she touched his hand. "I didn't realize how their attention toward me must've made you feel. Your people do need you. You're their strength. You're what keeps them together . . ."

He grabbed her hand. Unexpectedly, he plunged headfirst into the full swell of adrenaline sweeping through his veins. He yanked her to him. He could not help himself. The monstrous hunger—the fiendish passion—had finally overpowered him. If she had just stayed angry . . . If she had not softened toward him . . . If he had not lost all reason in the seduction of those enormous blue eyes, he might have been able to escape.

He caught her around the waist and crushed her to him. He forced his mouth against hers, penetrating the barrier of her lips with his tongue.

She shoved against him and jerked her head away. Stumbling back a step, she nearly collided with a large pine tree. "No! Don't!"

But he would not listen. A sweet fire swept through his limbs. He had to have this woman—now! It was as if he had turned into his animal spirit, the elk, and now the blood of the stag burned molten through his veins. His groin tightened—throbbing. He stepped forward.

Bracing her hands on the tree behind her, her eyes darted about like a frightened creature. She bolted to the side.

But Elk Dreamer was too fast. He grabbed her by the hips and whirled her around in his arms.

Fighting him, she twisted and turned, pulling his hair. "Don't do this to me—please!"

Elk Dreamer was deaf to her cries. Primal instinct guided his actions. Gripping her buttocks, he ground himself against her. His breath came hard and fast.

She tried to scream, but he silenced her attempt with the force of his own mouth.

He would not be stopped. The animal lust within him raged too strong—too powerful. The savage longing had stabbed him so sharply that he could not have restrained himself if he had wanted to. But suddenly he did just that. He stilled.

His stomach knotted. He felt her tongue press against his, timidly at first, then shamelessly bold. When had she stopped fighting him? She was kissing him back!

She moaned into his mouth a deep, throaty sound filled with physical torment and prolonged suffering.

He pulled back and stared at her.

Awash in sunlight, she lifted her face to his. Heavily lashed, her eyes opened to mere slits. They shimmered with tears, reflecting his own need in an anguished expression. She, too, had been overrun with desire and passion. She shuddered against him. Her hands slipped up to his hair. She leaned into him. "Please," she whimpered against his mouth. "Don't stop."

Now it was Elk Dreamer's turn to tremble. What had he done? He had thought she was afraid of him. During their previous encounters, he had thought her acceptance of his touch was only a means to insure her own safety.

But this was not a woman given freely to seduction—this was a woman who had been deprived of love for a very long time. He read the longing in her expression. It surprised him. It saddened him, yet aroused him even more.

Her eyes appeared to darken to a deeper shade of blue, tears brimming beneath her golden lashes. Her chest rose and fell, her breathing shallow. "Please," she begged again, her voice husky—tortured. Her hands splayed across his back, inching up to his neck.

Stunned, Elk Dreamer hesitated.

Entwining her fingers in his hair, she kissed one brow, then the other. Her lips quivered. "Remind me what it's like to be a woman again."

He groaned. Hearing the sweet pain in her voice cost him the single measure of restraint he might have been able to summon. He palmed her buttocks, lifting her into his arms.

Wrapping her legs around his hips, she arced into him with a hoarse groan. She clutched his head to her bosom.

He swayed, then turned, slamming her back against the tree trunk.

Her breath rushed into his mouth with the force of the action, but still she clung to him.

Wrenching his lips from hers, he buried his face against her neck.

She tilted her head back, allowing him room.

He stroked her ear with his tongue, trailing it down across her throat. Finding the hem of her dress, he tugged, lifting it above her hips.

She shifted within his grasp and moved against him.

He reached under the buckskin and cupped one breast.

Holding him tighter, breathing wildly, she cried out, her nails biting into the flesh on his back. She writhed as if on fire, pressing her hips harder against his loins, smothering herself against him.

Rougher than he had meant, he squeezed the fullness of her breast, then pinched her nipple. Heaven and hell, she felt closer to both than he had ever imagined anything could. He groaned.

His mind raced, oblivious to all but the want— the need—of her body's surrender to his. He could not stand it any longer. Bathed in the fiery passion, he could almost feel the very real flames scorching them both.

Reaching down, he freed the leather thong securing his breechcloth and let it fall to the ground. His maleness sprang upward, jutting against her belly. Hot and hard, he was all muscle and sweat. Tameless energy slammed through his groin. He had to take her—now!

Unable to control himself, he plunged into her.

"Oh, God!" She breathed out the words. She caught hold of his shoulders and reared back, thrusting to meet his entrance. Her muscles clutched at him, coaxing him higher. She gasped, a sweet, pitiful cry of pleasure.

His heart constricted, but he could not stop. He had

not wanted their joining to be this way, but he needed her as much as she needed release.

She was so beautifully responsive to his every movement. With each forceful shove, she met him with a like push. Fingers tangled in his hair, she pulled him to her breast. Her heart hammered in his ear.

Hands spanning her naked buttocks, he rammed forward. He rocked her hard upon the tree, crushing her backside against the pine, scraping the skin on his knuckles. He plunged deep inside her and quickened the pace.

Her legs tightened around him.

Unable to hold back, he grabbed the sides of the hardwood and planted his feet apart. He dug his grip into the bark and arced into the heated sweetness of her flesh. Thunder crashed in his ears. Lightning bolted through his body.

Vaguely, he heard her scream his name. Their bodies collided one last time, and he unleashed his seed. With the last vibrating throe, he fell against her and shuddered, gasping for air, mingling his sharp moans with hers.

Locked as one, they remained entwined until his legs started to shake from exhaustion. Heavy upon her, he thought he must be crushing her, yet no sound escaped her but her labored breathing. He tried to back away, but she would not release him.

Then it started. A soft trembling at first, followed by a catch in her throat. He listened. Heart-wrenching, the sound of the woman's suppressed sobs broke the spell.

No sharper pain could have pierced his soul than the sudden realization of the inexcusable act he had just committed against this woman. A serpent's belly could not have touched as low as he now felt. What could he say to her? How could he explain?

He groaned inwardly. No explanation could justify his crime. *He* was supposed to protect women, not attack and all but rape them. He pulled away and tried to speak, but no words formed. He looked down at her.

Sheened in a fine mist of perspiration, lashes still lowered and drenched with tears, Gretchen lifted her face. "I—" Her bottom lip quivered. "I'm sorry, Elk Dreamer."

What? Was she apologizing to him?

"It's been so very long since any man's looked at me the way you do . . . and when you touched me . . ." She raised a shame-filled gaze.

He could not stand the torment that registered in her eyes. *He* had been the one that had rushed in on her. "Gret-chen. Do not say this—"

"Shh." She pressed her fingers to his lips. Slowly, she released her hold on him and lowered her feet to the ground. "You were right. I did come out here hoping to see you. I shouldn't have sought your attention. I didn't mean to. It's just that . . . when you look at me, and touch me as you have—" Her voice strangled on a whimper, and her eyes brimmed with tears. Her gaze lowered to his chest, and she began to cry in earnest.

Gored by the meanest charge of any buffalo, he could not have felt more pain than he saw in this woman's face. She had undoubtedly been in need so long that she had somehow turned his crime into hers.

Tipping his head back, he pulled her to him. He shot an angry glare through the pine boughs. Why had he been so careless? Why could he not have controlled his sexual appetite this time with this woman when he had on so many occasions before with others?

Hands tucked beneath her chin, she leaned into him like a small child.

Her sobs nearly broke his heart. He would have liked nothing better than to have the man, Garret, trapped within the strength of his hands so he could squeeze the life from his body. It was good that he was dead.

How could any man have caused this beautiful woman such torment? How could he have thought her undesirable, then tortured her into believing it herself?

The sound of her pain cut Elk Dreamer to the very marrow of his bones. No woman—not even Fawn— had ever confused him so. Reaching down, he slipped his hand beneath her buttocks and scooped her into his arms. "Do not cry, Gret-chen. You have done no wrong." He carried her back to where he had left his pony blanket.

He had to comfort her. He had to soothe her spirit. He had to prove to her that she was not just a female needed to sate the hunger of a man's madness. That she could—no, should—expect love in the most beautiful sense of the word. He would demonstrate how desirable she was.

Lowering her onto the blanket, he kissed the tears away, then gazed into the depths of her eyes long and hard. "I *want* you, Gret-chen." He had no other words to prove the truth of it. He only hoped his actions would show her his heart.

Gently, he pulled her arms from around his neck and laid her back.

Tensing, she shied away from him.

He shook his head and leaned across her, bracing himself upright with one hand on the ground beside her.

Like a scared child, she shivered, staring at him.

Moving slowly so as not to frighten her more, he stroked the inside of one wrist, then trailed a gradual path up the inner side of her arm with his fingers. He found the lacing binding her dress closed across one shoulder. He pulled it loose, first one seam, then another, until the rawhide string tugged free.

She stiffened.

Softly, he crooned to her in his own language, caressing her face with his eyes. Lowering his head, he eased the buckskin cloth away from her skin, uncovering one breast.

He heard her breath catch. "Do not be afraid," he murmured, his tone soothing. This time she would know how captivatingly beautiful she was. This time he would *make love* to her. And this time it would be *all* for her . . .

THIRTEEN

Snow Dancer's eyes burned with all the fury of a raging inferno. Her heart pounded as she peered out through the trees and watched Gretchen basking in the pleasure of Elk Dreamer's touch. It should have been her lying in his arms—not that yellow-haired cow.

Tears blinding her vision, she tossed down her basket of roots, then turned away and clutched her arms across her chest. She could not stand to see any more. The white woman had seduced Elk Dreamer. How could the man be so blind? Could he not see the evil in her? Gretchen was doing as all whites had done with Indians. She was playing him for a fool.

Snow Dancer had seen this coming from the first. But she had thought she would be able to rid herself of the woman before anything like this could happen.

Now what was she to do? Her plan was not moving as quickly as she had hoped.

In the distance, the sounds of the couple's love-making floated on the breeze.

Snow Dancer held herself still. It hurt so badly to think of Elk Dreamer wasting his affection—just as he had with Fawn. Still, she could not really hold him responsible. After all, he *was* just a man. And the white woman was no more than a cow high in season.

To save herself, she would lift her tail into the wind for any man to catch the scent. Elk Dreamer could not help but be enticed. Yet Snow Dancer could not let this happen again.

Gripping the tree behind her back, she banged her head against the trunk and gritted her teeth. And to think of the hours she had put into being nice to that woman.

She had done everything as she and her white cohorts had decided. She had fought the bitter hatred she felt for Gretchen and kept it in check. She had even befriended the woman, hoping to relax the strain between them enough so that she could lull her into a comfortable relationship. And so far, it had worked.

But no longer. After witnessing this vulgar display of seduction, Snow Dancer would never be able to continue the ruse of friendship. She would have to hurry her plan along if she were going to get rid of the yellow-hair. Elk Dreamer had already proven his weakness under the influence of Gretchen's female charms. Something had to be done—now!

But she needed help from one of her own kind. Her mind whirled. Buffalo Calf. Maybe there was still a

chance to manipulate him into her ploy. She was not
without influence with him. He had made that clear
enough. He wanted Snow Dancer, and she knew it.
Yes. He would listen to her. Then he would have no
choice but to help her get rid of the woman. Now if
only she could just bend him to her side.

She smiled wickedly. Oh, yes. She had almost forgotten about the little precaution she had taken. She
had just the thing to persuade him. And if that did
not work . . .

She arched a brow. No. She shook her head. She
could not think of doing such a thing. Never would
she deliver herself up like that again. She had to save
herself for Elk Dreamer. The information would be
enough. She was sure of it. She would make Buffalo
Calf see the danger the woman presented—she just
had to.

Pushing herself away from the tree, she dashed
through the thick underbrush of the forest, back
toward the encampment. She did not stop until she
reached the lone aspen that abutted the back of Elk
Dreamer's lodge.

She peered around. No one had either observed or
cared about her feverish haste. Reaching up through
the quaking leaves, she retrieved a leather pouch from
a cleft of branches where she had hidden it for safe-
keeping. It was the same bag the soldier had been
carrying the day she discovered the white renegades.
It was good the men had not taken it.

Opening it, she pulled out the wrinkled paper Palmer had so thoughtlessly discarded. She glanced over
the writing. This would be her proof. Buffalo Calf
could not read the white writing, but he would trust

Snow Dancer to tell him the truth. And she would.

She tried to make out the handwriting for herself, but could only manage the simplest of words. Still, she remembered everything that Palmer had told his men the letter contained. She could pretend to read it as it was written.

Palmer would not have lied to his own men. He would have had no reason to do so.

She organized her thoughts. As far as the troopers at the surrounding forts knew, her people *were* responsible for all of the raids on the coaches—not to mention the other trouble that had recently begun with the white miners looking for the yellow iron.

Good. Satisfied with her recollection, she dipped her head. Once she told all of this to Buffalo Calf, he would be the first to help change the people's minds about *dear sweet Gretchen*. He would not allow the fact that she had saved his life to interfere with his loyalties.

Besides—Snow Dancer raised her brows smugly—her saving his life had only been a stroke of good fortune—an accidental advantage that could never happen again. But even *that* was about to change.

Snow Dancer smiled. She folded the document carefully, then replaced it in the pouch. Flipping over the leather flap, she fingered the letters U.S. ARMY tooled into the tanned hide.

Buffalo Calf would be impressed with her loyalty. This pouch would insure that what she told him was the truth. Feeling almost giddy with her newly found confidence, she chuckled to herself.

She would even suggest that he have Gretchen read the paper to him. But he would not have the woman do it. He would trust Snow Dancer. His warrior's heart and stubborn loyalty would not permit him to believe an outsider. The white woman was a threat. He had to see that. She would make him.

Even Elk Dreamer would not be able to justify the woman's staying. Gretchen would have to be sent back to her people.

Snow Dancer's happiness blossomed into glee. Then her plan to have the white woman killed could be carried out.

In the dimness of Elk Dreamer's tipi, Gretchen turned toward the firelight and read the crumpled paper she had just been handed by Buffalo Calf.

Arms folded tightly over their chests, both Elk Dreamer and Buffalo Calf stood in silence, watching her.

Gretchen shook her head. How could this be true? The army thought that it was this band of Sioux that had committed all of the raids on the stagelines? Yet what else were they to believe? Upon her initial confrontation with them, she, herself, had thought as much. Looking up, she shifted a questioning stare between the two men. "Where did you get this?"

"Snow Dancer brought it to Buffalo Calf," Elk Dreamer replied.

Gretchen looked at the woman sitting off to the side in silence. She appeared to be totally engrossed in making an ermine fur vest, but Gretchen had a feeling she was listening intently. "Where did she get it?"

"She has told us that she found it by a dead soldier

near Lodgepole Creek, when she was out searching for roots today."

Gretchen turned a suspicious look on the woman. She remembered the discarded basket she and Elk Dreamer had discovered near a tree at the edge of the meadow earlier that afternoon. It had been half full of the same kind of groundnuts Gretchen had gone out searching for.

She narrowed her eyes. Snow Dancer had been carrying just such a basket when she had gone out with Gretchen and Ponders-as-she-walks Woman. She did not know why, and could not prove it, but Gretchen was sure Snow Dancer was lying. Maybe not about where she had found the pouch, but definitely about *when* she had found it.

"It is true?" Elk Dreamer interrupted her thoughts. "These are the words of the soldiers?"

Gretchen glanced down at the dispatch and scanned the company stamp. "As far as I can tell, it is. I've never really dealt with the military, so I can't be certain. But this looks official enough." Elevating her gaze, she hesitated before continuing. "Do you have any idea what this says?"

Elk Dreamer nodded. "Snow Dancer has told us."

Gretchen frowned. "She reads English?"

"Not good, but enough to say that the soldiers at the Laramie Fort are coming to look for us."

"*Huka!*" Buffalo Calf slapped his fist into the palm of his other hand. "*Takpe was'icun!*"

Gretchen flinched at the fury in his voice. She was not certain what he had said, but she was afraid whatever it was, Buffalo Calf meant business.

"*Ptehinc'ala!*" Elk Dreamer spoke his friend's name

harshly. He glared at the man, then softened his expression, pointing him toward the fire. "*Ta ta iciya wo.*"

Buffalo Calf grumbled something unintelligibly, but crossed to the flames and sat down as he had apparently been instructed.

Elk Dreamer offered Gretchen a smile, then shrugged. He moved up beside her and took her hand.

Immediately, her gaze shifted to Buffalo Calf, then Snow Dancer.

Glowering at the fire, the man obviously had not witnessed Elk Dreamer's gesture of affection, but Snow Dancer did.

In the flash of a look, Gretchen saw the unmistakable sign of hatred—or was it jealousy? But why? Snow Dancer was in love with Buffalo Calf. Was she not?

"His blood is made hot quickly," Elk Dreamer said quietly, drawing her a step closer to him.

Gretchen glanced down to where his dark skin touched her paler hand. He did not seem to care if anyone knew of their secret. But she did. It had only been a few hours since their lovemaking, and she was still just a little too uncomfortable with Elk Dreamer's attention. She was not sure how to handle it—or how it had even come about for that matter.

She tried to smile, but her face heated with embarrassment instead. Clutching the pouch in one hand, she pulled out of his grasp, then moved to sit opposite Buffalo Calf. "Do the rest of your people know about this?" She knelt and sat back on her heels.

"We have told no one."

"But you are going to." She hoped he would not, but knew he would.

He nodded.

"What do you think they'll say?" For the first time in many days, Gretchen felt a tremor of fear for her own well-being. What if the people retaliated and used her to wage their revenge on?

"There will be much talk—much anger." Elk Dreamer sat beside her. He shook back the length of his hair, then looked at Buffalo Calf. Though creases of worry etched his features, he did not look overly concerned. "The council of elders will decide what is to happen."

Gretchen read the missive again. She had expected Elk Dreamer to be a bit more upset by all of this than he appeared to be.

"You are troubled, Gret-chen?" He tipped his head to one side and raised his brows. "There is no need. The council will listen to me. You will not be harmed."

Gretchen's stomach knotted. He had read her thoughts, yet his manner was all too calm. Just exactly how much of this letter did he truly know? "What did Snow Dancer tell you about this dispatch?" She waved the paper.

"She says that your being here will cause great trouble. That the soldiers know that you are with us and believe us to be keeping you against your will."

Gretchen looked across the room to Snow Dancer.

A weak smile played across the Indian woman's lips, and her eyes rounded a little.

What was going on? There was nothing in the paper that had even mentioned Gretchen—or any other woman for that matter. Snow Dancer had lied again. Did she not believe that Gretchen would tell them the truth? "That isn't exactly what this says."

Beyond Elk Dreamer, Gretchen saw Snow Dancer shake her head.

She stared at Gretchen, with an almost pleading look.

"There is more?" Elk Dreamer appeared puzzled. His gaze flitted to Snow Dancer, then back to Gretchen.

Apparently curious as well, Buffalo Calf leaned nearer.

Gretchen hesitated. Over the past few days, she and Snow Dancer had managed to strike up what she hoped was a good friendship. She had no wish to ruin that now. But how was she to handle this? It was not her nature to lie.

"Gret-chen?"

"Actually, it doesn't say anything here about your people holding me hostage at all. In fact, it doesn't mention anything about *any* hostages. I doubt they even know about me." She glanced up at the Indian woman.

Dropping the furs into her lap, Snow Dancer began gesturing to Elk Dreamer with frantic motions.

Gretchen could not make out all that the woman said. She watched intently, but the Indian woman was signing so fast, Gretchen could only make out the barest of details. Something about the driver of the stage. Cable? But he was dead. No. He was alive. Studying Snow Dancer's motions, she continued to watch.

Apparently Cable had made it out of the mountains and had told the soldiers about the stage attack.

"Ask her how she knows about the driver," Gretchen said.

But Snow Dancer only grunted, then gestured to Elk Dreamer with a flourish of frenzied hand signals.

By the time she had finished, Gretchen had deciphered that the woman had just assumed Cable had informed the soldiers about Gretchen. But there was something missing. Too many pieces to make the Indian woman's story believable. How did she know about the driver? She had not been at the scene of the attack that day. Gretchen watched Elk Dreamer's expression for any sign of doubt.

He held his features stoic.

Maybe *he* had witnessed Cable's escape and had recounted the incident to Snow Dancer.

"*Was'icun Zuya!*" Buffalo Calf threw a stick he had been holding into the flames, then made as if to rise.

Elk Dreamer stayed the younger man with an upheld hand. "The whites cannot make war on us if they cannot find us," he said in his Lakotah tongue. He shifted his gaze from Buffalo Calf to Snow Dancer. He seemed to be examining her for some reason.

She held his stare, but there was a visible clue of nervousness in the rapid-blinking of her eyes.

Elk Dreamer turned from the Indian woman, and looked at Gretchen. He did not speak for a long moment. He appeared to be sizing up the two women. "Tell me, Gret-chen. What *does* the soldier's writing say?"

Snow Dancer stiffened.

Gretchen cleared her throat. "Well . . . um . . ." There was no holding back now. She would have to tell him the whole truth. She cleared her throat.

"It seems that Chief Sitting Bull and—"

Buffalo Calf's head whipped up. "*Tatanka Yotanka*?"

Elk Dreamer rocked back on his heels, then sat down and crossed his legs like a pretzel. He pointed to the paper. "The writing speaks of *Tatanka Yotanka*?"

"Is that Sitting Bull?"

"Sitting Bull." He grunted with a nod.

"You know him?" Gretchen asked. It was a stupid question. Since news of the massacre at the Little Big Horn, there were very few who had not heard the chief's name.

"He is our leader over Gall," Elk Dreamer answered. "We have been waiting many moons to meet him, at the time of the gathering of our people, when we join the other nations of the plains." He paused. His gaze darted from Gretchen to Buffalo Calf, and back again. Obviously, he had not meant to tell her this much.

Gretchen swallowed. She stared down at the dispatch. Her throat tightened. She had been afraid of something like this. How could she read this to them now? How could she tell him that their scheme had been discovered? And that the information on this single sheet of paper would cause them to have to forfeit everything they had been living and planning for these last two years?

Moreover, *should* she tell them? If she did, she might be putting the lives of her fellow whites in further jeopardy by letting the Indians know what the army was up to. And what would happen to her once these people knew?

"Read us the soldier's words of *Tatanka Yotanka*,

Gret-chen," Elk Dreamer commanded. He arched a brow.

Still as yet uncertain if she should read the document, she hesitated.

"Gret-chen?" Elk Dreamer's tone became serious.

Wetting her lips, she peered up at the men one last time.

"How does it read?" He tilted his head and peered down at the paper as if he thought to interpret the writing himself.

She had no choice but to read as he had instructed. She had stalled as long as she could. Without further prompting, she took a deep breath and began.

20 May, 1878

Major Julius W. Mason
3rd Cavalry
Fort Laramie, No. Wyoming Territory

Sir:
     Be advised—This dispatch will put you on Alert:
     In compliance with orders forwarded from the Department of the Platt, Omaha, Nebraska, I am obliged to inform you that Sitting Bull and Crazy Horse are noted to be in Canada stirring up another outbreak of war. It has been brought to the attention of the Department that one of their lieutenants has trapped himself and a small group of Sioux in the Laramie Mountains.
     They are reported to be well equipped with the latest improved arms captured in raids on nearby ranches, frontier settlements, mining camps, and the like. It is further represented that this single wild band is solely responsible for the many attacks

and murders of civilian travelers. These renegades are believed to be saving their confiscated weapons and ammunition to carry into the interior of the Indian country. It is speculated they will try to meet up with these two war chiefs and the other Indian nations that have not as yet surrendered.

They must be stopped at all cost. Telegraph lines over the Laramie Mountains have been cut. Further communication between posts must be transferred by courier. Cannot string new wire until hostiles are captured, or destroyed.

Lieutenant Colonel Luther P. Bradley
9th Infantry
Fort Sanders, So. Wyoming Territory

Slowly, Gretchen lifted her gaze. She looked at Elk Dreamer. She knew he was angry.

His body was visibly taut, his features hard. "They think *we* are attacking the whites."

She answered him with a single nod. She did not know what to say.

"*Ece.*" Buffalo Calf jabbed Elk Dreamer's arm with his elbow, then pointed to the paper. Obviously, he did not understand and wanted to know what was in the dispatch.

Elk Dreamer shot the younger man a silencing glance, then looked back at Gretchen. "So that is why they hunt us down." He shook his head. "We have outwitted ourselves."

"What do you mean?" Gretchen asked softly. She had no wish to incite his anger.

"It is as the soldiers say. We are trapped. For two winters we have been in these mountains, cut off from our world. We have waited in silence for word from Gall." He poked a finger at her. "But we have hurt no one."

Gretchen swallowed. Her throat closed. She could not help but feel sorry for him. Although she had not known him very long, she knew him to be an honorable man. And she knew it had not been these Indians that had attacked the stage.

"We wish only to rejoin our people." There was a distant, a kind of forlorn pain in his voice.

"And when you get back to them—what then?" Instantly, Gretchen wished she had kept the question to herself.

Elk Dreamer pierced her with a savage glare. He looked as if he could kill her.

She tried not to shake, but her body trembled traitorously.

His eyes remained fixed and unyielding for a long moment. "Then . . ." He pursed his lips, and slowly his posture relaxed. The fierce glint in his eyes dimmed a little. "We follow Sitting Bull. Only he can say what we are to do."

"So . . . what happens now?" She really did not want to know, but something drove her to ask.

"Now we talk."

"Talk? We don't have time to talk." Gretchen could not believe what she had heard. Did he not understand the very real danger they were all in? "Don't you know what the army will do to you when they find you?"

"What would you have us do?" He snorted. "Attack?"

Gretchen pulled a face. "Of course not. But you

can't just sit back and let them—"

"What?" he demanded, stinging her with a hard look. "We cannot tell them the truth. They will not listen. We are *savage hostiles*." He gestured to the letter. "They have no wish to hear the truth. They want only to see our blood spilled onto the earth."

Panic rose like bile to choke Gretchen. He was right. The army would not listen to these people. She had to think of some way to help them. "I can tell them."

"They will listen to you?" Elk Dreamer sounded doubtful. "Why would the soldiers believe a woman who has stayed with Indians?"

"I'd tell them how you cared for me. I'd tell them—"

"They would think you touched by the Great Spirit." He tapped his head with his fingers.

"No. I was a passenger in that stage attack. I know who's really responsible. I'd tell them the truth."

"You would tell them it is white men that kill the travelers?"

"Yes." Gretchen was desperate. These people had done no wrong—at least not here. She could not just let the army destroy the entire village. And it would come to that. Elk Dreamer would never surrender.

"*Ece.*" Buffalo Calf questioned Elk Dreamer about the contents of the dispatch and the couple's argument.

In a lowered voice, Elk Dreamer explained.

Instantly his friend's expression mirrored his own, then it grew ugly—angry. Buffalo Calf leapt up and in a fit of rage yelled something that Gretchen could not make out. "*Takpe was'icun!*" He repeated his earlier threat, shaking a fist at Elk Dreamer.

"You can't kill them all," Gretchen interjected.

Standing, she faced Buffalo Calf head-on. She had understood that statement well enough. Buffalo Calf wanted to kill all whites. Was she included? She felt she had to defend the soldiers' reasoning. "What else would the army think? There are men out there dressing like Indians and murdering innocent people."

"*Takpe was'icun!*" The words slid through Buffalo Calf's teeth like a knife. He leaned toward her.

"How will you do this?" She did not want to make him angrier, but she had to get him to listen. "There are as many white men as there are . . ." She grasped at the first thing that came to her mind. "As many as there are stars in the sky."

Elk Dreamer glared at her. Standing, he flexed his hands. For a moment, it looked as if he were going to hit her. He leaned over to his friend and whispered something, his eyes never wavering from Gretchen's.

The younger man faced off with Elk Dreamer. It appeared as if he were going to challenge his friend. But after only a few minutes, he relented. He signaled Snow Dancer to follow him, glared at Gretchen one last time, then stalked from the tipi.

Snow Dancer peered at Gretchen for a brief moment before taking her departure. She had a strange glimmer in her eyes. She flashed a look of apology, yet beneath the surface of her eyes something just short of contempt reigned.

There was something very wrong with all of this— something that Gretchen felt sure was connected with Snow Dancer.

Once the couple was gone, she turned her attention back to Elk Dreamer. She stiffened her spine. She knew that she had overstepped her place. She was a visitor here—and one that was just short of being an enemy at that.

She should not have spoken as she did, but it was too late for that now. She would not back down. She would just have to make Elk Dreamer understand. "I'm sorry I angered Buffalo Calf. I know women aren't supposed to speak out like that, but—" Why was she making excuses for herself? She had every right to say what she thought. "Surely you didn't just expect me to sit here and listen to him—"

"Do not talk!" Elk Dreamer brushed past her. He moved to the opposite side of the tipi, and picked up the beaded bag that contained his pipe.

Eyes wide, Gretchen stared at the man's back. His impudence struck her temper like a match to flame. "Who do you think you are, mister?" she demanded. She was not going to let him get away with ordering her around. Rage instantly replaced common sense. She set her hands on her hips. "Look, I'm not your little squaw. And if you think just because we made love—"

Elk Dreamer whirled around. His dark eyes stabbed her with the sharpness of cold steel.

She bit back the rest of her statement. The moment she had said the words, she was sorry. Their time was still too near and warm—too precious and lingering in her mind.

"You are right, Gret-chen." He snapped a lock of hair back from his eyes with a flick of his head. "You are not my *squaw*. You are not my woman. You are nothing to me—not even my friend. You do not want to be anything to any man."

Anger and hurt sliced through her like a knife to

flesh. "Only a friend would offer to do as I have done. How dare you say that to me!"

Elk Dreamer crossed the room in three easy strides. He stared at her, his gaze reaching in and shaking her soul with its force. "I dare much with you. Yet you dare nothing. You are afraid."

"I'm not—"

"You *are* afraid—afraid to be a woman. You ask me to make you remember what it is like to feel as a woman. When I do, you cry." He grabbed her hand. "When I touch you in front of others, you are ashamed. You do not go to the army for us, but for yourself."

Gretchen's heart hammered in her chest. How could he say this to her? "Myself? You're crazy! What good will my going there do me?"

"Do you think I do not know?" His eyes narrowed. "When you have told the soldiers, what will you do then? Will you return to me?" He shook his head. "You will run—run like you did from the memory of your life with your husband."

Gretchen shrank back. "That's a lie! I've never run from any—"

"It is you that lies, Gret-chen. Look at how you are." He swept a gaze over her Indian garments. "Now, here with people who have cared for you and taken you to their hearts, you stand ready to attack. Why?" He snatched the paper from her grasp and shook it in her face. "You do not know these soldiers. Why do you defend what they do? Would you see *my* people killed?"

Gretchen gasped. "Certainly not! I merely wanted Buffalo Calf to know that there are too many for your people to fight."

"You believe *your* people have the right to take our land away from us and set us up like old men and women on some—what is it that you call them—a reservation?" Elk Dreamer's jaw tightened. His body trembled with the fierceness of his anger.

Gretchen shook her head. "No, of course I don't. I didn't mean to—"

"We are not like cattle on your ranches. Without our freedom, we are nothing. Your people have stripped the buffalo from the plains for their hides and tongues alone, then left the meat to rot in the sun. Like the coyotes, they slink into the sacred Black Hills of the Great Spirit and tear the yellow iron from the heart of the mountains. They do not ask to have these things. They take what they want, then throw the rest away." His chest heaved.

Gretchen stepped back a space. She had only seen Elk Dreamer this angry once before, when Snow Dancer had defied him the day of her arrival. He had frightened her then. He frightened her even more now.

"You will see that Indian men are not the cowards your white men are. *Your* man was such a coward. He took you, then left you to waste." Elk Dreamer seized her arm roughly.

Gretchen did not like the insinuating tone of his words. Looking into his eyes, she saw a glimmer of savagery she had never seen in him before. Uncontrollably, she shivered beneath his stare.

"Do not think to treat me as he did you. I will not let you throw us away. *I* will keep what *I* want. *I* will not be wasteful." He yanked her hard against him and crushed her lips with his. Then, just as quickly, he released her with a light shove backward. "You *will* become my woman! You would do well to know this, Gret-chen. It is what you want." His eyes bored into hers. He lowered his voice in a husky threat. "It is what you need."

FOURTEEN

In the wake of Elk Dreamer's departure, Gretchen stared at the shadows caused by the firelight, dancing on the hide walls of the tipi. Their frolic seemed to mock her frayed emotions. Dumbfounded, she shook her head. Elk Dreamer wanted to make her his woman?

Oh, Lord. She slumped down to a sitting position. She had not meant for this to happen. She had not meant to let things get so out of her control. She had simply gotten swept away by the man's magnetic allure. His statement had taken her by complete surprise.

Not that she had not found him attractive. He was young and strong, with a body that was beautifully formed. And she liked him—truly liked him—but that was not enough to sustain the kind of relationship he was talking about. Besides, could he not see that she was older than he was? Too much older. Actually, she had no idea how much older she was, but it was enough—she was sure.

She was flattered that he had wanted her, but she was not ready for anything like this. Since Garret's death, she had not so much as thought about being with another man. Except for Elk Dreamer, she had not even looked at a man—at least not with any kind of desire.

The flap whipped up on the tipi and Ponders-as-she-walks Woman entered. She hovered at the opening, staring at Gretchen for a moment before she waddled over to where the animal bladders hung on a support pole. Then, with a basket tucked in the crook of one arm, a water bag in her other hand, she crossed to the fire and sat down with groan of exertion. She did not speak. Except for the single look she had afforded Gretchen, she did not acknowledge the younger woman's presence at all.

Gretchen watched as the old woman dug out a few roots from inside the woven container and poured the clear liquid over them. She rubbed the dirt off with a soft antelope-skin rag.

"Where is Grey-eyes?" Gretchen asked, suddenly realizing that the lodge was unusually quiet for this time of evening. It had become her custom to play with the child a little at bedtime, then tell him a story before sleep.

"He is in the lodge of friends. They have a boy close to *Is'tahota*'s years. They played hard, then fell asleep."

"Mmm-hmm." It might have been the truth, and more than likely it was, but to Gretchen it seemed overly convenient.

Ponders-as-she-walks Woman offered her a root.

Accepting it, Gretchen peered at the bulb as if it held the answers to her many troubles. Ponders-as-she-walks Woman was up to something. What did she want? Gretchen had gotten to know her pretty well over the last few days—well enough to know that when Ponders-as-she-walks Woman came to someone in silence, there was something of importance on her mind. "You didn't come in here just to give me this, *Wiyukcan Maniwin*?"

The woman lifted her small shoulders. "You have not eaten this night."

"I wasn't really hungry." Gretchen shifted her stare to the fire. She lowered her hands to her lap. "I'm still not." Her mind swung back to Elk Dreamer. She had to figure a way out of this mess. She could not let him think that he could just bully her into becoming his *woman*, as he had put it. She was too far beyond being dominated now to ever let that happen again. She was her own person, and she was going to stay that way.

"You have great feeling for my grandson?"

Ponders-as-she-walks Woman's question hit Gretchen like a club. Raising her gaze to meet the woman's, Gretchen blinked. "What?" she asked as if she had not heard her correctly. But she had—all too clearly.

"I would know if your blood warms when you are near *Hanble Hehaka*."

Gretchen felt her face heat red. How was she supposed to answer such a personal question? Could she have been wrong about the basket she and Elk Dreamer had found in the woods? Could it have been Ponders-as-she-walks Woman's instead of Snow Dancer's? Could the old woman have observed their lovemaking? A flight of butterflies swarmed in her stomach. She bit her bottom lip.

"It is so hard to answer, Gret-chen? I would not ask, but when I was outside, I heard Elk Dreamer's words before he left."

Gretchen swallowed. She did not want to get into this. She sought to change the subject. "Do you know where he went?"

The old woman's lips pulled into a thin smile, and she nodded. "The men have gone into the council lodge. They will be there a long time."

Gretchen pressed the topic. "Do you know what they're discussing?"

"The women know—all of the people know."

"They told you?" Gretchen did not think the two men had had time to speak to anyone about the dispatch yet.

The old woman shook her head. "Snow Dancer told us. She says the soldiers are coming. That they are looking for you. That they think that we are holding you against your will."

"But that's not true."

"This I know. We only wanted to see you well—"

"No, that's not what I mean." Gretchen hesitated. Should she trust the old woman? Should she take her into her confidence? She touched Ponders-as-she-walks Woman's hand.

The older woman frowned, her features etched

with concern. "What troubles you, Gret-chen? It is Elk Dreamer?"

"No," she lied, though it was more truth than she cared to admit. Still, it was not her main concern at present. "It's Snow Dancer."

"*Wahinhan Wacipi*? What has she to do with you and Elk Dreamer?"

Gretchen's stomach clenched. They were back to that again. "Nothing—I mean—I don't know exactly."

"I do not think I understand."

"I'm not sure I do," Gretchen said honestly. "But Snow Dancer hasn't been completely honest about that dispatch." She scanned the floor of the tipi until she came across the wrinkled paper Elk Dreamer had snatched from her and tossed to the ground. Stretching out, she retrieved the letter, then retook her seat and looked up at the old woman.

Ponders-as-she-walks Woman peered down at the paper.

"It doesn't say anything in here about the possibility of a hostage." Gretchen handed the note to the woman as if she thought she could read it for herself. "Something's not right. Snow Dancer seems to know more than this says."

The old woman glanced up. Her expression grew hard—almost angry. "You think she lies?"

How would the woman react to Gretchen's suspicions? Would she take Snow Dancer's side? She had to know. Wetting her lips, she took a deep breath. "Yes—well—maybe not outright lying, but she definitely knows more than she's trying to lead us all to believe."

Ponders-as-she-walks Woman cut a glance toward the lodge flap, then looked back at Gretchen. "I think this, also."

"You do?" Gretchen was surprised. She had thought the woman would be against her.

"There was another such time as this with *Wahinhan Wacipi*."

Shocked, Gretchen's brows shot upward. "When? What happened?"

The old woman scooted closer. "She knew too much about the white men who killed *Tacincala*. She called one by name." Ponders-as-she-walks Woman lowered her voice. "No one else noticed but me."

Gretchen was shocked. "You don't really think she had anything to do with Fawn's murder, do you?" She felt certain that Snow Dancer was a little deceitful, but—no, surely not a murderess. This was the woman's own sister they were talking about.

Ponders-as-she-walks Woman shrugged, but the look of mistrust in her eyes was enough to display the truth of her heart. "The cut, too, was not so deep and bad as she pretends that it was." She touched her own throat in the place where Snow Dancer had been wounded.

Gretchen tried to visualize the younger woman's scar. It was embedded in a crease in her neck. It would be hard to know how badly the wound had been without actually having tended it herself.

"I have come across her when she does not know anyone is near, and I have heard her speak."

"What?" Gretchen shook her head. "You must be mistaken, *Wiyukcan Maniwin*. No one could pretend a thing like that for over two years."

"I have heard her," Ponders-as-she-walks Woman insisted.

"But why—why would she do such a thing?"

Again, the woman shrugged. "I am not certain." She looked toward the flap as if she were expecting someone. "I believe she wants *Hanble Hehaka* for her husband."

"But I thought it was Fawn that was supposed to—"

The old woman lifted a knowing brow and nodded.

"You mean, you think she might have conspired with the men that killed Fawn so she could have Elk Dreamer? Why haven't you told him?"

"I am old. My mind is feeble. I cannot say this to be true for certain."

Gretchen snorted loudly. "*Wiyukcan Maniwin*, your mind's about as feeble as a baby's lungs." She caught the old woman's wrist again and squeezed it gently. "So if you're not able to prove any of this, why're you telling me now?"

Ponders-as-she-walks Woman patted Gretchen's hand. She smiled, then brushed an errant strand of hair from Gretchen's face. "I did not think my *Hanble Hehaka* would ever find love again after *Tacincala*. You are a good woman, Gret-chen. My heart is glad for him—for you."

Gretchen flinched. Why was she destined to keep coming back to this? She pulled her grasp away. "*Wiyukcan Maniwin*, I can't." Tears threatened her vision.

"You have not found this same love with my *Hanble Hehaka*?" The old woman appeared concerned.

Gretchen fought against the disturbing emotions

stirring inside her. She looked away and stared at the fire.

Ponders-as-she-walks Woman touched Gretchen's chest. "Your heart pounds even now. Your eyes rain with tears at the mention of his name." She paused. Caressing Gretchen's chin, she gently lifted her face. "Does the one called Garret still haunt your heart?"

Gretchen blinked. Her stomach somersaulted at the mention of her late husband. "How do you know about Garret? Did Elk Dreamer tell you?"

The old woman shook her head. "When you first came to us, you cried out many times in your sleep. They were not happy dreams."

Gretchen swallowed and looked away. Guilt flooded her heart, pounding at her soul like a torrential downpour. She had all but forgotten about Garret, and her reason for leaving Reno. Not once over this past week had she thought about the man she had been married to.

"Do you still love this man?" Ponders-as-she-walks Woman persisted.

Love? Gretchen shook her head. No, love had not been a part of her and Garret's life for a very long time.

"Tell me about this man. *Hanble Hehaka* has told me he was not among the dead when you were found hurt."

"No, he wasn't," Gretchen offered in a shaky voice.

"He was not good to you?"

"He was at first . . ." Although Gretchen had not known Ponders-as-she-walks Woman for very long, she felt a kind of motherly comfort emanating from the old woman. Before now, she had not been able to confide in anyone about her troubles with Garret—not even Winter Magic. She had known her Indian friend was aware of the problem, but Gretchen had not felt at ease to speak with her about it. "I guess neither of us was very good to the other," she said.

"Do you run from him now? Is that why you traveled alone?"

The old woman's soothing voice coaxed Gretchen into telling of the tragic circumstances surrounding her marriage and, finally, Garret's untimely demise.

"Garret and I had only been married a couple of years when I was out riding by myself and was captured by Bannock." She shuddered. "I won't bore you with all the awful details about that incident. But when I finally escaped and was brought back to him by some friends, Garret believed that just because I was taken as a slave, I'd given myself to them in lieu of being killed. He hated the idea of another man having touched me. And nothing I said would convince him it didn't happen. He just wouldn't listen to reason, and finally I stopped trying."

Ponders-as-she-walks Woman nodded her head in an understanding manner.

"After that," Gretchen continued, "he grew more and more hateful toward my Indian friends. In fact, that's how he came to be put in jail. He tried to kill my best friend, Winter Magic." She looked away for a moment and shook her head. "I sent him there you know—to prison, I mean. It's my fault he's dead."

"You killed him?" The old woman frowned.

"No, but I was a witness to his crime."

Ponders-as-she-walks Woman stared at her. "I am not a man. I do not know their feelings. But this I do know . . ." Cupping Gretchen's chin, the old woman urged her to face forward. "*You* did not kill your man—*he* did."

Though Ponders-as-she-walks Woman's words were few and her wisdom not unlike the assurances of Gretchen's other friends, somehow hearing it now from this woman made it feel right. She felt strangely released, free of the blame and remorse she had been carrying around in her heart for the past couple of years.

"There is no shame in your leaving that place, Gretchen." Ponders-as-she-walks Woman smiled at her with an understanding expression. From within an old and sun-wrinkled face, deep-set brown eyes still young and full of caring reached out to her.

"Women must endure much with their men. It is not often we find one that has the strength to love a woman without imprisoning her somehow. I do not know." She lifted her shoulders, as was her custom. "I am only a woman . . . but I think it must be very hard sometimes to be a man."

Lashes wet from crying, Gretchen peered up at the old woman in confusion. She knew Ponders-as-she-walks Woman was trying to make a point, but for the life of her she could not see what it was.

The woman lifted a crooked finger. "I cannot say for certain, but it is my belief that men hold their women as great prizes—greater than even their ponies or rifles." She winked. "They do not say this thing, but I believe it is so."

Gretchen chuckled. The old woman had a flair for statements like this. And more times than not, she was right. But why was she telling this to Gretchen?

"I believe this to be true of my *Hanble Hehaka*." She chucked Gretchen under the chin. "He has found love again, and he is afraid. He holds you as his greatest prize, but you are not yet his."

Gretchen shook her head. Here we go again. "*Wiyuk-can Maniwin*," she started with a shaky voice. "I just don't know how I feel about him. We're strangers, and—"

"And?" The old woman leaned down and peered up. "You will know each other soon enough if you allow it to happen."

"But I can't—it wouldn't be fair to him. I told you. I'm going home."

"I did not hear *home* in the telling of your travels, Gret-chen." She tipped her head to one side. "You told me you were going to visit your sister. You said you did not know where you would go, or what you would do after that."

Gretchen squeezed her eyes closed, then opened them again. She stared hard at Ponders-as-she-walks Woman. God, but she hated to have her own words thrown back at her.

"Did I hear you wrong?"

Clasping her arms across her chest, Gretchen shook her head. "No."

"So you could stay with us if you wanted to?"

Pulling a corner of her mouth to one side, Gretchen sighed audibly. "*Wiyukcan Maniwin*, please." Her voice quivered. She felt drained. Her head drooped, as did her body. "I just can't."

Ponders-as-she-walks Woman's brows knitted.

"I can't think about Elk Dreamer and me . . . not together, not now. It's too soon."

The old woman patted Gretchen's cheek with a work-roughened hand. "There is time still."

Gretchen nodded, yet in her heart she felt sure that her time with these people was almost up. The army would not wait, nor would they back off from their pursuit. They would track this group down and slaughter them all if need be. But she could not let that happen. She had to do something to help them. But for now, she needed sleep. She was too tired to think.

Curling up by the fire, she lay down and closed her eyes. Before long, she felt someone stroking her head. She glanced up and smiled.

Ponders-as-she-walks Woman unbraided the length of Gretchen's hair and combed her fingers through the long strands, humming all the while.

Tucking her arms under her head, Gretchen relaxed beneath the old woman's gentle ministrations. It felt good to have someone taking care of her. It seemed that until now, *she* had always been the one seeing to everyone else's troubles. Her friends, both Indian and white alike, had always depended on her for strength and guidance. But now she had nothing to offer—not even to herself.

She was so confused. She had been through so much over the last couple of years. First it was her capture by the Bannocks, and Garret's mental torture. Then it was Winter Magic's attempted murder by Garret and his prejudicial friends, and now all of this. Where and when would it end? She needed to go home and feel safe again.

Yet would she? What was actually waiting for her in

Iowa? A farm she had not been back to since her marriage to Garret? An older sister who would undoubtedly find fault with everything Gretchen had done since her departure? How could she think of putting herself through all of that?

Except for the first couple of days, in these two short weeks, she had felt more at home here with understanding people she hardly knew, than she had in all the time she lived in Reno. Nothing was expected of her here. No one wanted anything from her—excluding Elk Dreamer, of course.

And what about him? He had asked nothing of her that he was not willing to give back in return.

Lulled by the warmth of the fire, and the comfort of the old woman's soothing touch, Gretchen drifted off to sleep. But her mind grasped at the unresolved worries crowding it.

Distant, yet clear, Garret's voice attacked her slumber. "You let those savages take you! No upstanding white woman would have ever allowed such a thing to happen. She would have killed herself first." His eyes burned red like fire in her memory.

"But I didn't—I swear," Gretchen cried. "I was a slave—no more than that. Not once did any of them touch me—not like *you* think." She reached out to Garret, but Gretchen's defense went unheard.

He pushed her away. "You think I'd ever have anything to do with you like that after you've whored yourself out to save your pitiful excuse of a life? It sickens me just to look at you."

Gretchen shivered in the wake of his fury. Tears stung her eyes. "Please, Garret, just listen to me—"

"I don't want to hear anything you've got to say."

After facing many hours of torturous insinuation and disgusted looks, Gretchen held herself up to his ridicule with a broken heart. She had to face the fact that she had lost Garret's love. "Then I'll leave. I don't want to bring you any more shame than I already have."

"You're not going anywhere!" he railed.

Grasping at any small chance of hope, Gretchen covered her trembling lips with one hand. Maybe he did love her after all. "You mean, you still want me?"

Garret glared at her with disdain. "Want you? Are you deaf, woman? Didn't you hear what I just said?"

"But I thought—"

"I could give a happy rat's ass what you thought."

"But you just said you wanted me to stay."

"Did I?" He grinned wickedly. "You're deluding yourself, darling. I don't *want* you—nobody would *want* you after what you've done."

Gretchen blanched. Why was he doing this to her?

"You think I want this town gossiping about us any more than it already is? Hell, woman, I've built myself a nice practice here. I've got a good reputation. People like me, and I like them. I'm not about to let you run off on me and cause me more grief."

He shook his head, then raked the full length of her body with his eyes. He moved up close, assailing her with his whiskey-heated breath. "No, darling. You're going to stay right her and be the fine, upstanding wife I took you into marriage for."

Gretchen could not believe what he was saying to her. If he hated her so badly, why didn't he just let her go?

"No matter what else, you've got the looks and

the quality manners that people find attractive. No.
I think I'll keep you around for a while—at least
until things die down and I can find a discreet way
of separating myself from you in a more . . . uh . . .
suitable fashion." He snorted loudly.

She did not like the way he had said *more suitable*.

"Tell you what. You like Indians so much, you can
just take care of them." He tapped her nose roughly.
"They're always skulking around with some kind of
illness or another. As a doctor's wife, it'd be your
civil duty to see to them in place of your busy husband. Besides, it'd make us look as though we were
magnanimous in our forgiveness of what's happened
to you."

Gretchen pulled away from him. She could feel the
hatefulness of his hideous and unfeeling heart clawing
at her. She had never known he could be this cruel.

He grinned again, even more treacherously than
before. "And if you should contract some deadly disease . . ." He feigned a sigh of remorse. "Who could
hold the loving husband responsible for not being able
to save his darling wife?" He laughed then, loudly
and viciously.

The sound rang in Gretchen's ears. The vision of his
face rushed her senses.

"I don't want you." His words flew at her from the
depths of a nightmare's dusky cloud. "Nobody would
want you!"

"I want you." The words suddenly changed, con-
fusing her mind. Not so distant in her thoughts, a
familiar voice moved in on Garret's. She fought the
cruelty of her past and ran toward a gentler space in
time. Like the warm chinook whispering across her

skin, Elk Dreamer broke through the mist. "It is what you want, Gret-chen. It is what you need."

"I can't," she heard herself answer. She backed away from the passion-infused glimmer in his dark eyes. Standing on the edge of her dream, she lost her balance and fell.

Eyes flying open, she bolted upright. Her chest heaved. Damp with perspiration, her hair clung to her face.

Tossing back a buffalo robe she did not remember from the night before, she peered around the tipi. It was morning, and she was alone. She groaned.

Though her sleep had been fitful, she had not woken. She swiped back the errant strands of hair from her eyes. The passing of the night seemed to have taken an eternity. She did not remember everything, but she knew Garret had stalked her in a nightmarish mist— and Elk Dreamer. He, too, had been there.

"Oh, God! What's happening to me?" She covered her face with her hands and shivered. She had thought that once she got away from her old life everything would change and she would find happiness. But this—whatever it was—was very far from any kind of happiness. Even in death, Garret had found a way to torture her.

Lowering her hands, she took a deep breath. She had hoped that by morning she would have been refreshed enough to concentrate more clearly on the matter of dealing with the army and the impending demise of these people. But her mind was far from being clear.

Night sweat covered her skin. She felt uncomfortably sticky and hot. She thought of the river, and of the sparkling pool not so far away. She needed to feel clean, and free of the nightmare. She had to get both Garret and Elk Dreamer out of her head—at least for a little while. On shaky legs, she struggled to her feet. What she needed was a very long, indulgent bath.

FIFTEEN

Arms folded across his chest, Elk Dreamer leaned against a thick-trunked pine near the bathing pool and watched as Gretchen strode out of the water and moved to where she had left her clothes. The sight of her nudity sparked a flicker of desire, yet as much as he would have liked to, he could not give into it.

He rubbed his tired eyes. He had not yet slept. He could not. His mind was too full of worry. Sounds of the churning river matched the upheaval agitating his system. He had to tell her the council's decision.

They had argued and talked throughout the night. There had been much anger, some of it directed at Gretchen, because she was white. But when the meeting had finally ended, all appeared satisfied with the outcome—all that is but Elk Dreamer.

Yet even he had to agree that they had no other choice but for Gretchen to be taken to the Laramie

Fort. She, alone, had a chance to convince the soldiers to the truth about the raids.

He watched as she rolled up her bar of soap in a cloth, then unpinned the length of her golden hair and let it fall against the slender curves of her pale hips. He brushed away the bead of sweat above his lips. He could almost feel the inviting softness of that tempting cascade taunting his fingers. He moved around to the other side of the tree.

Lost in the self-indulgence of her solitude, she appeared completely relaxed and at peace for the first time since he had met her. Slowly and deliberately she sprayed the entirety of her body with the perfume she had brought with her, then rubbed it into her skin.

His groin slammed tight. He inhaled, remembering the sweet springtime fragrance and the way it mingled with her own soft female scent. How could any woman be so alluring and not know her own power? Gretchen was not a maiden. She had known the secrets of love between a man and a woman. And he knew a little of her abuse at the hand of her husband, yet her despairing innocence continually surprised him.

In every other situation he had seen her in, she seemed well equipped to handle herself—whether she was afraid or not. Yet intimate circumstances left her overwhelmed and insecure.

He sighed. How could he have managed to lose his heart to her so quickly? When she had spoken of going to the soldiers, it had angered and frightened him at the same time. He had not had enough time to consider his feelings for her, much less the thought of her leaving.

In the back of his mind, he had always known she would be returning to her own people, but the full realization had not really hit him until last night. And then it had been too late. His fear had triggered his desire for her, and the words had tumbled out before he had a chance to think about them.

Now, it truly was too late for them. It seemed everything was against their being together—the spirits, the soldiers, the people—everything. And even if they did not have those things to consider, there was still the ghost of this Garret between them.

He rubbed his hand across his mouth again. No sense delaying the task at hand. She had to be told. Pushing himself away from the tree, he stepped up behind her just as she slipped her dress over her head.

She tensed visibly, even before he spoke.

He cleared his throat.

Keeping her back to him, she bent down and retrieved one moccasin. "Did you enjoy watching me?"

He stared at her in surprise. She had known he had been observing her? "Did *you* enjoy it?"

She whirled around and faced him, anger sparking in the deep color of her eyes. She shook her head. "You always have to make me feel dirty, don't you?"

He stiffened his spine. Why did she constantly test his temper? "Then I was right last night. You *are* ashamed of what we shared yesterday?"

Hopping on one foot, she tugged the moccasin onto the other and pulled it up her calf. She snatched up the other moccasin and glared at him. "I don't want to talk about it!"

Their eyes met in a battle of wills.

Then, without a single word, she wheeled away from him and marched over to a pile of boulders. Sitting, she yanked on the remaining moccasin.

Elk Dreamer followed close behind. He took a seat next to her. For now, he would let the matter drop. Leaning back, he crossed his ankles, then clasped his arms over his chest. "Good." He dipped his head in agreement with her statement. He did not want to talk about it either. He was afraid of what she would say. "There is another thing we must make talk on."

After securing the top of the moccasin just below her knee, she peered up at him. This time when she spoke, her voice came softer. "You were up all night with the council, weren't you?"

Elevating his gaze, he looked at the treetops swaying in the breeze and nodded.

"Were they very mad?"

"Mm. Much anger."

She pulled her hair around to spill over one shoulder, then braced her hands atop the boulder and leaned forward. "Did you tell them about my offer?" she asked, her voice sounding more than a little uneasy.

"I did not have to."

"You didn't?" Her head snapped up, and she stared at him.

He lowered his hands to his knees, matching her posture. "They have decided that you should go to the soldier's fort and tell them what you know."

She straightened. Her eyes rounded. "They did?" She hesitated. "Good! I'm glad." She jumped up and strode over to her things. "When do I leave?"

He did not answer her right away. He did not know if she was prepared. "*We* leave with tomorrow's dawn."

"*We?*" Squatting down, she gathered her soiled dress and soap. "You can't be serious."

"It has been decided."

Standing, she shook her head. "Not by me, it hasn't." She frowned, true fear shining in her eyes. "Surely you know what kind of danger that would put you in. Why, the army's liable to shoot you first, and find out the truth later."

"The elders have made the decision."

"But *you're* suppose to be their leader. Can't you tell them what might happen?"

He dipped his head. The men had taken every objective into consideration. It was better to lose only one man, instead of many. "*I* am the one who made the final decision."

"You?" She stared at him in disbelief. Her body began to shake. "Damn it, Elk Dreamer! We're talking about your life here."

Startled, he glared at her. He had never heard her use an obscene word before. Indians did not say such things—not even when they were angered. Besides, she was challenging him again. Rising to his full height, he pinned her with a defiant look. "It has been decided."

"No it hasn't." She stalked the space between them with angry steps. "Why do you have to go—why does anyone but me have to go? It'd be better for all of you if I went alone." Her cheeks blushed pink with the force of her temper.

"You have been to their Laramie Fort?" He wanted to touch her. She was so arousingly beautiful when her blood was stirred. But he did not. He had to remain in control if he was going to get through this.

"No! You know I haven't."

He shrugged. "There is no other way. I must take you."

"Look, just because I tell them what happened, and that who they really need to be after are white men—that doesn't mean they'll believe me." Her chest heaved. "There's nothing saying they will. And even if they do, they'll more than likely interrogate you to try and find out the location of your camp here."

He stepped back from her. Her words held more truth than he would have liked. "This is so."

"So you think that just because you march into that fort and sacrifice yourself, those men are going to forget about the rest of your people?" She shook her head and looked at him as if she thought him crazy.

"You know they won't. Even if you don't tell them where your people are, they'll come after them. And then what? I'll tell you *what*. If they truly believe that your people are responsible for the murders of the travelers, and the raids throughout these mountains, they'll slaughter them down to the last child. Tit for tat—tenfold." She took a breath, and her voice pitched louder, filling with disheartened anger. "And they won't wait to hear the truth before they do it either!"

"We have thought this, also."

"Then why, for God's sake, do you want to do this?" She sounded desperate. "Why don't you just pack up your camp and get your people out of these mountains while there's still a chance?"

"That *is* our plan."

"What?" Her expression registered confusion.

"It will take time for so many to cross out of the mountains, and through the vast territory between here and the Canadas." The breeze blew a wisp of his hair across his eyes. He studied her from behind the strands. "*I* will give them that time."

Shock cut through her angry expression. "You mean *you're* going to act as a diversion?"

Unsure of the word, he frowned.

"Bait—you're going to set yourself up as bait to the army?"

He nodded. "It is a good plan. The soldiers will want the leader."

"It's a lousy plan," she railed, throwing her hands up. "Did you consider the fact that they might just kill you, then hunt down your people anyway? The army's not quite the fools you might think them to be."

"You will help us," he answered calmly, matter-of-factly.

"You know I will. I told you that, but they've got orders to see that you don't join up with Sitting Bull. They'll never let your people through."

He sighed resolutely. He knew that there was more than a good possibility that the tribe would never make it as far as the Canadas, but they had to try.

"And why does it have to be you that goes with me? Wouldn't you serve your people better by staying with them?"

"It is my place—my risk."

"But why can't someone else take me?" She sounded as if she were struggling with her voice.

A twinge of excitement plucked at his insides. He had been right all along. She *did* care for him. Until now, no amount of goading had tempted her into telling him, but he would know. He had to hear her say it. He moved in closer and took her shoulders between his hands. "Why, Gret-chen. Why should I send another in my place?"

She did not attempt to move away, but remained poised within his grasp. "Because—"

He heard the unmistakable catch in her throat. He pressed her for the answer. "Tell me."

"Because you're their leader—they need you."

He arched a brow and eased a little closer. He slid his hand up to her cheek and caressed her lower lip with his thumb. "*They* need me?"

She opened her mouth as if to speak, but remained silent. Her eyes darted back and forth as she looked into his.

Sunlight filtered through the trees, dappling her face with shadow and light, causing her features to appear even more distress-drawn. Her eyes darkened to a deeper shade of blue. There was a war going on inside the woman. He could feel it—he could see it in her expression.

"I can't, Elk Dreamer," she said, her tone low, husky, threatening to break.

The slight tremor in her voice added to his urgency to know. "What?" He plucked her lip gently.

She groaned, closing her eyes for a second.

His body reacted. He felt himself grow hard. He had her trapped. She would have to tell him she cared for him—that she wanted to be with him. "What can you not?"

He knew he was pushing her into admitting something she was not quite ready to accept, but their time together was waning fast. They could not afford the luxury of taking it slow. He slid his hand around to the back of her neck and down her spine.

"Please," she whispered breathlessly. "Don't do this to me. I can't think when you touch me like this." She quivered beneath his hand.

"Do not think," he murmured against her mouth. He palmed the small of her back and pressed her up against him. He stroked her cheek with his other hand. Feather-light, he nuzzled her nose, then brushed his lips across her face to her ear. He breathed the heady aroma of woman and fragrant mist, and a bolt of excitement shot to his loins. He teased her earlobe with a flick of his tongue. "Tell me why you do not want me to go, Gret-chen."

She swayed into him with a shudder. Still as yet unwilling to yield, she clenched her hands into fists against his bare chest.

He knew she was waging a losing battle. He could feel her wall of resistance crumbling, her fortress of strength falling away with the passing of every breathless second. She was slipping uncontrollably toward him, toward the arousal she so desperately needed to know. "Tell me what I want to hear."

She shook her head, still fighting herself and him. "Don't do this to me, please," she whimpered. She sounded so helpless, so irresistible, so frightened, and yet so wonderfully inviting at the same time. "I can't . . ."

Like the crack of a whip, something snapped within him. He groaned, real pain clutching at his insides. He wanted this woman—more than any he had ever known—even Fawn. But he could not torture her into an admission. He would be no better than the man Garret if he did.

But instead of using bitterness and hatred, as had Garret, Elk Dreamer was using love and passion to bend Gretchen to his will. He could not take her like this. When she was ready, she would come to him. In the end, he felt certain, she would. He would have to give her the time she so desperately needed.

He pulled her into his arms and held her until the tremors subsided within her, until the spasms faded within him. It would take them three days to reach the fort. That was all the time they had. He prayed that it would be enough.

Snow Dancer jumped down in back of the fallen tree she had been hiding behind. She could not let Elk Dreamer see her. He would be angry if he knew she had been observing him and Gretchen. She watched as he stalked past.

Deep lines of worry drew his face taut.

She had heard him ask *Wiyukcan Maniwin* for the white woman's whereabouts, and had seen him leave. He had looked troubled, so she had followed him out to the river, hoping to discover the council's decision, but she had learned more than she had bargained for.

The council had helped her with one part of her plan. They were getting rid of Gretchen—and that would have been enough, if it were not for the fact that now Elk Dreamer actually thought he had found *love* with the woman.

Snow Dancer waited until Elk Dreamer was out of sight before she dared to move. Once he was gone, she looked back at Gretchen. Seething with anger, she growled, a low, deep sound like a stalking animal. The pale-faced cow had managed to maneuver her way into Elk Dreamer's heart. Snow Dancer dug the full grip of her hands into the decaying bark of the trunk. She would have to work even faster now.

Scowling, she bared her teeth. She knew if she did not see to the woman's death, Elk Dreamer would do everything in his power to keep the yellow-haired cow. If that happened, he would be lost to Snow Dancer forever. No. She would never allow that to happen. She would have to take complete control of the situation.

She lifted her gaze and stared at the point to the east where sky met mountain ridge. She would have to get in touch with Palmer and his men. They would have to be told of this new development—that their plan would have to be pushed forward.

Looking back at Gretchen, she took a deep breath and stood. She smoothed her braids and picked off the few sprigs of grass that had clung to her dress. If she were going to pull this off, she was going to have to have the woman's cooperation.

She arched a brow and smiled to herself. That should not be too hard. The white-faced cow had ensnared herself in Snow Dancer's ploy to gain Elk Dreamer's attention. The woman had not saved herself at all. She had simply given Snow Dancer the means to the woman's assured demise.

Stepping out from her hiding place, she walked toward Gretchen as calmly as if she had been out for an afternoon stroll and had just happened upon the woman.

Eyes still red with foolish tears, Gretchen looked up with a start.

Feigning concern, Snow Dancer stole up to her cautiously. She smiled sweetly.

With a heavy sigh, Gretchen turned her gaze askance. She sniffled. "Are you looking for somebody?" she asked, a hint of sarcasm edging her voice.

Inside, Snow Dancer smoldered. She would have liked nothing better than to slap the willowy cow's face. She hated the sight of the woman. It would take every ounce of strength she could muster to be kind now, after all that she had witnessed between Gretchen and Elk Dreamer. "Are you feeling ill?" she signed, leaning around to the woman.

Gretchen shook her head. "It's nothing."

"I would like to help if I can." Snow Dancer was determined to win the woman's trust—she had to.

Gretchen shot her a sidelong glance. She appeared to be studying her.

"Tell me what troubles you." Snow Dancer moved her hands fluidly. Over the last two years, she had become more fluently graceful in silence than most were in speech.

"Not now, *Wahinhan Wacipi*." Whirling around, Gretchen strode to the pile of boulders bordering the pool and sat down. "I want to be alone for a while."

Narrowing her eyes, Snow Dancer squared her shoulders. She would not give up that easily. The woman was not about to put her off. She forced a smile on her lips and ambled up next to her. "You are unhappy?"

"Please, *Wahinhan Wacipi*. I'd really like to be left alone if you don't mind."

Standing in front of the white woman, Snow Dancer nodded complaisantly. "I thought you would be happy to be going back to your own kind."

Gretchen looked surprised. She squinted up at Snow Dancer. "How did you know about that?"

Snow Dancer pursed her lips, then took advantage of the first answer that came into her mind. "As soon as the council meeting broke, the news spread throughout the encampment like a swarm of honeybees to flowers." She moved beside the woman and sat down. "This does not bring joy to your heart?"

Gretchen shook her head, then smiled ruefully. "You can stop the playacting, *Wahinhan Wacipi*." She narrowed a piercing look on Snow Dancer.

Puzzled by the woman's statement, Snow Dancer tossed one braid back over her shoulder and peered at her with an innocent expression. "I do not understand," she signed truthfully. Surely the white woman could not know anything of her scheme.

Gretchen pulled her mouth to one side and snorted. Standing, she folded her arms across her chest, then turned back to face Snow Dancer. She shook her head again. "You know, you're good. In fact, you're *very* good."

What could the cow mean by that? It appeared that the woman had shifted her upset with Elk Dreamer onto Snow Dancer. Still as yet confused, Snow Dancer frowned and lifted her hands.

Gretchen scratched her temple, then gestured toward Snow Dancer with an accusing wave of her hand. "I just can't figure how, or why for that matter, you've kept this sham of yours up for such a long time."

Completely baffled, yet overwhelmingly intrigued, Snow Dancer pursued the subject. What exactly did the woman think she knew? "I do not understand," she insisted.

"Oh, stop it, *Wahinhan Wacipi*. I know you can talk."

Snow Dancer's stomach cinched tight. How could this white-faced cow know that? She had been careful. She had not so much as uttered a word in or around the camp since the woman's arrival.

Eyes wide, she glared up at her. Except for that one time—at the sight of the stage attack. She gave herself a mental shake. Gretchen could not know anything about that. She had still been ill from her wound. She decided to keep up the pretense. The woman was simply guessing. Touching the scar on her throat, she shook her head.

"I know you can. People have heard you."

Snow Dancer leapt to her feet. No one could know. She had been too careful. "Who has told you this lie?" She moved her hands furiously.

Smiling with an uplifted brow, Gretchen crossed her arms over her chest and tucked them into place. "It doesn't matter." She leaned nearer. "It is the truth, though, isn't it?"

Snow Dancer tried to remain calm. She had to think of how to handle this. She was cornered. Even if the woman did not have anything to go on but speculation, it might be enough to spoil whatever chances she had of winning Elk Dreamer.

No. She could not risk Gretchen exposing her secret. She took a breath. With practiced effort, she forced a tear to her eyes, and a quiver to her bottom lip. She opened her mouth as if she were about to speak, then slumped back to her seat on the rocks and began to sob. She turned away from the white woman just enough to shield the deception she now employed. "I—" She paused for effect. "I am so ashamed."

Gretchen remained silent.

Choking on a whimper, she continued. "The people will be angry when they see that I have tricked them." She sniffled loudly.

"But why?" Gretchen asked, sounding concerned. "Why would you do such a thing?"

Snow Dancer darted a glance toward the water and smiled wryly. Good. It was working. She shrugged. "You will not tell anyone, will you?"

"Apparently someone else already knows, or I wouldn't."

"Elk Dreamer will have me beaten," she wailed, trying to sound as pathetic as possible.

"Surely you must've known you would be punished if you were found out, *Wahinhan Wacipi*?" Gretchen sounded as if she might be softening. "Why would you do such a thing?"

Like a frightened child, Snow Dancer pulled farther away and shook her head. What should she say? Maybe if she offered the foolish woman a small piece of the truth, it would be enough to manipulate her into the trap. "You will not tell?"

"I don't know, till I hear the reason."

"I am so ashamed," Snow Dancer moaned again.

She would have to play the woman like a fish on a line if she were going to accomplish her goal.

"Look," Gretchen began. She moved up to sit by Snow Dancer. "Tell me why you would do such a thing. Maybe it's not so bad as you think."

Slowly, Snow Dancer lifted a gaze to the woman. She pretended to start to speak, but then shrank back to her original pose. She clutched her arms over her middle and began to shake. "No," she cried out in Lakotah. "Please don't make me."

Gretchen did not speak.

Snow Dancer waited, but the white woman remained silent. She would have to dangle another tidbit in front of the old cow. She shuddered. "I wanted Elk Dreamer to love me."

"You what?" Gretchen sounded shocked.

"Do you know of my sister?"

"Yes. *Wiyukcan Maniwin* has told me of her."

Snow Dancer narrowed her eyes. So that was who had told Gretchen about her. It had to be—no one else could have known. Holding onto the pretense of distress, Snow Dancer continued. "It is not good to speak of the dead, but I will tell you of the tragedy . . . then I will speak of her no more. After she died, I was left alone. I had no living relatives. No one wanted me. I would have been made to live with the old widows of the tribe. I was desperate. My only chance to be taken in was by *Hanble Hehaka*."

"Oh, my God! You did—" Gretchen appeared to catch herself.

From behind the cover of her hair, Snow Dancer cut the woman a quick look. "What?"

Gretchen cleared her throat, then straightened her

posture. "Did you . . . have anything to do with Fawn's death?"

Like a badger's jaw, Snow Dancer's stomach clamped tight. How did she know about that? This was something Snow Dancer had not counted on. Still, maybe she could make it work for her. She gasped audibly. "No! No!" she wailed in her native language. "I loved *Tacincala*. She was my sister! Who has accused me of such a lie?" She forced a showing of tears.

"I-I'm sorry, *Wahinhan Wacipi*." The white woman touched her back, sympathy spilling from her mouth like sweet mountain water.

Snow Dancer sighed, though not from regret, but relief. She covered her mouth to keep from snickering out loud. She had the woman now. She shrugged. "It is understandable, I suppose. I *was* with *Tacincala* when she . . . was killed. It was a miracle that I survived." She lowered her voice. She had to draw the woman in tighter. "I lost more than a sister that day."

Gretchen pressed a little closer. "Yes, I know about *Is'tahota*, too. It must've been terrible for you." The woman actually sounded as if she cared—as if she were sorry for the white man's crime committed against Snow Dancer so long ago.

Now was her chance. Snow Dancer raised her head and wiped away her tears. "I know I should not have deceived the people, but I found that I had trapped myself into a world of silence. My voice was lost for a time. It was many months before I could speak well again. I, too, was surprised at the return of my voice. But if I had allowed *Hanble Hehaka* and the rest of the people to learn of my secret, he might have cast me out of his lodge." She shivered, quite honestly this time, at the uncertain prospect. "By then, it was too late for me."

"My God!" the woman gasped. "It's true then." For a moment, Gretchen appeared perplexed and unable to continue. She toyed with the fringe on the edge of her sleeve. When again she spoke, her words came soft and hesitant. "You're in love with Elk Dreamer, aren't you?"

Snow Dancer kept her face concealed. This would set the blade in place just above the heart, then Snow Dancer could shove it in. Arching a brow, she nodded, a crafty smile spreading across her face.

Gretchen did not speak for a long moment. "I don't think he would've thrown you out." Her voice held a pathetic note of melancholy. "I've found him to be a gentle-hearted man—even understanding at times."

It sickened, yet delighted Snow Dancer to hear the woman speak of Elk Dreamer so intimately. But at least she knew she had the white-faced cow where she wanted her. "You, too, have much fondness for *Hanble Hehaka*." She looked up shyly.

Gretchen blanched. Her posture stiffened. She appeared shocked, dumbfounded.

"I understand." Snow Dancer hurried on before the woman could deny the truth. "I believe him to care for you, also."

Gretchen only blinked.

The silly female. Did she think their *love frolic* had gone unnoticed? "It is good that he has finally found love with another." She nearly bit off her tongue telling that tale. She pressed herself to the limits of her endurance and patted the white woman's pale hand.

"I believe that my sister smiles down with happiness for *Hanble Hehaka*—and you, also."

Gretchen's shoulders slumped, and she began to tremble. She peered at Snow Dancer as if she were trying to see if she could trust her. The white woman's eyes grew wet and red. "Oh, *Wahinhan Wacipi*. I don't know what to do. Elk Dreamer is determined to take me to Fort Laramie himself. But if he does, the soldiers will surely take him prisoner—maybe even kill him. I don't know how to find the place myself, but I can't let anything happen to him either."

Snow Dancer squeezed her hands into fists. It had worked. She had gained control of the situation. And now she had Gretchen all but leaping in front of the knife that silently awaited the woman's heart.

She clasped Gretchen's hand with forced but gentle reassurance. "*I* know the way to the Laramie Fort of the soldiers." Wetting her lips, she moved in for the kill. "And for a promise of keeping my secret . . . *I* would be most happy to take you there."

SIXTEEN

Gretchen stood on the top of the ridge and looked down on the sleeping camp of the Sioux. Her breathing came fast and short from the climb she had just made. In the moonlight, she scanned the many tipis until she found the one with the single file of elk symbols painted on it.

Her throat closed. A little over a week ago, she had been afraid of these people, but now she found herself missing them even before she had gone. She had become overly fond of each and every one of them, but especially Ponders-as-she-walks Woman and Grey-eyes . . . Her heart felt as if it had just been sliced in two.

Now, if all went as planned, this would be the last time she would ever see Elk Dreamer again. Her mind struggled with the thought. Why had she not been able to tell him how she felt yesterday? Bittersweet, the threat of tears stung her eyes. All she would have had to do was give in to her feelings, and let her emotions carry her through. It would have been so easy. But she could not do it. It had been too long since she had felt anything even remotely close to love for a man.

"Come, Gretchen." Sharp and demanding, Snow Dancer called out to her. "The moon will lend us little time before it gives up its power to the sun. We have no time for remorse now. Elk Dreamer will come after us when he discovers that we are gone."

Blinking, Gretchen only nodded. With one last regretful glance down, she wheeled around and trod after the Indian woman. "How long do you think it will take for us to get to the fort?" she asked after a few hours of travel.

"Two, maybe three days if we walk fast and talk little."

At that point, Gretchen noticed a change starting in Snow Dancer. Subtle at first, it became more blatant with every passing hour.

Picking her way over the stones and underbrush, Gretchen struggled to keep up with her companion's rapid pace. Over the course of the short while they had been together, Gretchen had seen the woman's gentle and caring demeanor shift to a surly and unbending disposition. She appeared driven by some great force.

Many times during the passing of the night, Snow Dancer had pressed on ahead. And once, while they were crossing an open meadow, the Indian woman had even vanished from sight for a few minutes, managing to enter the surrounding forest before Gretchen could catch up. Whether or not it was intentional, Gretchen did not know.

Unsure of her whereabouts, and even more wary of her surroundings, Gretchen had been more than a little fearful. She had called out to Snow Dancer, but had gotten no response until she reached the edge of the trees herself.

"You must keep up," Snow Dancer had commanded in a harsh tone from the shadows.

It had startled Gretchen. Then and there, she had decided not to allow Snow Dancer more than a few steps' lead—no matter how difficult the path might be, or how tired she, herself, might become. She found herself almost hoping Elk Dreamer would catch up with them.

Even now there was a good chance that he would overtake them. Gretchen shuddered at the thought of his anger when he discovered their absence. And there was not a doubt in her mind that he *would* come after them. He had been defied, and she knew what that would do to him. She had borne witness to his rage too many times where that was concerned. Their only chance was to keep to a fast and steady pace, and beat him to the fort.

After climbing what seemed to be the hundredth slope since their departure, Gretchen slumped down onto a tree stump and gasped for air.

"Why do you stop?" Slightly bent, bracing her hands against her knees, Snow Dancer turned back. She appeared to be just as out of breath as Gretchen, yet she wore a look of determination. She lifted a hand toward the sky. "The sun is high. By now Elk Dreamer will have left the camp."

Gretchen held up a hand. "We need to rest. We haven't stopped since sunrise." She swallowed back the dryness in her mouth. Lifting the water bag slung over her shoulder, she took a long drink. Cool and refreshing, the liquid eased the burning in her throat. After quenching her thirst, she noted that Snow Dancer did not let the moment pass without giving in to her own need for water.

Wiping her mouth with the back of her hand, Snow Dancer looked at Gretchen. "We go now."

"No." Gretchen shook her head. Shielding her eyes with her hand, she glanced up at the sun. "It's near noon. We should eat something."

Snow Dancer glared at Gretchen. "You have dried deer meat in your pouch. That will be enough for now."

Gretchen's stomach grumbled. Knowing she would be leaving the friends she had made among the Sioux, as well as Elk Dreamer, she had not eaten much at the previous night's meal. They had not been able to gather anything but a few turnips and some mushrooms while they walked. Gretchen had only brought her medical bag and the small pouch of venison. The women had allowed themselves few provisions, hoping the lightness of their burden would insure greater speed of travel.

But now the lack of food had caused Gretchen to feel light-headed. "I need to eat some real food. I'm hungry." She hated to complain, but she could not help it. She was not used to needing this kind of physical endurance. And, too, Snow Dancer's temperament was starting to get on her nerves. "Why didn't we take at least one horse? We'd be able to travel much faster."

"The horses will be needed by the people when they leave." Snow Dancer shook her head as if she were amazed by Gretchen's statement. "I did not think I helped such an old woman. I knew that you were beyond my youth, but I did not think you were so feeble and delicate." She stiffened her spine. "You must remember Elk Dreamer. Remember what the soldiers will do to him—"

"All right—all right! I'm getting up." Snow Dancer was goading her and she knew it. And unfortunately it was working. Being told that she was acting old, not to mention being reminded of what might happen to Elk Dreamer in the clutches of the army, was just the thing to spur her into action. Forcing herself to stand, she snatched up her medical bag and shot the younger woman a haughty look. She would keep up with this *child* if it was the last thing she did.

They walked on for endless miles and countless hours, until Gretchen thought she would surely drop from exhaustion. But still she pressed on, paying little attention to the time of day or their direction.

Finally, in late afternoon, Snow Dancer stopped.

Panting, Gretchen halted beside her and peered out across the land. "What's wrong?" From where she stood, she could see a great distance.

Backs toward still another slope, they were at an altitude above most of the other peaks.

Gretchen searched the horizon below her. "Do you see something?" She held her breath and prayed, hoping it might be so.

"We will spend the night here."

Gretchen looked at the Indian. "What about Elk Dreamer? Aren't you worried that he'll catch up to us?"

Snow Dancer shook her head. "We do not follow the path to the fort."

Gretchen swallowed, trying to catch her breath. Lifting her water bag from around her shoulders, she lowered herself to the grassy floor of a small ravine and drank deeply. She emptied her animal skin of its contents. She would have been concerned if she had not heard the sound of a waterfall in the distance behind her. She focused her attention on the Indian woman. "What do you mean, we're not following the path to the fort?"

Snow Dancer did not answer right away. Instead, she, too, took the moment to finish off the contents of her water.

"Snow Dancer, I asked you a question." Gretchen became suspicious. "Where're you taking me?"

After downing the last of the liquid, the woman glanced at Gretchen with an air of indifference. At last she smiled. "I have white friends another day's walk from here." She pointed in an easterly direction.

"But I thought you were going to—"

"Like Elk Dreamer, I cannot go to the soldier's fort. They would treat me no better than they would him."

Gretchen peered at her with skepticism. What was the woman up to?

Snow Dancer lifted her brows innocently. "You would not have me taken against my will again . . . would you?"

Gretchen studied her. She knew Snow Dancer was trying to use guilt to wield her power. Lord in Heaven, she should have never placed her life in this woman's hands. If she had not been pressed to do this while she was still so vulnerable from Elk Dreamer's advances, she would have given thought to other options. But as it was, she had little choice now. She had to trust the Indian.

"My friends will take care of you. They will see that you get to the fort safely enough."

"These . . . uh . . . *friends*, how long have you known them?" Gretchen chose her words carefully. If Snow Dancer were up to some kind of deception, she did not want the woman to become suspicious. She would have to play along with her until she could determine exactly what was going on.

"Since our coming into the mountains." She moved around the shrubbery and began to gather dried grasses and twigs.

"Why didn't Elk Dreamer tell me of these people? Why didn't he think of taking me to them?"

Snow Dancer shrugged. "He does not know of them. Elk Dreamer has been very wary of all whites. He does not like whites—" Her head snapped up, and she flashed Gretchen a winning grin. "Except for you, of course."

Gretchen smiled back.

Snow Dancer suddenly appeared stricken with surprise. "Gret-chen. You do not think I would let anything happen to you?"

Gretchen held the woman's stare a moment. Then with a resigned sigh, she shook her head. "No, *Wahinhan Wacipi*."

The younger woman's face beamed in the waning sunlight. "That is good." She jumped up, moved to a spot void of grass, and began to pile all that she had collected in a clump.

Gretchen had to continue to trust Snow Dancer. She had come too far to turn back now. Taking out another piece of jerked venison, Gretchen took a bite, her eyes remaining fixed on the Indian.

After all, she could not keep up false pretenses forever. Sooner or later, if she were playing Gretchen falsely, she would have to let her guard down. And then Gretchen would have her dead to rights.

Then, another thought struck her. What about the woman's ruse of muteness? She had managed that for almost two years. Gretchen, you fool, you. She cut a wary glance toward Snow Dancer and observed her movements as the woman built a small fire.

Once the embers glowed, then leapt into small flames, Snow Dancer pulled what looked to be a sling from the pouch fastened at her wrist. She tugged at the leather pocket, smoothing it open with expert fingers. "Now I will see if I can find us a rabbit or maybe even a grouse." She made as if to leave, then turned back. She tipped her head to one side, then offered Gretchen an angelic expression. "You will be all right until I return?"

Although Gretchen was quite certain the look was meant to relax her, it did just the opposite. She felt a prudent quiver race up her spine. She rubbed her arms and moved nearer the fire, feigning what she hoped was an air of nonchalance.

"Good." The woman's teeth flashed bright against her brown skin. "I will try to be quick."

Once Snow Dancer had gone off to hunt, Gretchen stared out at the purple-rose hues painting the western horizon. All around her, imposing black peaks marked the skyline. She glanced back in the direction of the Indian's departure and hugged herself.

She thought of Elk Dreamer, and how worried and angry he must be. God help me. She shook her head. She should have listened to him. She should have done as he had planned. At least they would have been together for a few more days . . . and nights.

Oh, the nights. Bending her knees, she tucked her feet under her thighs like a pretzel and rocked back and forth. How might they have spent their evenings if only she had listened to him? She could almost feel the warmth of his arms. She tossed a couple of larger sticks onto the fire. Tiny embers shot up into the air with a pale wisp of gray. She inhaled. She could almost smell the mingled scents of wood smoke and soap weed that always clung to his skin.

She shuddered against the impending outcome of what had started out to be a simple trip, but now had turned into a fearsome adventure. During the passing of the day, she had almost wished that he would find her. After the hellish ordeal she had endured today, she would gladly have borne his anger.

But there was no chance of that happening now—not with Snow Dancer leading her off to God only knew where. Elk Dreamer could not come after them if he did not know their direction. Now he was surely lost to her.

Somewhere off in the distance, she heard the sound of a coyote calling for a mate. She inched closer to the fire. How sad it sounded . . . how desperately lonely.

She gazed out into the shadowy void. How long had Snow Dancer been gone? As the blackness of night enveloped her in its cloak of darkness, she began to feel as though she had been abandoned—as if she were the only human left on the face of the earth.

She focused on the fire. Within its dancing flames, she could almost picture Elk Dreamer, his glittering black eyes, his chiseled features. The way his dimples cut into his usual stoic expression. She should have told him of her feelings for him. She should have confessed how much she wanted him. But she could not. It would not have been fair to either of them.

Both of them knew the eventual outcome. She had to leave. If it had not been now, it would have been later. Still, they would have at least been able to share a small time of love together.

The animal howled again.

A despondent sigh escaped Gretchen's lips. It was an anguished echo of the yearning in her heart.

Oh, Gretchen. A tear slipped from her eye, trickling down her cheek. What have you done to yourself?

SEVENTEEN

From out of the darkness, a sound like a gasp rushed at Gretchen from behind. She flinched. Body tense, she whirled around. Heart pounding, she searched the shadows, but could see nothing. Her pulse leapt. Was it an animal?

Rising up on her knees, she leaned nearer the fire. As long as she had the security of the flames, she would be safe from predators. Then, another thought struck her. What if it were the men that had attacked the stage?

She looked around. Oh, God. She had nothing to protect herself with. Snow Dancer had the only knife, and she had taken that with her. She squeezed her eyes closed for a second. Why had she not prepared herself better? She had no real food, limited water, and no weapon. It seemed that she had made one mistake after the other. She should have thought to bring a rifle at least.

Then she heard them, or, rather, felt their presence. Squinting into the blackness, she reached down and grasped the end of a thick limb sticking out of the fire. She held it as if it were a weapon of great magnitude. "Snow Dancer?" No response. She knew someone was out there. She could feel their eyes upon her. "Come— come out where I can see you."

Something snapped just outside the firelight.

Rising to her full height, Gretchen grasped the stick with trembling hands. She swallowed, trying to fortify her courage. "Look, I know somebody's out there—I can see you," she lied. She held herself rigid, waiting for an attack. Her nerves skittered beneath her sweat-dampened skin. Why did whoever it was not come into the open? "I'm not alone here. I've got friends—" Her breath caught.

A figure, clad in buckskin, moved into the light.

Snow Dancer's face came into view.

Gretchen went limp. She clutched her chest with relief. "Snow Dancer. Thank God it's you." She tossed the stick back into the fire. "You scared me half—" She tensed.

Grasping the Indian woman by the back of the neck a hand came into focus, followed by an arm, a body, and finally a face.

"Oh, my God!" Gretchen's heartbeat bolted again.

Like one of the many grisly masks used in ceremony, Elk Dreamer's rueful countenance loomed before her.

For a moment, her heart soared. She could not

believe it. Her prayer had been answered. He had found her. She was so glad to see him. She took a step toward him. "Oh, Elk Dreamer—"

"*Hiyu wo*," he said between clenched teeth, then shoved the woman forward.

Gretchen stopped short.

He appeared angry—angrier than she had ever seen him.

She looked at Snow Dancer.

Head down, body stooped slightly in submission, the woman stole a glance up at Gretchen. A drop of red trickled from one corner of her mouth.

Gretchen cut Elk Dreamer a quizzical glance. She darted to the woman's side. "What happened?" She tried to wipe the blood from Snow Dancer's mouth.

The Indian woman flinched, and brushed Gretchen's hand away. She glared up at Elk Dreamer from beneath furrowed brows.

Gripping his rifle tightly in one hand, he moved up beside them, halting only an arm's distance away. Beneath a thick fringe of gleaming black hair, his firelit dark eyes glowed almost demonlike against the russet-brown of his skin and the golden hues of his tanned vest and leggings. He moved up closer. He looked as if he were daring the woman to say anything in her behalf.

Gretchen shifted a stare between the two Indians. Had he done this to her? Like a lioness with her cub, she turned on him. "I know you're mad, but did you have to hit her?"

Elk Dreamer glowered at her. "I did not know it was *Wanhinhan Wacipi*." He flexed his jaws, causing the creases in his cheeks to become even more pronounced. He took another step nearer. "You should not have run away."

Gretchen shook her head scornfully. Her eyes narrowed. She could not believe his impertinence. He did not even care that he had hurt Snow Dancer. "Is that all you care about—that I shouldn't have run away?"

His eyes leveled on something behind her, and he nodded.

Turning, she nearly jumped out of her own body.

There, not two feet behind her, Buffalo Calf stood holding his rifle in one hand, cradled against his other arm. His waist-length hair hung in disarray around his shoulders, and his body glistened with sweat as if he had been running. He said something to Elk Dreamer that Gretchen could not quite grasp, but it was something about them being alone.

Elk Dreamer stiffened his posture, then turned toward Gretchen. "Where are you going? You do not take the path to the soldiers' fort."

Gretchen glanced at Snow Dancer. Should she tell him the truth? She caught a frightened look in the woman's eyes, and a glimpse of her blood-smeared lip. If their leaving had upset the man enough for him to hit Snow Dancer, the discovery of their change in destinations would probably incite his full wrath. Still, she had to tell him something. "We didn't want the soldiers to find us before we could get to the fort and talk to the commanding officer."

He frowned as if to say, I still don't understand.

"We decided to make our own route," she rushed on. "We didn't know if they'd already sent out a detail of troopers."

Out of the corner of her eye, Gretchen watched for any sign of denial from Snow Dancer.

She did not so much as blanch at the lie.

Of course she would not. Gretchen was probably saving her from a severe beating. She peered up at Elk Dreamer. Did he believe her? She could not tell.

"Why did she leave you alone?" Elk Dreamer gestured to Snow Dancer.

"We didn't bring any food with us." Remembering the jerky, she smiled, then lifted up a piece from her pouch. "Well, almost none anyhow. She was hunting for something for us to eat."

Elk Dreamer scowled and shook his head. "Yet she comes back with nothing."

Gretchen noted that Snow Dancer's sling was nowhere to be seen. It was true. She had not brought anything back with her. Had she lost it in the scuffle with Elk Dreamer? No. He would have mentioned it if she had.

Snow Dancer said nothing in her defense.

"I should beat you." Chest heaving, nostrils flared, Elk Dreamer took a step toward her. "If you were my woman I would cuff you."

Gretchen's blood instantly heated, yet she moved back a space. Who did he think he was? Her face flamed with fury. "Beat me! Look, we've been through this before." Her voice pitched into the air like the sparks from the burning wood. "I'm not your woman! And if I were, you'd draw back a stump trying to beat *me*, mister."

Elk Dreamer's gaze darted between the man and the woman standing off to the side, before he returned a stalwart glare to Gretchen. He looked as if he might explode. "We will see!" Then, without another word, he grabbed Gretchen's wrist, and stalked out into the darkness, yanking her along behind him.

"Let me go!" she shrieked, true fear marking her tone.

He did not release her.

Stumbling along after him, she flailed and kicked, screamed and railed at him.

But still he would not let her go. Like a beast maddened with hatred, he tramped over the underbrush. In and around the pines and aspens, he marched into the forest, picking his way through the night as easily as if he had the eyes of an animal.

Following blindly behind, Gretchen snagged her foot on a bush and fell.

Elk Dreamer caught her under the arms and jerked her up to her feet, slamming her hard against his chest plate.

In the dappled light of the moon, their eyes met.

His were full, black, imposing.

Hers challenged him with a mixture of fear and rage. "Let me—"

"*Wanyaka, tuwena!*" He jabbed a finger in her face and stared at her a moment longer. Then, without warning, he turned away and weaved an intricate path through the wilderness.

"What do you mean, no one acts like this? *I* act like this." She slapped at his arm, but her strike drew no more attention from him than a fly. "Where're you taking me?" Gretchen could hear the sound of the waterfall growing louder with each step. Did he truly mean to beat her? "Look, Elk Dreamer. I don't know what you think you're planning—I don't want to know—but you can't just whisk me off somewhere and—"

He stopped short and whipped her around to face him. A lock of dark, damp hair clung to his forehead. His eyes pinned her with an unholy and wicked glint. "I can *do* anything I want." His fingers pressed into the flesh of her arm.

She tried to twist away.

He held on firmly.

For all of her efforts, she could not do anything to free herself. He was too strong, too powerful, too fearsome. At that moment, she was truly afraid of him, but she could not let him know it. "If you let me go now, Elk Dreamer, I'll—"

"You will what?"

Staring at him, she could see that he meant business—although she was not quite certain just what kind—or maybe she was, and that is what frightened her the most. "Look," she started, then stopped. Her throat felt suddenly dry. She moistened her lips with her tongue. It was her first mistake.

His gaze slipped from hers to the subtlety of her movement, his eyes nearly glowing red-hot in the darkness. His hand moved to her waist. He squeezed it.

"No," she breathed the word aloud. Now she was truly frightened. She had seen that look in him before. And as badly as she might want him, she could not let this happen again. She pulled away.

Just as quickly, he drew her back, hard against him. His mouth came down on hers, searing her lips. His tongue probed into the recesses of her mouth.

She felt his fingers on her shoulder, loosening the

lacings of her dress, and she groaned. She swayed into him. Her mind fought against what her body would not. She had to stop this—now—before she lost her will to his. Palms against his chest, she shoved with all her strength. That was her second mistake.

He ripped her buckskin garment.

Gretchen was free of his grasp, but the cloth tore open.

The coolness of the evening air whispered across her heated flesh. She gasped and glanced down. Still secured at her other shoulder, the tanned cloth had fallen open, exposing one breast. She shot a look up.

Shards of black cut through the night, stabbing her with the sharpness of his heated stare. Elk Dreamer took a step toward her, lust reigning heavy in his expression.

Her heart slammed against her chest. She needed no further prompting. She knew she was in trouble. Snatching up the gaping cloth, Gretchen turned and dashed away from him.

He growled like an angry cougar, and darted after her.

She screamed.

He grabbed her hair.

Yanked backward, she lost her balance and fell, but managed to jump back up in escape when he reached for a better hold.

"No!" she shrieked. But who would come to her rescue? Buffalo Calf? Snow Dancer? No. She would have to save herself. With every ounce of energy her weary body could summon, she pounded her feet on the ground. She would have to outrun him—he was too far gone, too lust-crazed, to hear her pleas.

She sprinted toward the roar of the falls. She chanced a look over her shoulder. In the darkness, she lost sight of him. She stopped and listened, but the thunder of the tumbling water drowned any sound the man might have made.

She had to keep going. Her only chance was to get back to the others. Coming upon a fortress of huge boulders, she climbed over and around them, weaving and circling through the maze of stones. Her breathing came heavily.

As she rounded a huge wall of rock, the gaping mouth of a cave yawned, dark and ominous. She jumped back, pressing herself against the cool stone. She held her breath. Was he in there? Was he waiting for her—ready to pounce? She strained to hear over the sound of the rushing falls.

Nothing.

She peeked around. All she could see was blackness. Taking one cautious step after another, she inched her way inside—ready, knowing that at any moment she might have to take flight. Fingers probing the damp rock, she worked her way to the back of the cavern.

It was small, maybe twenty or thirty feet through the center. It smelled stale, dank, and musty from the surrounding dampness.

Arms spread, she leaned against the wall directly in front of the opening. If Elk Dreamer passed by, she would be able to see him in the moonlight. She waited, trying to slow her heart, swallowing against the dryness in her throat.

Glancing around, she searched for a means of escape other than the front entrance—just in case. Then, she heard something.

A chirping, almost yapping, noise.

She froze. Wide-eyed, she peered around the interior, trying to use to her advantage whatever meager light she could.

It sounded again—closer—just to her left.

Oh, God! She scarcely allowed herself a breath.

Two eyes glowed in the darkness. It was an animal. It looked small, but what kind was it? Did it matter? Even little creatures could be dangerous if they thought they were cornered.

She should have known better than to go inside a cave. "Okay," she whispered. She stepped away from the wall. Whatever this was, right now, *it* was more frightening than Elk Dreamer. Slim as it might be, she felt certain she would have a better chance with him. "I'm leaving."

Ever so stealthily, so as not to disturb the beast any more, she backed toward the opening. When she stood in the moonshine spilling in at the cave mouth, she turned. But she had only taken a couple of steps before a shadow blocked her path.

She screamed. She had all but forgotten her reason for taking refuge in the cave in the first place. Fear slammed hard in the pit of her stomach.

The animal behind her growled and barked.

She risked a look over her shoulder.

It darted at Gretchen.

Leaping forward, she screeched.

The little beast nipped at her heals.

Two arms clamped around her, lifting and swinging her around at the same time.

"Hai!" Elk Dreamer yelled, stamping his foot. He

pulled Gretchen around behind him. *"Hai!"* he hollered again.

Yipping with ear-piercing shrills, the ball of red fur bolted past them and out into the forest.

"Oh, my God—what was that?" Gretchen clung to Elk Dreamer's back, her earlier fear of him replaced by fear of the little beast.

"A little dog," Elk Dreamer answered, amusement marking his tone. He turned in Gretchen's grasp to face her fully. He slipped his arms around her waist and smiled down at her.

Gretchen frowned. "You're telling me that huge noise came from a fox—a little fox?"

Grinning, Elk Dreamer nodded.

Gretchen gulped a breath and released it in a whoosh. "He nearly scared the life out of me."

"Little dogs are good warriors. It is good it was a male. A female with little ones would not have been so easily frightened away." Fingers splaying along her spine, Elk Dreamer drew her even nearer.

The action reminded Gretchen of her original fear. She stilled. Her heart set up a flurry of beats. She was trapped. Would he try to force her to his will again? Cautiously, she stole a glance upward.

Now, smiling as he was, his face appeared softer than it had before. His eyes still glittered, though not so fiendishly. "You should not have angered me, Gret-chen."

Temper sparked inside her again. "*I* should not have—"

"Do not set your storm on me again, Gret-chen." His voice was hushed, though still a little raspy from his bout of running. He tossed back his head, causing the quill circle woven into his hair to clink lightly against the tiny beads dangling inside the hoop. "I did not follow you to fight."

Awash with moonlight, Elk Dreamer appeared almost to glow, like a ghost—a link between the physical and spiritual worlds. He bent lower, feathering her cheek with his breath. "I came after you—"

"No, Elk Dreamer." Gretchen pushed gently against his chest. She knew what he was about to say. "We can't do this. It's not fair—" She swallowed, trying to hold her emotions in check. "To either of us."

"What is this *not fair*? I do not understand." He sounded almost childlike, hurt and confused. "I want you. Do you not want me?"

She squeezed her eyes closed and held to silence. Why did he continually bait her with this subject?

"Gret-chen. You would not answer me by the pool." He pulled her nearer.

She knew she should, but she did not try to stop him. It felt so wonderful to be in his arms again.

"I would hear your answer now." He nibbled on her ear.

She shivered, all memory of their earlier battle fleeing from thought. What was she supposed to say? Yes, Elk Dreamer—I want you? I want you so badly I ache all over when you're not around? "Please. I— we can't do this anymore." She could not think clearly when he held her like this.

Pulling back to look at her, he frowned. "I do not understand. You have told me this many times, but you do not tell me why."

Gretchen pushed back the aching lump in her throat.

She had to make him realize what they were doing to each other, once and for all. But how to go about it? She had numerous reasons—all of them sound, all of them detrimental.

"Come. Sit." He swept a hand toward a large, flat rock near the water. "I will hear your reasons." Without waiting for a reply, he strode to where he had pointed. Turning back, he looked at her. Hands at his side, he stood in silence, apparently waiting for her to join him.

She took one precautionary look at her dress where it had been pulled open. Though it still gaped, she had secured the material back up enough that it concealed her breast. She did not dare draw his attention to the garment by relacing it now.

She looked up.

He was still waiting.

Clasping her hands together, Gretchen felt the dampness from her palms. Whether or not it was from nerves or the mist churned up by the tumbling water, she could not say. She did not want to think about it. She started slowly toward him, her mind jumbling with all the logical arguments.

She stepped up beside him and drew in a calming breath. She had to get this over with fast, before she lost her nerve. Careful to avoid eye contact, she plopped down on the rock, then drew her knees up to her chest, encompassing them with her arms. "Look, Elk Dreamer, you don't want me—not really."

He sat down beside her.

"I'm . . . well . . . I'm too old for you." She cringed at her choice of words. She had never before thought of herself as being *old*, and hated the thought of using it as a means of escaping the situation now—however much she felt it to be true. She touched his cheek. Heat seared her hand. "You need someone . . . a little closer to your own age." Her mind flitted back to the Indian woman's confession. "Someone like Snow Dancer."

Elk Dreamer grimaced. "*Wahinhan Wacipi* is my *hankas'i*."

"No—not really." Gretchen fought against saying the only woman's name she thought might grasp his attention. She had to force him to see the truth. He would be better off with one of his own kind. "You never married Fawn. Snow Dancer isn't truly your sister-in-law."

He grunted, then flipped up his hand, dismissing the reference to Snow Dancer. "You are not a maiden, this is true, but you are not old." He drew a finger lazily across her cheek to her chin. "Your eyes shimmer with youth. Your body is smooth and strong." His hand eased downward. He trailed it down her arm, and crossed to her stomach. He pushed lightly against her abdomen. "Your woman's seed still blossoms—"

"Please," Gretchen whispered, though she was not sure he heard her over the roar of water. She felt her face heat red. "Can't you see? Tomorrow, or the next day, whenever we get to Fort Laramie—" She lifted her gaze to meet his and nearly drowned in the liquid-black depths of his eyes. "Once we've told the army who the culprits really are, we'll go our separate ways. You with your people, and I'll go on to mine."

His hand stilled, and he scooted closer. "Is that what you want?"

It was a simple question really, so why could she

not answer him? She held his stare, unable to utter the word *no*—unwilling to say *yes*. "It's the way it has to be. You can't live in my world, and I can't live in yours."

"Why?"

Startled by his candor, she blinked.

"Have you not been living in my world these last seven suns?"

"Wh—yes, but—"

"Have you not been happy with my people?" He began to massage her shoulder again, inching his way up to her neck.

"You know I have."

"And what of *Is'tahota* and *Wiyukcan Maniwin*? Will you not miss them?"

Gretchen felt another tug at her heart. She would miss both the child and the old woman very much. Although she had not known them very long, she had grown to care and—yes—even love them. She nodded, the swell of traitorous tears blinding her vision.

"And Elk Dreamer? You have not spoken of him. You do not answer his words." He paused. "I will ask you once more, Gret-chen. Do you not want him"—he brushed a finger lightly across her ear—"as a woman wants a man . . . as a wife wants a husband?"

"Please." It seemed to be the only word that could escape her lips. She could not think rationally. Where had all of her logical arguments gone to? She tried to nudge his hand away with her chin. "No good will come of this."

He paused a moment. His voice became hard. His eyes darkened. "It is still this *Garret* that haunts your heart?"

Gretchen sighed. The mist from the falls felt heavy,

making her feel even more weighted with what must be said. She would have liked to reassure him by telling him it was not, but she could not. It was true—at least partly—though not for the reasons Elk Dreamer believed. "I don't love him anymore—if that's what you mean."

His expression lifted, and the soft glimmer in his eyes returned.

All the shame and guilt of her past relationship with Garret suddenly rushed to the surface. Like a rainstorm out of control, it flooded her being, gouging away at her pride, tearing down her defenses.

"Don't you see? Garret's dead because of me." Tears burned her eyes. "*I* testified at his trial. *I'm* the one that sent him to prison." Giving into all of the self-accusations she had been hiding within her, she began to cry in earnest. "He tried to kill my best friend, Winter Magic. He almost ruined the lives of many wonderful people. I couldn't just let him get away with that. I had to tell what he had done." She lifted swollen eyes and shivered. "But I never meant for him to die. Oh, God, Elk Dreamer. I never meant for him to die."

Taking her into his arms, Elk Dreamer held her close, soothing her with soft utterances in his native tongue, holding her until she had spent the last of her tears. After a long while, he cupped her chin and lifted her face. "You are not to blame for your Garret's death, Gret-chen."

She shook her head. She raised sodden lashes and peered up at him. "You don't understand. I was his wife. By white law, I wasn't forced to testify—"

"What is this *tes-ti-fy*?"

Gretchen sniffled. She lifted herself back, stretching the limits of his embrace. "It means, I didn't *have* to tell them what I'd seen Garret do."

"But you said you *had* to tell."

"I had to for me." She swallowed back the ache in her throat. "The friend he tried to kill was Paiute— *Coo-yu-ee Pah*."

"Indian." He gazed into her eyes, a look of admiration flickering in the dark recesses of his stare.

She nodded. "The only other people who knew what had happened were another friend, and the friend's brother."

"Were they of the *Coo-yu-ee Pah*?"

"No." She shook her head. "They were white. But Lance was Winter Magic's lover—everyone knew this. They mightn't have believed him, or his brother, if I had not added my truth to theirs."

Elk Dreamer smoothed away the last of her tears, and smiled at her. And when he did, it was like the rainbow after the storm. "You did nothing wrong, Gret-chen. The shame lies with Garret. You are a good woman." He kissed each eye in turn. "A woman any man would hold up to the world with pride."

His thumb set up a circular pattern on her bare shoulder. "Garret was a fool. He could not see the love you would bring into his life, for the hatred that filled his heart." He bent his head and brushed the fullness of her lips with his. "You would do well to know this, Gret-chen. You would do well to see, also, that *I* am not such a fool as he."

EIGHTEEN

Encompassed as she was in Elk Dreamer's arms, Gretchen did not dare move. To do so might spark the passion she saw smoldering just below the surface of his stare. Why could she not just let go with him? She had done so before—yet had she really? It had been him pressing her.

She had not taken the initiative, or actually participated. She had merely succumbed to her need. She wanted him—more than anyone she had ever known. She wanted to experience every nuance of his soul, explore every inch of his body, but she could not seem to find the courage to indulge wholeheartedly in the encounter. What was she truly afraid of?

Lashes slightly lowered, she scrunched a handful of fringe on her dress. This was silly. She was not some nervous school girl at her first dance. She was an experienced woman—one who had been married and knew the expectations of a man's desire.

Elk Dreamer held himself poised just outside her touch. He had not so much as kissed her, and she could already feel her body's response.

Her breasts tightened against the soft buckskin cloth. She tried to calm her breathing, but it quickened despite her effort. Her blood surged, warming its way through her system, lighting a low fire in the pit of her stomach, spreading, inciting a pulse in the heartbeat of her need.

She watched his mouth. Why did he not move forward? Did he not know the torture he was putting her through?

She hesitated a moment longer. She could not do this. It was not fair. Once they were at the fort, and had seen to the business of the renegades, he would rejoin his people, and forget her. It was not fair that he had come into her life only to leave her more desperate, more yearning than when he had found her. It was not fair that he had awakened her womanly passion—not when she knew she would have to give him up so soon.

She felt herself slip toward him. Her eyes lifted to his, then lowered, almost closed. Her instincts collided with her conscience. To hell with fairness. She wanted him, and he wanted her. Even if it were only for this one night, she had to have him.

His black eyes held her entranced. It was as if he were commanding her to let go—to come to him—to take what she so desperately wanted.

Should she? Could she? She felt defenseless against his power. Before she had time to think, she touched him. Timidly, she stroked the hard curve of his inner thigh. "God, help me. I do want you, Elk Dreamer." She exhaled a breathless shivering sound.

He grabbed her hand, expelling a throaty groan.

"I-I'm sorry—" Shocked by her own sudden boldness, she tried to pull away.

He held her palm still against his taut leg muscle.

Within a shaft of mellow moonlight filtering down through the trees, she saw him squeeze his eyes tightly closed. He shook his head.

She held herself rigid, a painful gulp of air suspended in her throat. What had happened? Had she read his intentions wrong?

Finally, he drew in a ragged breath. "You will wait here," he instructed her even before he looked at her.

Her body filled with anxiety. He was leaving her? He had aroused her, and now he was leaving her? In a flush of humiliation, she reached up to his face, but withdrew her touch in midair. She should have known better. She should have never given in to her wanton desires. "I'm sorry," she said again, her voice a quiver. "I shouldn't have—"

He opened his eyes and gazed into hers, the hint of an anguished smile playing across his lips, deepening his dimples. He took her hand and kissed her fingers. "Do not be sorry, Gret-chen. I am not."

It was her turn to be confused. "Then why—"

Still holding onto her, he tipped his head back. His eyes glazed. His expression remained unmoved. Yet, barely audible, the unmistakable sound of a broken moan gave him away. He rested his hands, one on top of each thigh, and shifted, just slightly enough to draw her attention to his discomfort.

She glanced down. Her stomach clutched tight as she caught sight of the effect her touch had had on him. There was no hiding the fact that he was just as aroused as she. Surprised, her gaze bounced up to his.

His smile spread across his face, and his eyes melted into dangerously stirring dark pools. "I will be back." He stood then, and was gone before she could question him further.

What was he doing? What was *she* doing? She felt suddenly giddy with excitement, and a little wicked. But it did not matter. If only for this one night, she would set her cares aside.

Somewhere way up in the highest boughs of the trees, two owls set up a chorus of hoots. Drawing her knees up to her chest, she wrapped her arms around them and listened. Her heart thrummed pell-mell within her breast as the birds continued to call out to each other.

She breathed deep, a flood of anticipation causing her to feel dizzy, a rush of exhilaration warming her body. She tucked an errant strand of hair behind her ear, then glanced down at herself. God in Heaven, she must look a sight.

With hurried movements, she pulled her braids loose and combed her fingers through the full length of her hair. She had to make herself more presentable before he returned. She looked back in the direction he had taken.

Barely visible through the forest, the tiny fire where they had left Snow Dancer and Buffalo Calf winked suggestively at her. Settling her hair around her shoulders, she clutched her arms around her legs and leaned back her head. She peered up at the twinkling sky and giggled, a deep, throaty sound. No matter what came of tomorrow, she would have this night to remember forever, and she was going to enjoy every second of it.

A prickle of hairs stood up on the back of her neck, and she froze. She could feel someone's eyes on her. Slowly, she turned. Lifting her gaze, she met a tender, yet hungry look in Elk Dreamer's eyes. She shot a fevered gaze over his appearance.

Visibly proud of his prowess, he stood only in his breechcloth, holding a fur bundle. Somewhere between the distant camp fire and herself, he had removed his clothing. He was so ruggedly handsome and exquisitely well formed.

Liquid fire shot through her limbs. He nearly took her breath away. She felt instantly wet with the want and need of him.

Wordlessly, he outstretched his hand to her.

She needed no other prompting. Without hesitation, she rose, extending her grasp to his. She came close, so close she could feel the heat radiating off of his body.

"Take off your dress," he commanded softly, releasing her hand.

Lifting her chin, she tethered her eyes to his. She felt the power of the woman within her surge through her veins. This time there would be no shame in her stare, no shyness in her touch. Nothing he could ask of her would be denied. Head held high, she lifted off the garment.

His eyes shimmered, though they did not leave her own. Still watching her, he then snapped the bundle loose, spreading it down atop the plush carpet of calamus and sweet grass at the edge of the water.

"Tonight, Gret-chen, I make you mine." He gathered her hand in his and moved toward the liquid depths that pooled below the rumbling falls. Standing hip-high in the mountain pool, he began a soothing song, and though the words were unintelligible, the lilt was erotically stimulating.

Gretchen shivered in the snowmelt. Still she did not question his actions.

Stepping around behind her, he pushed her hair to the side, drawing it up to drape one shoulder. As he continued to sing, he lifted a handful of water from the pond and let it trickle onto her skin.

"Ooo." She wriggled against the light sting of the water.

He smoothed it over her neck and back, massaging her muscles with pleasure-heightening strokes.

Ignoring the cool temperature, Gretchen allowed her head to slump forward, relaxing under the kneading, experienced fingers of the man. Set adrift on a cool sea of icy water and heated skin, she became lost in the luxury of his gentle hands on her, caressing her, coaxing her deeper under his spell.

Elk Dreamer moved in front of her, his voice a hushed murmur above the loud drone of the falls. "Look at me, Gret-chen. I want to see you."

On command, she raised her head and gazed up at him. Shamelessly, she smiled. She could not believe her boldness. Where was the shy woman she had always been where lovemaking was concerned? She should look away, but she could not. She was drawn to him. She wanted to see what he saw when he looked at her.

Dark and luminous like water ablaze with fire, his eyes shimmered down on her, flickering hot across her body. He scooped up more water and held it for a minute, then spilled it onto her skin.

A tiny cry escaped her throat. She clutched herself tight, expecting the frigid liquid to stun her. But it did not. He had cupped it until it warmed enough to remove the initial chill. He was so gentle, so tender, in his handling of her. It surprised her that a man, a warrior of such strength, could be so tender.

The warm breath of the night air blew across her skin, and her breasts pulled achingly tight.

He thrummed his fingers across her nipples—first one, then the other, drawing them up into rigid puckers.

Moisture flooded the ache between her legs, and she trembled. She wanted him to touch her there. She wanted to feel him inside of her again. Remembering the possessive way he had pounded into her, she swayed toward him. He was driving her mad with the sweet pain of desire.

And all the while, he continued to sing, lulling her deeper into his irresistible seduction. He lifted one breast and pinched the nipple lightly.

She moaned, a high fever gripping her body.

One hand on the small of her back, he slipped the other lower, over her stomach, spiraling tiny circles downward. Each movement brought him nearer to the throbbing juncture of her womanhood. He brushed the curls, his fingertips toying with her sensitive flesh. With each pleasure-filled stroke, he dipped deeper into the folds. Slow and easy, almost as if he were inviting the water to rush in and touch her, too, he urged her legs apart. Then spreading the moist lips open, he slid a finger inside.

Gretchen clutched his forearms. She could not steady herself upright any longer. As hot as she felt, she was sure the cool surge would give rise to steam. She moaned, from the bottommost point of her being, low and sultry, dying with need.

He pulled up and looked at her.

Beneath a profusion of lashes, she saw him. She shook her head and grabbed his hand, returning it to the spot.

He found her pulsing bud and rubbed it gently, feeding her system with soft thunderbolts and warm shock waves.

"Oh, God," she whimpered, throwing back her head. She dug her nails into the hard flesh of his arms. Never had she found such pleasure with so little effort. With Garret, it had always been fast and rough, and all for him.

But not so with Elk Dreamer. He was working her into an unhurried maddening frenzy.

Her muscles flexed, tighter with every stroke. She scrunched her toes into the muddy earth beneath her feet and pulled him nearer. She had to have him close. She squirmed against him, wanting to feel his body next to hers.

Swept up in an ocean of warmth, a sudden infusion of heat swelled through her, holding her suspended above its crest. She arced against his grasp, and the wave ripped through her. "Oh, God," she screamed.

He answered her. A low male vibrating sound spilled into her mouth as he locked his lips to hers, then plunged his tongue inside.

Unable to respond, Gretchen drowned in the current of spasms ravaging her body. She had never known such erotic pleasure. It shocked her. It drained her strength. Clinging to him, she floated, drifting on the tides until they were mere ripples lapping at her soul.

But Elk Dreamer did not allow them more than an ebbing moment before he lifted her into his arms and carried her from the water to the buffalo hide on the grass. After lowering her atop the finely brushed robe, he urged her to lie back. Then, in one quick movement, he loosened the leather thong securing his breechcloth and tossed it to the ground beside them.

She swallowed hard. Never before had she seen a man so comfortable with his nakedness, or so blatantly displayed. Her eyes slipped to his arousal.

Full and erect, he stood above her for a moment, his eyes devouring every inch of her flesh. Then, kneeling between her legs, he lifted one of her feet and kissed her instep.

She flinched, her nerves still raw, still jittering just below the surface of her skin. She watched as with his tongue he drew a thin wet line up to her inner thigh. Her heartbeat quickened again. She reached down to him.

"Not yet," he said in a husky murmur. "I must make all of you mine." When he looked at her this time, there was a new fire burning in his eyes. He bent down to her and tasted the innocent secrets of her body.

A flash of heat lashed at her. No one had ever touched her in such a private manner. She clutched his head, pulling him harder against her.

As if he were trying to find the flame that burned deep inside her, he dipped into the moist recesses and stroked her with his tongue. He rekindled the embers of passion, each stroke fanning the brushfire that smoldered inside her. He was driving her, burning her, with the heat of his desire.

Hotter than before, the rush of passion engulfed her, searing her body. She screamed his name. Her thoughts went wild, setting her soul ablaze so bright it seemed it could be seen for miles. She was out of control. Nothing could save her from the raging fire spreading inside her—nothing but the man that clutched her to him.

And just when she thought she would explode, he bolted upright and grabbed her buttocks. His eyes were emblazoned with a primitive luster she had never seen before. He lifted her up to meet his entrance, then plunged deep, groaning with the force of the impact.

An almost violent pang of excitement tore through her with his thrust. She groaned. Reaching down, she clasped his legs just below his buttocks and arched to meet his push. Engulfed in his fire, burning with her own, she writhed nearer and nearer the flames.

He drove into her again, hard and fast, each collision deeper, wilder, more furious than the last.

In the last throes of passion, they came together in a roaring, thundering firestorm of undisguised pleasure, smothering all but the tiniest embers, hidden, glowing, waiting until the next time.

Doubled up in front of the camp fire, arms clasped around her knees, Snow Dancer dug her nails into the soft flesh of her palms. She knew what was happening between Elk Dreamer and Gretchen. She had heard their love cries echo through the night air, and she did not like it. The thought of them writhing together, like some rutting beasts in the forest, sickened her. It drove her mad with hurt and frustration. She had to end this now—once and for all.

Catching a movement out of the corner of her eye, she looked up and saw Buffalo Calf toss another limb onto the flames, a knowing smile playing across his mouth. He looked up. Immediately, his face colored to a deeper shade of red. He glanced away. Obviously embarrassed by his thoughts, he feigned a sudden interest elsewhere.

Snow Dancer snorted. His innocence always amused her. Did he think he was the only one that knew what was happening between Elk Dreamer and the white woman? Her gaze flitted over his regal and unspoiled countenance.

Though he was not quite as tall or well formed as Elk Dreamer there was no questioning the man's appealing looks. He was an innocent where women were concerned, yet his warrior's eyes, dark and foreboding like shards of onyx, were enough to cut through any female's defenses. As he picked up one of the animal bladders he had refilled from the nearby stream, his long black hair brushed the ground.

Snow Dancer inhaled sharply. She watched as he lifted the bag and drank. If it had not been for the deep emotions stirred within her breast by Elk Dreamer, she just might have considered Buffalo Calf for a suitor. But as it was, she could never do that—not while her medicine man still drew a breath of life.

"You should not have left with the yellow-hair," Buffalo Calf said when he looked at her again.

Startled, she stared at him. It was the first time he had spoken to her since the men's arrival. "I thought I was helping." She made the signs with her hands. Having been able to speak to the white woman made her long to use her voice again.

"Why did you do it? You knew you would be punished. You knew it would anger Elk Dreamer."

"I did not want him captured by the soldiers." It angered her that Buffalo Calf had suddenly chosen to chastise her now. "The yellow-hair would have gotten him killed."

Buffalo Calf arched a brow. "Elk Dreamer is a warrior. I have seen him in battle. He would not be killed so easily as you might think."

"But the yellow-hair—I know her. She would have lured him into their grasp." Her hands flew up in a flurry of movements. "She is evil, Buffalo Calf. She will not stop until she has seen him dead."

"I do not think you know Gret-chen well enough. I do not believe she would intentionally see Elk Dreamer hurt." The man's gaze lifted to the forest, and he smiled. "Still, there may be more truth in your words than even you know."

Snow Dancer grimaced. She shivered with the force of her anger.

Gathering a blanket, Buffalo Calf rose, then walked over to her and sat down beside her. He lifted the covering around her shoulders and encompassed her body with a protective arm. "Let us not speak of Elk Dreamer and the white woman. They do not need our words this night."

Wide-eyed, she peered over at him. Not again. She cringed inwardly. If only she could hurry this plan along and get rid of the yellow-haired cow, then she would be free to work her way into Elk Dreamer's heart as she wanted. Then she would never have to fend off this man-child's advances again.

"Snow Dancer," Buffalo Calf began as he had on so many occasions before. "When will you accept me as your husband? I have eight good ponies waiting to be given to Elk Dreamer. I am a proven warrior, skilled in hunting and stout of heart." He puffed out his chest in a display of pride. "The people know of my feelings for you. They appear to think us a good match. Why do you hesitate? Why do you not present me with a gift of love?"

Snow Dancer lowered her gaze. She thought of the beaded moccasins she had fashioned as a wedding gift for Elk Dreamer. She longed to flaunt them in Buffalo Calf's face, and tell him she loved another, but she could not—not just yet.

"Talk to me, Snow Dancer. Tell me of your reasons," he persisted. He nuzzled her ear. "Tell me why you do not shiver beneath my stare when you know I am looking?"

Snow Dancer's heart quickened, though it was not from excitement, but rather hostility. How was she going to get out of this? She pulled her lower lip between her teeth. She would have to change the subject, and fast. There was no one here to keep Buffalo Calf to a brave's proper decorum.

She turned to face him and showered him with her most radiant smile. "You must know the song of my heart." She signed a circle over her breast.

"There will be time for us when we return to the people. But for now, we must concern ourselves with protecting Elk Dreamer from this shrewd white woman."

"Elk Dreamer!" Buffalo Calf bolted to his feet. His eyes bored into hers with all the fury of a spurned lover. "Always when *I* speak of us, *you* talk of Elk Dreamer."

"He is our leader, and my guardian." She fought back the grin twitching the corners of her lips. She could see the jealousy sparking hot in the man's eyes, and somewhere in the pit of her belly, she felt a surge of joy aching to burst forth. "There is no need for envy or resentment."

It gave her a wicked kind of pleasure to incite Buffalo Calf's wrath. Whereas she knew Elk Dreamer was not, she knew the younger man *was* in love with her, and that he would never harm her. She reveled in the feel of the near-maiming power it gave her over him. Never did she miss a chance to use it when she could.

Oh, she liked Buffalo Calf well enough, but not enough to marry—never enough for that. But somehow having Elk Dreamer's closest friend in the palm of her hand made her feel closer to him. Maybe even a little in control of the medicine man himself.

"Woman!" Buffalo Calf startled her from her musings. "If I did not hold fast to your beauty, I would cut the eyes from your head so that you could never look upon my friend again."

Snow Dancer slithered up beside him. She narrowed a sultry gaze on his face. "You would hurt the woman you wish to marry?"

His eyes darkened to a dangerous glimmer. "Do not play the game of seduction with me now, Snow Dancer. I am too angry." He wheeled around and strode to where he had been sitting before, then snatched up his rifle.

Seeking his attention, Snow Dancer slapped her shoulder repeatedly.

He glared back at her.

She was not finished with him yet. She had to drive the knife deeper in search of the thrill. "You will leave me alone?" She lowered her head in shame, though she kept an enticing look leveled on him.

Buffalo Calf glanced off in the direction of the forest where Elk Dreamer had disappeared hours ago. His nostrils flared.

She knew that, like her, he had heard the numerous screams of passion the white woman had expelled. She could see the man's lust had been triggered. She knew the high moral standards he placed on himself. He would not take her, even if she signaled him of her acceptance. It was a game she played often, but dare she taunt him over the edge now, while there was no one near to stay his advances?

She smiled to herself. "Do not leave me, Buffalo Calf," she signed with a slow sweep of her hand. Then, provoking him further, she tilted her head back and followed the edge of her collar with a finger, tracing it to the lace bindings at her shoulders. Arching a brow, she toyed with the end of the leather tie.

He watched her movements with narrowed eyes, his top lip curled upward in a tormented snarl. Then, without so much as a disgusted grunt, he whirled around and slunk off into the night like a wounded animal.

A low, deep rumble of laughter rose up in Snow Dancer's throat. The torture of a man's ego. It was the second best stimulation she had ever known.

NINETEEN

Lying on the buffalo robe, Gretchen rested her head atop Elk Dreamer's shoulder. With the night's increasing chill, he had drawn up one corner of the fur over them, and now, taking full advantage of its warmth, she snuggled down deeper beneath the heavy blanket.

Exhausted from their lovemaking, and thoroughly sated, she sighed blissfully. Never had she felt so completely at peace. She would have liked nothing better than to remain like this, in the man's arms forever. But like it or not, she knew their forever was only a few hours away. She chose, however, not to think about that at the moment. Reality would impose on them soon enough. Turning her head, she looked at him.

His eyes were closed, long sooty lashes feathered

across the high arc of his cheekbones. His breathing came slow and even. And though he had not spoken for a long while, she was not quite certain that he slept.

She tested him in a whisper. "Elk Dreamer?"

"Hmm?" The resonant sound vibrated through him to her.

"Did I wake you?"

One arm clasped around her, he pulled her closer. He shook his head and smiled.

Like a contented feline, she nudged his shoulder with her nose. "Why did you sing to me?"

He opened one eye and peeked at her.

Reading his unasked question, she glanced toward the pool and raised her brows. "Earlier." No longer enraptured by her sexual desires, she felt a little shy and embarrassed again. "You know."

The creases in his cheeks deepened into a knowing smile. He settled his lashes closed again. "It is Lakotah tradition."

Her curiosity sparked. She poked his shoulder playfully. "Tradition as in . . . why?"

"It is part of the ceremony." He kept his answers brief.

Intrigued more, Gretchen squinted at him. He was not going to give her any more than what she asked for. He was going to make her worm every tidbit of information out of him. Surely he could see that she was interested, so why the game? Okay. She grinned. I can play, too. "Oh," she said, resettling herself as if she suddenly did not care.

She waited a long time, hoping he would wonder why she did not press him further.

But with most men, she'd found, when you wanted them to do something, they didn't. Elk Dreamer was no exception. He did not stir.

Finally, unable to contain herself any longer, she rose up and dug her chin into his chest. "Okay, you win. I can't stand not knowing. What ceremony?"

He chuckled out loud. "When curiosity flutters within a woman's breast, no man's knowledge is safe."

"Oh, you!" Scowling, she nipped at his bare skin, and jabbed him roughly. "Tell me."

He turned to face her, his eyes alight with mirth.

"I'd really like to know." Thrusting out her bottom lip, she flashed him a pouty expression.

He stared at her a moment longer. He eased his hand up to her head and gently pushed it back down to his shoulder. Filling his lungs with the brisk mountain air, he glanced up at the night sky. "When a Lakotah man takes a woman in marriage, there are certain rites he must follow."

"Marriage?" Gretchen's head snapped up. Ogling him, she let her mouth fall slightly agape. "Are you trying to tell me we're—"

He forced her head back down, silencing her with the action. "A woman is made by the Great Spirit to be soft and yielding to a man."

"Yielding!" She feigned an insulted voice, but it did not appear to dissuade him.

"*Most*," he said, punctuating the word with a gentle squeeze to her side, "do not understand this, and so it is up to the man who becomes the woman's husband to teach her." He began to comb through the long strands of her hair with his fingers.

Relaxing under his ministrations, Gretchen turned in his arms just enough so that she, too, could gaze up at the sky.

"Once the woman has accepted the man in marriage, the husband must know her in all ways so that he may teach her to obey him, so she will *want* to obey him." He took in a deep breath, causing his chest to rise. "At first, it is only natural that the woman should be shy and resistant. That is why the Lakotah men sing to their women. It is a quieting song meant to dispel her alarm, to give her strength, for this is a time when she will feel weak and powerless."

Thinking back to the scene in the water, Gretchen smiled to herself. She had to admit it had worked.

"White men do not do such things for their women?" Elk Dreamer raised his head and peered down at her with questioning eyes.

Gretchen thought back to her own wedding night with Garret. She grimaced. Except for the gaslight streaking in from the street lamps, it had been pitch black in their hotel room. He had come to her, whiskey-drunk, and tossed her onto the bed. Then, without a single word of comfort for a virgin's fears, he had jerked up her nightgown and forced himself upon her. In answer to Elk Dreamer's question, she shook her head.

"That is how I believed it to be."

Puzzled, Gretchen glanced up at him. "What do you mean, *believed*? How would you know about marriages in the white world?"

He peered down at her, his eyes alight with warmth and understanding. "You responded to me tonight as a maiden, yet you had a husband."

Gretchen could feel her face heat red. She felt as though she should defend herself, but she had no words to use. He was right. Pulling her gaze from his, she turned her attention back to the sky and watched as a pale wisp of a cloud sidled up to the moon.

"You have never known a man's touch such as I have shown you this night."

She did not reply. She was not sure if he had posed a question or made a statement. In any event, it was true. And she was still too raw with passion's tension to speak about it.

"After my first vision quest," he began again, "I was told the secret of a man's power over a woman by the ceremony makers."

Gretchen held her usual sarcasm to silence. She wanted to hear just exactly what these *ceremony makers* had told him.

"A man must perform upon his woman an irresistible act, they told me. He must let his tongue know her in the same way as the organ of his life seed. His breathing must fan her, his mouth touch her, and his tongue taste her. Then, with tenderness and guidance, he must lift his head and raise his body above hers and enter her with his hardness of purpose." His voice was as soft and cool as the fine spray misting from the waterfall beyond the pool. "He should enter her only then, with gentleness to remember, not the forcefulness of pain."

Listening to him, Gretchen's body went warm inside. Her heart set up a tempestuous beat. She could feel the strength of his words begin to arouse her. She stirred within his embrace.

With seeming casualness, his hand slipped down to

her breast, and he drew light circles around her nipple with his fingertips. "In this way a man was created by the Great Spirit to pleasure a woman, so that she, in turn, may obey him in all things, in all ways, so that he, in turn, may be pleasured. In this way does she learn that her life with the man is an act of submission that she chooses, not one he demands."

Gretchen felt a catch in her throat. Her stomach tightened. She turned so that her back was against his side, then nuzzled against his forearm, pulling his palm back up to her breast. Nothing had ever been explained to her before with such logic, and such immense strength of emotion. The way he told it, it made perfect sense. Men and women *should* pleasure each other.

The whisper of a cool breeze drifted beneath the fur blanket, stroking her warm skin with its teasing breath.

She shivered.

Moving onto his side so that he hugged her back, Elk Dreamer tugged the robe up around her neck.

No other man had ever cared for Gretchen as this one now did. She felt loved and wanted, for nothing more than herself alone.

"I wanted to do this thing for you in the meadow ... but it was not right. I was not sure if you would accept me for a husband." He thrummed her taut nipple, pulling and pinching it softly.

Moisture instantly rushed to the heated juncture of her thighs. She could not speak. Grasping his free hand, she pulled it below the coverlet and gloved it with hers atop her other breast.

He kissed her ear. "Will you accept me, Gret-chen?"

Gretchen exhaled a quivering breath in one long sultry moan. She did not trust her voice. She wanted to say yes, but she could not. They only had this one night—tomorrow and reality was only a few hours away. And she would not have their time together ruined with promises she knew they would not be able to keep.

"Gret-chen?" He almost sounded hurt that she had not answered him yet.

Overcome with impatient desire, she moved against him. She wanted him again, and by the growing hardness pressing against her buttocks, she was certain he felt the same. "Make love to me again, Elk Dreamer."

He slipped a hand lower, flattening his palm on her stomach, and pulled her hard against his groin. "In all ways, Gret-chen. I want you for my woman—my wife." He grazed her ear with his tongue. "*Tecihila,*" he murmured.

He loved her? Did he know what he was saying? Or was he simply caught up in the moment of passion?

"Did you hear me, Gret-chen? *Tecihila.*"

She drew in a sharp breath. This was something she had not expected. Once might have been a slipup, but twice? She moaned with the bitter sweetness of his pledge. She had waited a lifetime to know the true impact of emotion that came with the sentiment. But the cruelty of fate being what it was, they had been brought together too late.

Tears stung her eyes. "Oh, Elk Dreamer . . ." She shifted in his arms and framed his face with one hand. She studied the sincerity in his eyes. It was no mistake.

His dark gaze shimmered with emotion.

Oh, God. Why? It was not fair that after all of this time she should discover a man she could trust with her heart. Her aching soul gave up its guard. "I love—"

"Well, now." A loud voice attacked them from the shadows.

Gretchen gasped. She looked up.

Grinning wickedly, a scruffy-faced fat man moved into the light, a huge knife wavering in his hand. "Would ja jist looky here at what I found?"

Elk Dreamer bolted upright. He leapt to a crouch.

Sitting up, Gretchen snatched the robe around her. Her heart slammed against her chest, its impact jarring her entire system. With a blink, she darted a glance from the intruder to Elk Dreamer.

A gleam of instant blood lust lit his eyes. Battle-ready, the epitome of a naked savage, he rose to a hunched position.

"Red boy?" Another voice, softer than the first, encroached on their haven, a hollow, clinking noise announcing the man's approach. From out of the darkness of the trees, a tall, formidable fellow with bushy muttonchop sideburns walked out into view. He held up Elk Dreamer's breechcloth. "You lose something?"

Masculine laughter rose up from the recesses of the forest, signaling the approach of others.

Elk Dreamer constantly shifted, keeping himself as much between the leering men and Gretchen as possible.

Fear clawing her throat, Gretchen clutched the fur robe tighter against her chest. At the sound of footsteps behind her, she turned within the folds of the heavy covering.

Two more men, one old, the other a younger replica of his cohort, entered into the shards of moonbeams lighting the area.

The boy-faced man with red hair pointed at Gretchen, then whispered something, his tiny eyes glowing lustfully in the darkness.

Gretchen winced. Her mind whirled in fear. Who were these men and what did they want?

"Relax, red boy. You're outnumbered." Sideburns tossed the garment at Elk Dreamer. He looked at Gretchen. "He speak English?"

Gretchen flitted a nervous glance at Elk Dreamer, then back to the tall man.

"I speak English." Giving up his readied posture, Elk Dreamer rose to his full height. But instead of covering himself as the man had commanded, he gripped his breechcloth tightly in his hand at his side.

"I'll be a soldier's bastard!" The fat man moved up closer to Gretchen. He eyed Elk Dreamer up and down with a scrutinizing scowl, his astounded stare coming to rest just below the Indian's waist. "Would ja look at that, Palmer? He's built like a son-of-a-bitchin' ruttin' horse!"

The younger man scurried up beside the heavyset guy and snickered like a little boy gawking at some saloon harlot. He cut Gretchen a suggestive wink. "Guess she thinks so, too, huh, Oren?"

"Knock it off!" The one called Palmer stepped up and faced off with Elk Dreamer. The man challenged the Indian with a volatile expression, his fingers flexing inside the lever of a rifle.

For a moment, Gretchen thought the two would surely go to battle.

Palmer's gaze darted to her.

She shivered beneath his perusal. In that brief few seconds, she almost imagined him to be Garret glowering at her in disgust.

"Get some clothes on," he ordered in a deadly tone.

Gretchen blanched. A tremor like ice water quivered up her spine. She wanted to look away, but the intense look of pure loathing he had leveled at her held her immobile.

"Did you hear me, bitch?" His teeth gnashed white in the night.

Elk Dreamer tensed.

Palmer snatched up his weapon. "I wish you would," he said, obviously wanting to provoke the Indian.

"Do what he says," Elk Dreamer commanded in Lakotah, his voice pitched low.

Palmer struck out. The back of his free hand cracked loudly against Elk Dreamer's cheek.

"No!" Gretchen bolted to her knees. Blanket clasped in one hand, she reached up to Elk Dreamer. Air crowded her lungs. They were going to kill them— she just knew it.

Nostrils flared, body tense, the Indian slowly turned his face back to Palmer. His jaw tightened. He looked to be daring the man to hit him again.

The white man did not so much as flinch. The two appeared to be waging a war of wills, with Palmer the victor.

"I give the orders around here." Lips drawn tight between the bristle of his thick sideburns, the leader narrowed his eyes on Gretchen. "If you need some help, I'm sure Oren or one of the other boys will be glad to—"

Gretchen did not wait to hear any more, before she jumped up and ran to the edge of the pool, where she had left her clothing. She was not about to let any of them get near her. And she knew if they tried, Elk Dreamer would kill them—or be killed trying to defend her.

"Harlan." Looking at the older man still standing in the shadows, Palmer nodded toward Gretchen. "Keep an eye on her."

"I'll do it," Oren offered in a guttural tone. He grinned, and even in the dusky light, his teeth flashed a nauseating decayed yellow color.

"I said Harlan," Palmer commanded harshly. Apparently he was not about to stand for any kind of challenge—not even from his own men.

Gretchen sent a thankful prayer heavenward. Bending down, she grabbed up her dress. If she had to be left with any of them, she would rather it be the old guy. He did not look quite as dangerous as the other three, and that included the youth.

She watched as the leader motioned for Elk Dreamer to move out ahead of him, ramming him in the back with the barrel end of his rifle. Shaking open the buckskin garment, she tried to pull it over her head, but she nearly dropped the buffalo robe. Immediately she looked up.

Grinning from ear to ear, the pimple-faced redhead nodded as if he were mentally coaxing the blanket to plummet from her grasp.

"Jefferson Lee!"

The youth whipped his head toward the older man left to tend her. "Yeah, Pa?"

Harlan directed the young man with an uplifted thumb. "You git yer ass over to the others like Palmer said."

Jefferson Lee licked his lips like a hound with a fresh bone.

"Now!" His father's tone brooked no defiance.

Lips spread wide over crooked teeth, the boy nodded, then loped after his companions.

Gretchen nervously peered over at her captor.

Rifle cradled across his chest, the man turned sideways, obviously trying to give her a small measure of privacy.

A marauder with scruples? Gretchen almost felt relieved. Still, she left nothing to chance. His courteous bearing might be a ploy to get her to lower her guard—not to mention the barrier concealing her nudity.

Scuffling sounded in the distance.

Gretchen's pulse quickened. What was happening? She could hear the men talking, but she could not make out what they were saying.

"You hurry up now, miss."

Needing no further provocation, Gretchen leaned over and stepped into the dress. She had to get back to Elk Dreamer. In one swift movement, she pulled the buckskin up and dropped the heavy robe. It fell to the ground with a weighty thunk.

Out of the corner of his eye, the old man glanced toward her. He wiped his hand across his mouth, then darted a look in the direction of his friends.

Gretchen did not wait to discover the meaning

behind that hungry look masking his features. She jerked the dress closed over her shoulders and quickly tied both sides securely. She tossed her hair over her back and grabbed up her moccasins. Hopping on one foot, then the other, she yanked them onto her feet.

When she was finished, Harlan gestured toward the glimmer of the camp fire still burning in the distance.

Oh, God! Snow Dancer. Buffalo Calf. In her fear for her and Elk Dreamer's safety, she had forgotten all about them. Hurrying forward, she kept her eyes downcast and rushed past her guard.

Oren's throaty scratch of a voice snatched at her attention as she walked up to the camp.

"So where'd this buck come from?" He did not appear to be directing the question to anyone in particular.

Gretchen immediately sought out Elk Dreamer.

Hog-tied, the Indian had been forced to lie on his side next to Snow Dancer.

"What about it, squaw gal?" Oren asked, squinting down at the Indian woman. "You told us it was just you and the white woman."

Gretchen shot Snow Dancer an accusing stare. What did he mean *told* them? Surely the woman was not in league with these men.

Silently, Harlan motioned for her to move over by Elk Dreamer.

Gretchen brushed past Snow Dancer and knelt near Elk Dreamer's head. She reached out to touch his face.

His lip was bleeding. Palmer must have carried out his threat.

Eyes piercing brighter than the flames leaping in the small fire, Palmer glared at her again before his gaze slid to Snow Dancer. "What about it, woman? Who the hell's this red bastard, and what the hell's he doing here?"

All eyes looked at Snow Dancer.

She appeared nervous and fidgety. She flitted a glance at Elk Dreamer.

Lifting his head, he peered up at her, morose anticipation marking his features.

"C'mon, squaw gal. We ain't got all night." Oren scratched his groin, then hitched his pants up around his waist. "We gotta git this over with. No tellin' when them soldier boys'll be comin'."

"What does he mean?" Gretchen asked. She could not stand not knowing any longer. "Do you know these men?"

Snow Dancer lifted a hate-filled glare on Gretchen.

"Oh, God, no." No need for the woman to answer— the look she gave Gretchen told her everything she needed to know. "Why, Snow Dancer?" A flash of memory sparked her brain, and she suddenly knew the reason even before the woman spoke.

"You would take Elk Dreamer from me." Snow Dancer spat the words in a seething whisper.

Hearing her, Elk Dreamer stared at the woman, a look of incredulity and loathing seeping into the contours of his face. "*Wins'ni!*" Elk Dreamer said in a low growl, a feral light flashing in the depths of his eyes.

Like the strike of a snake, Palmer kicked Elk Dreamer in the face. "Shut your damn mouth, red boy! Nobody's talking to you."

Gretchen screamed. Glowering up, she clutched Elk Dreamer to her breast. "What do you want from us?"

Muttonchop Face sneered wickedly. He dragged his eyes over Gretchen with an agonizingly slow sense of purpose. "We want you."

TWENTY

Wide-eyed, mouth slightly agape, Gretchen stared at the man. She could not believe what he had just said. Why would they want her? She did not even know them.

A low rumble of laughter vibrated up from the fat man's belly. He eased over to the leader, then jabbed him in the arm with an elbow. "Hell, Palmer, she ain't even got no idear who we are."

The clink in the man's steps drew Gretchen's attention. It sent a biting chill slithering up her spine. Why did that sound cause her so much discomfort? It was almost as if she had heard it somewhere before— Recognition sparked her memory.

Something flashed like metal.

Oh, God! She had heard the sound before. Her gaze fell on the unfastened buckles that clinked when the man moved. Her throat closed, squeezing the breath from her lungs. They were stitched onto the tops of boots. But these were not just any boots—these were *rubber*.

Palmer snorted, a thin-lipped grin plastering his face. "I think she's just figured it out. Look at her eyes."

"You're them—the men that attacked the stage!" Stunned with the sudden realization, she sat staring at them, unable to move.

"And to think . . ." Palmer joined in with Oren's amusement. He chuckled cruelly, bitterly. "All this time I thought this woman was stupid for laying with an Indian." He snorted, his features contorting into a mask of savage hate. He shook his head. "Nah. She's not stupid. She's just Indian-loving trash, that's all. Just like Lavinia Louise." The latter he said under his breath.

Gretchen shrank down over Elk Dreamer. It could not be. But that was the same name Ponders-as-she-walks Woman had mentioned when she spoke of the friend from her girlhood. Could this be the woman's jealous husband?

She lifted her gaze and studied Palmer's features. He looked to be about the same age as Ponders-as-she-walks Woman. Gretchen shivered uncontrollably. Had he killed his young wife so long ago? Is that why the old woman had never seen her friend again? "Why?" she asked, not knowing what question she wanted answered most: why he had killed his wife or why he was killing white travelers and blaming it on Elk Dreamer's people.

The man's lip lifted in an unmistakable snarl. "Because they're filth—no better than some devilish disease. They have to be wiped out—once and for all!" He gestured toward her with an angry flick of his hand. "Look at you. That red boy's afflicted your mind." His gaze traveled over the length of her body with a disgusted glower.

Gretchen cowered down, but just as quickly stiffened her spine. He was not going to make her feel ashamed for anything she had done with Elk Dreamer. He was clean and pure of heart, and she loved him—truly loved him—and he loved her, too.

"You're a white woman, for God's sake!"

Gretchen's heart pounded at the fierce volume of the man's temper, but still she held herself steady and unyielding. She would not let him see her fear.

He moved up beside her and jerked her to her feet. "How could you let that red bastard touch you?" He shook her violently, then slapped her across one cheek.

She fell hard on the ground. Her eyes, wide with true fear, met Elk Dreamer's.

His jaw tightened. His unflinching expression warned her of the smoldering anger he was holding back.

"Get away from that heathen devil." In one swift movement, Palmer reached down for her and drew back his hand.

Snow Dancer bolted up. "Not yet. She must be last."

Halting in mid-action, Palmer wheeled on the woman. He looked as though he could tear her in half. "You're not running this outfit."

Chest heaving, Snow Dancer pinned him with a look that should have knocked him off his feet. "Do not threaten me, white man."

"You backin' out on our deal, squaw gal?" Oren took a step toward her.

Quick to move, Snow Dancer jerked her knife from her moccasin and jabbed it at him in a menacing strike. She shifted her weight back and forth on her feet.

He laughed, causing his great girth to shake. "Seems to me I recollect you tryin' that once before . . ." He lunged at her. Grabbing her wrist, he yanked her up against him. He twisted her hand and wrested the knife free, knocking it from her grasp to the ground.

"Ooowee!" The redheaded youth began to jump up and down like a child on Christmas morning. His eyes moved over Snow Dancer's body with feverish interest. "Cain't we have're now, Palm?"

"*Petehinc'ala!*" She squirmed against Oren's hold. "*Petehinc'ala! Hiyu wo was'icun.*"

"What the hell's she yellin'?" Oren had his hands full with the Indian woman.

Even though she was overpowered, she fought with all her might.

"Hell, I don't know," Palmer hollered, his face still flaming bright red.

"Well, you're s'pposed to be able to speak all this—Ouch!"

Snow Dancer sunk her teeth into the hulking man's fleshy arm.

He whirled her around and slammed her back up against him. "Damn, but she's a feisty li'l squaw gal." In the squabble, the knife was kicked toward Gretchen.

She looked up. No one appeared to have noticed.

Palmer approached the wrestling couple. He snatched Snow Dancer's head up by her hair.

She went deathly still.

"You got you some brave out there somewhere close by, don't you?"

"What?" The older man, the one called Harlan, immediately became alert. He slammed the lever of his rifle forward and back, then wheeled around to face the darkness. "You sayin' there's another one out there, Palmer?"

"No." He leaned into the Indian woman's face. "She did."

Gretchen darted a terrified look at each of the men.

All but Harlan were turned on Snow Dancer.

Gretchen glanced at the knife still lying on the ground, then at Elk Dreamer. It was only an arm's distance away. She checked the men again.

Their interest still weighed heavily on Snow Dancer.

"Hey, quiet! I think I heard something." Harlan crouched and squinted into the night.

Palmer came to attention.

The other men, too.

With one last look at Gretchen, Palmer cocked his rifle. He moved up next to Harlan. "The girl only called out to one brave."

"Yeah, well, there could be more than that out there."

"I don't think so. If there were, they'd've been on us by now."

"What d'ya figure we oughtta do?"

Palmer turned back to Snow Dancer's captor. "Oren, you and Jefferson Lee stay here with the women," he whispered in a strained voice. He glanced at Gretchen. "Either of them make a sound . . . kill them."

"Sure thing, Palm." The youth grinned, his eyes feasting on the swell of Snow Dancer's heaving chest.

"If one them Injuns's really out there, he'll be fer tryin' to steal our horses, what'd ya bet?" Harlan gestured to the east. "I'm goin' this way."

Palmer nodded, then headed off in the opposite direction. "Yeah, well, keep awake. Don't let that heathen sneak up on you."

Gretchen waited for the two men to enter the darkness before she made her move. Then, eyes fastened on Oren and the boy, she stretched out and eased her hand toward the knife.

Snow Dancer twisted and turned, with heart-wrenching groans.

"C'mon, li'l squaw gal. Give ol' Oren a taste of that sweet juicy red meat you got tucked under that dress." He snaked his hand up under her buckskin.

She screamed, cursing them in Lakotah.

"Hey, save some for me. . . ." Jefferson Lee moved in.

Gretchen's fingers touched the blade. Her heart stopped, then lurched forward in a fit of fear-filled beats. She clasped the end of the handle, her eyes never wavering from the two men. She had it. With the knife fully grasped, she leaned back and draped her hand behind Elk Dreamer's back.

His gaze sought hers. A mixture of pride, anger, love, and hatred swam in the dark glimmer of his eyes.

Smiling tremulously, she began sawing through the thick rope binding his wrists and feet together.

A rifle shot echoed through the still of night. Followed by another. Then more.

"Son of a—" Oren immediately lost interest in Snow Dancer. He peered out into the black void, though he still held her firmly against him.

Jefferson Lee gripped his rifle. He grinned. "Hey, Pa? Did you get him?" He glanced back at Oren. "They got him!"

More shots echoed, closer than before.

"Hey!" Jefferson Lee yelled.

Fear lodged in Gretchen's throat. He had seen her. She did not dare look up.

The next few seconds were a dust-flurry of movements.

Gretchen cut through the ropes.

Elk Dreamer lunged to his feet. Clasping his hands together like a war club, he swung, connecting with the boy's jaw.

Jefferson Lee groaned. His feet flew out from underneath him with the force of the blow.

Snow Dancer stomped her heel into the shin of the big man holding her.

He released her, though not because of her frail attempt at escape, but to defend himself against Elk Dreamer's attack.

The Indian flew at Oren.

They locked in a deadly grip of brute strength. Groaning and snarling, each man moved in resistance to the other's force.

Still clutching the knife, Gretchen sat frozen. She could not seem to move. She could only watch.

Elk Dreamer twisted his arms one atop the other and gripped the big man around the neck. He wheeled away and yanked.

But Oren's greater weight held him planted firmly to the ground. One huge hand thrust beneath Elk Dreamer's groin, the other around his throat, Oren lifted the slighter man, then slammed him against his knee.

A whoosh of breath rushed out of Elk Dreamer. He collapsed at the feet of the man.

Gretchen bolted to her knees, the knife flashing in her hand. She was no expert with a blade, but she could not just stand by and watch Elk Dreamer killed.

But before she could manage to struggle to her feet, Elk Dreamer leapt to his. He ran at the hulking man, hell's fury raging in his eyes.

A movement off to the side caught Gretchen's attention. Too late, she saw the woman.

Snow Dancer's foot cracked beneath Gretchen's chin. She was hurled back on her bottom, and the knife flew from her hand.

Snow Dancer grabbed the blade. She flashed it in Gretchen's face. Her teeth gnashed. "Now I kill you, yellow-haired cow."

The battling men tumbled behind her.

Startled, Snow Dancer leapt out of the way just in time.

Neither man appeared to see her.

Turning her attention back to Gretchen, the woman looked confused about something. Plainly, she was afraid of the men, but just as obviously, she wanted Gretchen.

Narrowing her eyes, Gretchen fought to regain her balance. She pushed herself up, leaping at the Indian woman. She caught her around the ankles, knocking her into the dirt, then jumped to her feet.

Snow Dancer barely hit the ground before she came at Gretchen again.

This time, Gretchen was ready for her.

Snow Dancer charged forward.

Imitating Elk Dreamer's attack on the boy, Gretchen formed a club with her hands and buffeted the Indian woman backward. The force of the impact nearly threw her atop Snow Dancer, but she managed to keep her balance.

Lip bleeding, Snow Dancer recoiled. Her eyes burned hot. She lurched up. She looked down at the knife clutched in her hand and smiled.

Gretchen swallowed hard, but held her ground. She did not stand a chance against the weapon. Still, she had no intention of giving in to death. She crouched low.

But instead of attacking Gretchen, Snow Dancer stilled, her gaze moving toward the men.

Gretchen turned and looked.

Locked in a deadly grip of brute strength, Elk Dreamer lay naked on the ground. Squeezing his eyes tightly closed, he growled fiercely. Hands wrapped in the cord of his breech cloth, one leg thrown over his opponent's body, Elk Dreamer pulled on the leather tie around Oren's throat. Every muscle strained taut.

Gretchen paled. She had never seen such primitive anger in action. Behind her a sudden shuffle of footsteps grappled with her attention. Senses alarmed, she turned.

Snow Dancer bolted toward the forest.

No! Gretchen charged after her. She could not let her get away. Chasing after the woman, she ran as hard as she could.

But in the dusky shades of the growing predawn sky, the Indian woman had disappeared, blending into the maze of aspen and pine, swallowed by the light and shadow encroaching on the trees.

Halting, chest heaving, Gretchen strained to listen. She had to get her bearings. She could not run blindly through the forest. Snow Dancer still had the weapon.

A woman shrieked.

Oh, God, no! Harlan and Palmer. She had all but forgotten about them. Surveying her surroundings, she held herself to silence. Now what was she to do? The white men had undoubtedly killed Buffalo Calf and recaptured Snow Dancer.

Gretchen shook her head to clear her thinking. Her first instinct was to run back to Elk Dreamer. They had to get out of there—fast—before the men returned to the campsite.

Voices echoed up through the misty gray morning.

Taking a gulp of air, Gretchen hesitated.

"Let me go, Buffalo Calf." It was Snow Dancer. She sounded panicked.

Buffalo Calf? He was alive? Oh, God! Her heart soared. That meant he had defeated the white men. No. She could not be certain until she saw for herself.

"How is it you can talk?"

Unmistakably, the guttural sound of Buffalo Calf's voice caught Gretchen's hearing. She ran toward them and halted when she came upon them.

Standing in a small glade, nearly out of breath, Snow Dancer pointed toward her. Gretchen could only make out some of what the Indian woman said, but it was enough to instill true fear.

"Gretchen is with the white men. They will kill Elk Dreamer. Stop them!"

Feathers fluttering from one end of the rifle gripped in his hand, Buffalo Calf followed Snow Dancer's line of vision back to Gretchen.

Looking at the suspicious expression on his face, Gretchen felt certain that he was not totally convinced of her entanglement with the white renegades. But then, neither did he appear to be assured she was not with them. She shook her head, praying he could see that she was not the one at fault—and that Snow Dancer was lying.

"If you love me, Buffalo Calf, you will do this thing I ask." Snow Dancer was using every means of coercion she could grasp. "If you do this for me, I-I will accept you for my husband."

Apparently stunned, Buffalo Calf looked back at her. He held her stare a long moment, as if considering her vow. Then he shifted his attention back to Gretchen. He stiffened.

Snow Dancer swallowed. Her eyes filled with loathing as she, too, swung her gaze back to Gretchen. A secret smile pulled her lips into a thin line.

Buffalo Calf's stare remained riveted on Gretchen.

Apparently impatient, Snow Dancer tugged on the young Indian's arm, pulling him forward. "We must help Elk Dreamer. Kill her, quickly!"

Instinctively, Gretchen took a step back. Please, no, God. She sent a prayer heavenward. Don't let him believe her. She wanted to say something—anything to sway him to her side. But what? He would certainly believe the woman he loved over a woman whom he saw as his enemy. Gretchen held onto her one hope— *she* had been the one to save his life.

Suddenly, Buffalo Calf's posture relaxed a bit. His suspicious expression ebbed ever so slightly. "Why would this one deed now warm your heart to mine? Gret-chen has proved herself a friend." He veered around to face the Indian woman. "*She* has never deceived us."

"But she has. She is in alliance with the white men come to kill us."

He tipped his head to one side. "Is she?"

Twisting her hands, Gretchen held her breath. Please, God, please.

Snow Dancer nodded. "We must get back to Elk Dreamer. It is not safe to leave him. There are two others in these woods looking for you."

Buffalo Calf raised his weapon and arched a brow. "They look no longer," he stated flatly.

Snow Dancer blanched, then just as quickly flashed him a satisfied smirk. "Good. Then there is only the yellow-hair and the two at the fire."

Buffalo Calf held on to another moment of silence. With his back to her, Gretchen could not see his face. Did he believe the woman?

He suddenly turned toward her.

Shaking her head, she backed away. She watched a slow smile spread across Snow Dancer's lips.

The Indian moved forward.

But before he had taken more than a couple of steps, Snow Dancer's features contorted into a mask of hatred. She took a deep breath and puffed out her chest. In the next instant, she lifted the blade and flew at Buffalo Calf's back, yelling like a woman possessed.

"Gret-chen!" Elk Dreamer grabbed her from behind, nearly wrenching her off her feet.

"Look out!" she shrieked.

Buffalo Calf dropped to the ground.

Shocked, Gretchen shrank back into Elk Dreamer's arms. So transfixed by the horrible scene before her, she could not move.

Too late to stop herself, Snow Dancer collided with Buffalo Calf. She pitched over his curled body and gasped. A smothered groan vibrated up from her sprawled form. Then, silence, and she moved no longer.

Gretchen did not wait for the assured outcome. She ran to them and fell to her knees.

Elk Dreamer hurried behind her.

Lifting the Indian woman carefully, Buffalo Calf turned her over.

Her dark eyes rolled up to them. She struggled on a breath, then looked down. Imbedded to its hilt in her stomach, the knife stood erect, blood oozing from its entrance. Squeezing her eyes closed for an instant, she cringed with an agonizing moan.

"Oh, my God!" In that split second of time, Gretchen could not seem to remember any of the medical training she had learned. She waved her hands helplessly. "We've got to help her. Get me something—some rags—anything to stop the bleeding," she commanded.

"Do not touch me!" Snow Dancer ordered in a gurgling murmur.

But Gretchen did not back away. She had dealt with others before who did not want her help. She would do it now. Though a river of tears stung her eyes, her adrenaline surged into her brain, and suddenly she remembered her medical satchel.

Still shaking a bit, she gripped Buffalo Calf's hand. "My bag!" When, after she had commanded him to action, he still did not move, she glanced up at Elk Dreamer. "I need my bag!" No matter what Snow Dancer had done, she could not sit by and just let the woman die. But deep down, she knew it was already too late.

Gretchen worked frantically to apply pressure to the wound. She wanted to pull out the knife, but that might do more damage than good. She searched the area around her. She needed some packing of some kind, but she could not see anything that might work. "Elk Dreamer, please! The bag."

But instead of doing as she asked, he squatted down beside her and shook his head. He peered at her with sorrowful eyes. "It is too late."

Snow Dancer's face paled from the loss of blood. She tried to speak, but only managed to swallow instead. She lifted anguished, lusterless eyes to Buffalo Calf's, then clutched his forearm.

"Kill the yellow-hair," she begged in a strained, choking utterance. The hatred in her eyes flickered a little dimmer. Then, turning an enamored, yet pathetic gaze toward Elk Dreamer, she reached up to him. "Do not let her have my . . ." Her voice went shallow and slowly, pitifully waned, as did the Indian woman's life.

TWENTY-ONE

Gretchen raised a doleful expression past the whispering tree tops, to the sun-filled heavens, and sighed. Decorated with playful puffs of white clouds, its bright and boundless expanse seemed determined to appear each day bluer and more brilliant than the day before. Nothing in nature appeared to have noticed Snow Dancer's passing from the self-inflicted torture of her earthly bounds to the final release of her celestial freedom.

Elk Dreamer moved up behind Gretchen and squeezed her shoulders tenderly. "You think of her still?"

Caressing his hand with a loving brush of her chin, she nodded.

It had only been three days since they laid Snow Dancer out on a bed of pine boughs and placed her up in her final resting place, in the arms of a mighty evergreen.

"She must've truly hated me," Gretchen said hesitantly, still a little tired from their half day's hike through the mountains.

Elk Dreamer massaged the tight muscles at the base of her neck. "She was a woman in pain and great torment," he answered thoughtfully. Though he did not show it, Gretchen knew that, in his own way, the warrior grieved for the loss of the woman. He did not even appear to feel any animosity toward her.

"Mm," Gretchen murmured. "I suppose she was." She leaned back, enjoying the feel of his soothing touch on her neck. "I just can't believe she's really dead. None of it makes any sense."

"Her love—at least what she believed to be love—was most strong, and unguided."

Gretchen peered out a short distance below and watched the flowing current of the Laramie River sweep past the fort just north of them. They had only taken a brief respite before continuing on to Fort Laramie, and she wanted to make the most of her time with Elk Dreamer, yet she could not relax. Her gaze shifted to a grassy knoll where Buffalo Calf sat.

He stabbed a stick into the ground repeatedly, a look of forlorn loss marking his otherwise chiseled features.

"He's the one I feel sorry for. He truly loved her."

"Mm. He, too, is in much pain." Elk Dreamer slipped his hands around in front of Gretchen and crossed them over her chest. "But he is strong. He will learn, as I did. When the time comes, he will love again."

A horse snorted in the near distance.

Another answered, blowing loudly.

They reminded Gretchen of what was soon to be. She glanced toward the indifferent animals, letting her gaze follow the covered forms draping the beasts. So many deaths—and all for what? Prejudice? Greed? Where would it end? She shuddered to think.

Swinging her attention to the bent-kneed, red-haired boy resting his head in his hands, Gretchen took a deep breath and exhaled. "You think they'll believe our story—the army, I mean?"

Elk Dreamer nodded, the side of one jaw rubbing up and down against Gretchen's temple. "They will not want to, but the fire-hair will tell them the truth of the white renegades."

"Do you think the soldiers'll be able to catch up with the others? Jefferson Lee said there were at least twenty more miners in league with his father and Palmer."

"I cannot say." He sighed profoundly, though a bit reluctantly. "I will ask the Great Spirit to guide their path. He will help them search out the bad white-eyes who would see our people killed."

Gretchen smiled at his use of the word *our*, for she had come to think of them as *hers*, too, but her smile faded all too quickly. "What about the people? Once you speak to the soldiers, they'll want to know where to find them." Gretchen felt his muscles grow tense. She turned in his embrace, to face him. "Oh, Elk Dreamer. You can't still be thinking of fighting the entire army. They'll—"

"I have lived now two seasons without war." He scanned the rolling foothills with ever-moving, hope-filled eyes. "If it is the path the Great Spirit wishes me to continue upon, I will find a way to walk a small bit farther."

Gretchen nearly flew at him with joy. Hugging him, she felt as if a heavy weight had been lifted from her shoulders. But her fears had not been completely laid to rest. What if the army did not see it his way? What if after they were told the truth, they still wanted to imprison him for taking part in the massacre at the Little Big Horn?

As if reading her thoughts, Elk Dreamer pulled her tighter against him, enveloping her with his loving arms. "Do not worry, Gret-chen. It will be—" He pulled back and looked at her. "Okay?"

Hesitantly, she nodded. She would not let him see her true fear. She would see him through all of this, come what may.

"We must go now, Gret-chen." He looked down at the fort, his gaze traveling the length of the bridge spanning the width of the river.

Nodding, Gretchen lowered her arms from around his waist. She waited, watching the two Indian men gather up the ponies laden with the dead bodies of Harlan, Oren, and Palmer.

Buffalo Calf ordered Jefferson Lee to stand and mount the remaining horse.

Obviously unable to understand the man's com-mand, the youth reared back and visibly trembled, staring at him with a fearful expression. He glanced at Gretchen. "Wh-what's he want me to do, miss?"

Gretchen lifted a brow.

Jefferson Lee had been the picture of social etiquette since he had discovered that he was the only member of his small group still alive. It had been consistently *yes'm*, *no mam*, and *miss* since he had been taken a prisoner.

Buffalo Calf did not wait for Gretchen to translate. Instead, he snagged up the leather thong securing the boy's hands together, then yanked him to his feet.

Gretchen cleared her throat to hide a chuckle. "I think he wants you to get on your horse."

Buffalo Calf was not about to injure the one person who could tell the soldiers the truth. But Jefferson Lee did not know that. It was only too apparent that he was genuinely afraid for his life.

Grunting, Buffalo Calf nodded, then shoved the youth toward the waiting animal.

In only a matter of moments, they had descended the forested hill and were converging on the bridge. Aligned in pack-trail style, the horses' hooves clattered hollow on the iron-and-wood overpass, adding to the agitating sound of the river's churn.

Gretchen's own heartbeat thundered so loud with uneasy anticipation, she felt certain it could be heard above the other discordant noises around her. Once they had crossed over, she flitted a glance at Elk Dreamer.

Though his face was still battered and bruised from Palmer's abuse, he walked ramrod straight, with his head held high. The deep gash over his left eye did not even detract from his noble countenance.

In the distance, a trumpet sounded alarm.

"Would ya look at that?" Hushed voices arose from the settlement just outside the fort. "That's a white woman garbed in them buckskins and braids."

"Yeah, and ain't that Harlan Jethrops's kid them Injuns's got tied to that horse, there?"

Catching sight of the blur of faces leering in and out of her line of vision, Gretchen's nerves skittered just below the surface of her skin. She could feel the hatred and fear directed at her and the Indian men, but she tried to keep her focus on the fort just visible beyond the Laramie settlement.

The closer they approached to the fort, the clearer she could see the soldiers rallying to the natural-timbered walls encasing the post. She could hear them calling out in rapid succession, each sounding louder and more frantic than the next. Fear closed in around her, and she faltered a step.

"You are afraid, Gret-chen?" Elk Dreamer seemed to have read her thoughts again.

She would have liked to have been able to deny it, but she could not. The tiny quiver of butterflies fluttering in the pit of her stomach had suddenly been transformed into a raging swarm of bees. Pulling her lower lip between her teeth, she cut him a sidelong glance and silently answered him with a nervous smile.

"You have still not answered my question, Gretchen," he announced as if he had no other care in the world. He appeared to be trying to take her mind off of the upset that was about to take place.

Frowning, she tried to keep up with his long strides. "What question?"

His dimples deepened in that same boyish charm she had grown so quickly to love. "I asked you by the pool if you would accept me as your husband."

What? He was bringing that up—now? Embarrassed, she looked over her shoulder at Buffalo Calf only a few feet behind them.

He appeared not to have heard Elk Dreamer.

"I can't believe you're thinking about that right now," she said in a frantic whisper. "There're more pressing things at hand than our . . . uh . . ." Still as yet unable to think of a lasting relationship with him, she paused. "That question."

"I will have your answer now, or I will never have it."

What was he saying? Did he mean that if she did not comply, he would not accept her decision later? Or did he believe there might not be a *later*? Neither set well with Gretchen. Her fear of fairness in matters of love, or lack thereof, reared up to taunt her. She hesitated. What was really stopping her from answering him? She loved him—she knew she did.

She was torn between the future and the present. Yet how could she consider the time ahead? Nothing was for certain. She was living proof of that.

Seeking happiness, she had married Garret, expecting to have a long and fulfilling life as a doctor's wife, and that had not worked out. Wanting to escape his death, she had left Reno to return to her family home, in hopes of finding a new life, yet she had never made it there.

But had she found that better life? Could she be avoiding the very future she sought? She considered Elk Dreamer for a long, pensive moment. She could feel the pride emanating from his regal bearing.

He was *Hanble Hehaka* a *Cante Tinza Lakotah pejuta wicasa*, she reminded herself with a smile. A medicine man of the Brave Heart warrior society of the noble tribe of the Teton Sioux . . . and *her* lover.

She thought of the song he had sung to her the night by the falls. As it had done then, it did now. The memory of its power acted upon her, dispelling her alarm and giving her strength as he had promised it was meant to do. Her fear remained close, but she would not let it overtake her. Breathing deeply, she lifted her head. She had made her decision. "I would be proud to accept you as my husband," she answered in her feeble attempt at using his dialect.

Lifting a palm to her, he grinned roguishly. "It is enough for you to say *tecihila* . . . I love you."

Her answer had not even surprised him; he seemed to have expected it, in fact. Shaking her head, she took his hand. And feeling the inner strength of his warrior's touch, she offered him an engaging smile. Then and there she swore never to hesitate with him again. She had found her future—no matter how long or short it might be—in the man that walked beside her.

No longer would she worry over what might be, but would take whatever pleasure she could find in what was now. She vowed to live each day as if it were the only one allotted her. She loved Elk Dreamer, and she would tell him so every remaining day of their lives. "*Tecihila, Hanble Hehaka*. I love you." And for now . . . that was enough.

If you enjoyed WARRIOR'S TOUCH and would like to write the author, you can send your letters to:

Deborah James
P.O. Box 60631
Bakersfield, CA 93386-0631

Diamond Wildflower Romance

A breathtaking new line of spectacular novels set in the untamed frontier of the American West. Every month, Diamond Wildflower brings you new adventures where passionate men and women dare to embrace their boldest dreams. Finally, romances that capture the very spirit and passion of the wild frontier.

__NEVADA HEAT by Ann Carberry
    1-55773-915-3/$4.99
__TEXAS JEWEL by Shannon Willow
    1-55773-923-4/$4.99
__REBELLIOUS BRIDE by Donna Fletcher
    1-55773-942-0/$4.99
__RENEGADE FLAME by Catherine Palmer
    1-55773-952-8/$4.99
__SHOTGUN BRIDE by Ann Carberry
    1-55773-959-5/$4.99
__WILD WINDS by Peggy Stoks
    1-55773-965-X/$4.99
__HOSTAGE HEART by Lisa Hendrix
    1-55773-974-9/$4.99
__FORBIDDEN FIRE by Bonnie K. Winn
    1-55773-979-X/$4.99
__WARRIOR'S TOUCH by Deborah James
    1-55773-988-9/$4.99
__RUNAWAY BRIDE by Ann Carberry
    0-7865-0002-6/$4.99 (April)

Payable in U.S. funds. No cash orders accepted. Postage & handling: $1.75 for one book, 75¢ for each additional. Maximum postage $5.50. Prices, postage and handling charges may change without notice. Visa, Amex, MasterCard call 1-800-788-6262, ext. 1, refer to ad # 406

Or, check above books and send this order form to:	Bill my: ☐ Visa ☐ MasterCard ☐ Amex _____ (expires)
The Berkley Publishing Group 390 Murray Hill Pkwy., Dept. B East Rutherford, NJ 07073	Card#_____ ($15 minimum) Signature_____
Please allow 6 weeks for delivery.	Or enclosed is my: ☐ check ☐ money order
Name_____	Book Total $_____
Address_____	Postage & Handling $_____
City_____	Applicable Sales Tax $_____ (NY, NJ, PA, CA, GST Can.)
State/ZIP_____	Total Amount Due $_____

*If you enjoyed this book,
take advantage
of this special offer.
Subscribe now and get a*

FREE
Historical
Romance

No Obligation (a $4.50 value)

Each month the editors of True Value select the four *very best* novels from America's leading publishers of romantic fiction. Preview them in your home *Free* for 10 days. With the first four books you receive, we'll send you a FREE book as our introductory gift. No Obligation!

If for any reason you decide not to keep them, just return them and owe nothing. If you like them as much as we think you will, you'll pay just $4.00 each and save at *least* $.50 each off the cover price. (Your savings are *guaranteed* to be at least $2.00 each month.) There is NO postage and handling – or other hidden charges. There are no minimum number of books to buy and you may cancel at any time.

**Send in
the Coupon
Below**

To get your FREE historical romance fill out the coupon below and mail it today. As soon as we receive it we'll send you your FREE Book along with your first month's selections.

- -

Mail To: **True Value Home Subscription Services, Inc., P.O. Box 5235
120 Brighton Road, Clifton, New Jersey 07015-5235**

YES! I want to start previewing the very best historical romances being published today. Send me my FREE book along with the first month's selections. I understand that I may look them over FREE for 10 days. If I'm not absolutely delighted I may return them and owe nothing. Otherwise I will pay the low price of just $4.00 each: a total $16.00 (at least an $18.00 value) and save at least $2.00. Then each month I will receive four brand new novels to preview as soon as they are published for the same low price. I can always return a shipment and I may cancel this subscription at any time with no obligation to buy even a single book. In any event the FREE book is mine to keep regardless.

Name
_____

Street Address _____ Apt. No. _____

City _____ State _____ Zip _____

Telephone _____

Signature _____
(if under 18 parent or guardian must sign)

Terms and prices subject to change. Orders subject to acceptance by True Value Home Subscription Services, Inc.

988-9